She wants one night

Marcus lost interest in t[...] nuzzled his neck. He jerked [...] step back, but she held o[...] to stumble. His hands fell to her waist as they regained their balance. Damn, when had he become so clumsy?

"What's the matter Marcus? Can't you handle her?"

Marcus tried to locate the joker in the back of the room, but it was impossible with camera flashes going off. His anger once again rose to overshadow shock and embarrassment. He returned his attention to the cause of his humiliation. "Would you mind telling me what the hell you're doing?"

She smiled seductively, continuing to play to the crowd. "Paying you back."

His jaw clenched tighter. "For what?"

"Someone altered my bid." Her finger twirled around the hair at the back of his neck. "I'm thinking it was you."

Of all the things she could be paying him back for, that wasn't one of them. "Why would I do that?"

She leaned in close, her angry whisper betraying the sultry expression she presented to the crowd. "You tell me. You're the one who chased me down. You're the one who had his hands all over me in the closet."

"I already told you I followed you to apologize, and I seem to remember an invitation."

She glanced at his mouth, and her smile widened. "And I seem to remember how quick you were to accept."

The fact that he couldn't deny her statement pissed him off. He'd been a fool to let desire rule his actions. "That doesn't mean I can't put a stop to this farce right now."

Her blue eyes clouded then hardened. "Yes, you could walk away. We both know you're damn good at that."

Praise for Author

Darah Lace

BACHELOR AUCTION

"This storyline is an attention-getter and one hard to put down. The subordinate characters help make the book a poignant travel through the ups and downs of their relationship...I recommend this book as one which is explicitly written but also has a wonderful plot. Readers should rush out and get this book. You will not be sorry. Kudos, Ms. Lace!"

~*Brenda Talley, Joyfully Reviewed*

SADDLE BROKE

"Hold on to your hats, because *Saddle Broke* is hot enough to start a fire...For a sexy, arousing, and romping good time, don't hesitate to read Darah Lace's *Saddle Broke*. You won't be sorry!"

~*Natalie, Romance Junkies*

BUCKING HARD

"I got this one right as I was ready to fall asleep. Told myself I was just going to load it on my ereader and read it later. Didn't happen. Two hours later, I was still reading... This book is a very fast read, without a lot of the tiring running around in circles...Darah focuses on the characters and what they want...Oh, and the "hot, no-holds-barred sex" is excellent, too."

~*Emmarae, Romancing the Book*

Bachelor Auction
Preston Brothers Book Two

by

Darah Lace

This is a work of fiction. Names, characters, places, and incidents are either the product of the author's imagination or are used fictitiously, and any resemblance to actual persons living or dead, business establishments, events, or locales, is entirely coincidental.

Bachelor Auction

COPYRIGHT © 2010 by Darah Lace

All rights reserved. No part of this book may be used or reproduced in any manner whatsoever without written permission of the author or The Wild Rose Press except in the case of brief quotations embodied in critical articles or reviews.

Contact Information: darah@darahlace.com

Cover Art by *Diana Carlile*

Published in the United States of America

This book contains ambiguous consent
and might disturb some readers.

Be sure to check out the bonus chapter for

S.A.M.: Satisfaction Guaranteed

in the back of this book.

Chapter One

Marcus Preston stared at the straw in his hand, dread weighing heavy in his gut. He'd drawn the short end of the stick. Par for the course of his life these days.

Resisting the urge to loosen the bow tie that suddenly felt like a noose around his neck, he looked up at his brothers. All three waited for his reaction. "Anybody want to go two out of three?"

His younger brother, Avery, laughed as he strode across the country club manager's office to slap Marcus on the back. "With only three of the four of us taking part this year, that won't work. Unless you think Spencer should be included. Technically, he's still a bachelor."

No way in hell would his soon-to-be sister-in-law ever go for Spencer's participation in this mad endeavor.

"I don't think Melody would agree with you," Spencer echoed Marcus's thoughts from a wingback chair near the unlit fireplace. "Besides, I've more than earned a reprieve. I drew the short straw the last two years running."

"Hey," Avery said. "I volunteered to take your place last year."

Spencer rolled his eyes. "Until you found out it's not always fun and games."

Marcus ignored Spencer and turned hopefully to Avery, even knowing he'd never step in for him. Not after what Spencer experienced last time. Still, he had to ask. "So, you'll take my place this year?"

"Are you kidding?" Avery shuddered dramatically. "I'm older and wiser now."

"We could pull out altogether if none of us wants to continue," Nick, the oldest Preston brother, said from behind the mahogany desk across the room. "But let me remind you, Marcus, you were the one who suggested we do this in the first place to promote the company."

"That was back when we needed the PR."

Nick stood and made his way around the desk. "Yes, and the company's participation in the charity auction was instrumental in bringing new clients to the table. After the losses we've suffered the last few months, I don't think we should turn down the chance for positive publicity."

The air in the room grew somber as each of them pondered events leading to Preston Enterprises' current state of affairs. Though things had begun to come around, the effects of corporate espionage had taken a toll on the company as well as the family. Spencer had lived through hell when he suspected Melody of leaking information to their competitor, Reese Consolidated.

Marcus had his own regrets in the overall scheme of things. And the strains of the Texas waltz filtering through the closed doors only served as a reminder of one particular regret.

Spencer sat forward, running his finger around the inside of his collar. "Melody's already wishing she hadn't let Charlotte talk her into taking charge of this year's auction. She'd have my hide if you guys backed out. She's counting you to bring in the big bucks."

Marcus grimaced, his apprehension growing. It wasn't just that he would be placing himself on the auction block of Houston's Most Eligible Bachelor Auction that had him cringing. When he and his brothers joined the festivities of the charity benefit in progress, he would have to face Charlotte Reese.

He had to sooner or later. After all, they moved in the same circles of Houston's upper echelon. She was Melody's best friend and, as such, would serve as maid of honor when Melody and Spencer married next month.

He also owed her an apology.

"We'll just have to hope Marcus escapes the blue-haired old bat who won Spencer last year." Avery shuddered again.

"Bea wasn't so bad. We had a pretty good time on that mini-cruise. She wasn't all that demanding, and after the promos were done, I was free to do whatever I wanted."

"Or *whoever*," Avery rubbed his hands together. "You had all the pussy you wanted after grandma went to bed. At least, the women who didn't think you were a gigolo. Hey, Marcus, maybe Daphne Cohen will decide to go for another Preston and bid on you. That trip Spencer took with her year before last sounded awfully hot for December."

Marcus didn't want to think of a weekend spent with Daphne Cohen. Though she was beautiful, any interest he might have held for her died once she slept with his brother. He'd rather make the most of his predicament with someone like Beatrice Reynolds who only expected a weekend of companionship, not casual sex. If he was lucky, his final bid would come in low and his buyer's prize would consist of dinner only.

"Did you boys get your business taken care of?"

The four men turned as Melody glided into the room, her black satin gown shimmering in the harsh fluorescent lighting. Wisps of chestnut hair that matched smiling brown eyes framed her face and fell from some kind of twist to tease bare shoulders.

Spencer stood to greet her with a kiss that told Marcus all the Daphne Cohens and bikini-clad cruise babes were history. He knew he shouldn't envy Spencer's happiness, but at the moment, he doubted he would ever know anything remotely like it. He'd thought once maybe, but...

"So, who's the lucky bachelor?"

He held up the straw.

"Oh, thank goodness." Melody slipped from Spencer's embrace to give Marcus a quick hug and peck on the cheek. "The good-looking Preston."

"Hey now," Spencer said, drawing her back to his side. "Remember which one of us you're engaged to."

Straightening Spencer's tie, she smiled up at him. "I think I can tell you apart."

Marcus couldn't help the semi-smile that pulled at his lips at the good-natured byplay and Melody's choice of words. With similar features and the same jet-black hair, he and his brothers were often mistaken for one another, especially dressed alike as they were for tonight's black-tie affair.

Of course, the majority of their acquaintances didn't realize Avery stood six-foot-four, an inch taller than his older brothers. Nor did they take the time to notice that by some fluke of nature, Marcus's eyes were deep green, Nick's were blue, Spencer's gray, and

Avery's brown.

"Seriously," Melody said, turning to face him. "I can't tell you how much I appreciate you doing this."

Marcus shrugged. "No problem."

At least not yet. He had a feeling this auction would turn his routine life inside out and upside down. Yet maybe that's what he needed—to let go and have a little fun. He hadn't in a long time. In fact, he could remember the exact moment he'd lost interest in the playboy life he'd led.

That wasn't to say he had given up women. He simply didn't crave them, or to be precise, he didn't crave sex the way he had. Better make that meaningless sex. It left him hollow and needing something more than physical release. Dating had lost its appeal as a sport and became a search for his idea of the perfect woman. One who shared his values of home and family.

One who could erase the memory of the only woman he did crave.

"I'm just sorry I couldn't convince you all to volunteer." Melody's eyes gleamed with excitement. "I mean, can you imagine the coverage Preston Enterprises would get if all three of you were on the auction block?"

"Sorry, Mel," Nick said, shaking his head. "For all my talk of corporate image, I'd just as soon not be put on display like a piece of meat for a bunch of women to fight over."

"They do that anyway, Nick. You just choose to ignore them," Melody teased. "And speaking of women, there are quite a few out there wondering where the Preston men are. They want dance partners without two left feet. And they're dying to know which of you is on the block. Did you know there are bets on who it will be?"

Five years ago, Marcus would have been thrilled with the prospect of being fought over by dozens of beautiful women. But now, the thought of being cornered by the winner left him cold. Thank God, the auction was silent, and he wouldn't have to face the humiliation of standing on stage during the bidding.

Avery clapped his hands together once and headed for the door. "Well, I don't have a problem with women fighting over me. There's plenty to go around, and I'll gladly share."

Nick shook his head as he followed in Avery's wake. "Better go keep an eye on him."

Marcus hesitated, not necessarily eager to face the music, especially after Nick labeled him a piece of meat. Still, he couldn't hide any longer. At least not here. Not when Spencer's and Melody's hushed tones and close proximity indicated they would appreciate a few moments of privacy.

He exhaled slowly and started for the door.

"Marcus, wait." Melody laid a hand on his arm. "I have a favor to ask."

Surprised at her solemn expression, he glanced over her head at Spencer, who gave him no inkling as to what she wanted. Marcus returned his attention to Melody and tried to convey a casualness he didn't feel. "Sure. What is it?"

"Well, the thing is…" She bit her lip as if afraid to say more, then suddenly rushed on. "I know there's something going on between you and Charlotte, and since the night of the mayor's party for the governor last summer..."

He didn't hear her next words as the memory of that night and what he'd shared with Charlotte in the mayor's garden, clouded his brain. He hadn't meant to let things get so out of hand. Hell, the only reason he'd gone outside with her in the first place was to keep her from interrupting Spencer's plan to be alone with Melody.

And the only reason he'd kissed Charlotte was to distract her.

But at the first taste, after five long years of wondering what it would be like to kiss those sensuous pink lips, he had forgotten that Charlotte's father was stealing Preston Enterprises blind and that part of the suspicion fell on her. And he had forgotten her reputation was as tarnished as some of the trophies in the cabinet behind him. Or that she was a far cry from his ideal woman.

He had allowed that kiss to lead to more than he should have, but not so far as to satisfy his own needs. Hell, holding himself from Charlotte had been pure torture as he watched her beautiful body writhe with pleasure beneath his touch. Only the memory of her rejection years earlier had kept him from fucking her on that cold stone bench under the gently swaying willow.

Marcus knew he had been right to maintain control when, afterward, she passed off his efforts to please her as *a real treat*. As if they meant nothing more to her than a way to pass the time. In retaliation, he'd made a cutting remark, one he regretted the moment the words slipped out.

He still regretted it.

"…you two weren't exactly civil at the celebration for my promotion." Melody squeezed his arm, her brown eyes round with concern. "Anyway, I just want you to be nice to her tonight. This is her first public appearance since her dad's arrest, and I want all of us, especially you, to show everyone the Prestons don't harbor any hard feelings. If everyone sees we don't hold her responsible for her father's crimes against Preston Enterprises, then maybe *they* won't either. So, could you maybe ask her to dance?"

"Sure." Marcus swallowed hard. "No problem."

She beamed as she whirled and grabbed Spencer's hand. "See, I told you he'd be reasonable."

"That you did." Spencer wrapped his arms around Melody and mouthed the words "thank you" over the top of her head.

"We'd better get back." Melody hurried toward the door. "I need to get your picture in front of the bidding sheet."

Marcus watched Spencer and Melody stroll away, glad everyone was so damned excited when he couldn't muster the least bit of enthusiasm. Donating his time was one thing. His soul was quite another. Which was exactly what his promise to Melody would cost if he weren't careful. He had already planned to make nice with Charlotte, but only long enough to apologize.

Would she let him? Or would she put up her defenses as she had at Melody's promotion party, totally ignoring him and flirting outrageously with his brothers?

"Only one way to find out," he muttered and forced himself down the hall.

He entered the ballroom behind Spencer and Melody, and a flurry of commotion on the other side of the dance floor caught his attention. In the middle of it all was Charlotte. He'd recognize that silvery blonde hair anywhere. And, as usual, practically every male in the building, young and old, flocked to her side.

Marcus made his way around the crowded dance floor, his feet heavy and dragging. He hated the idea of vying for her attention, of giving her the satisfaction. Yet a promise was a promise and the sooner he fulfilled it the better.

One dance, one apology, then he was done.

Ten feet from the pack of wolves drooling at her feet, Marcus heard her laugh. His stomach tightened at the husky sound. He'd forgotten how her laughter carried a sensual quality that made him ache to be the lucky man she favored with a smile. A smile that came with a price.

His feet stopped of their own accord. He couldn't do this.

No, what he couldn't do was let the entourage surrounding Charlotte sway him from his purpose. After all, he only wanted a few words with her. He'd simply walk up, ask for a moment of her time, and get the *I'm sorry* over with. Forget the dance.

Once again, he forced one foot in front of the other with dogged resignation, and once again, he stumbled to a halt as the crowd around her shifted.

He'd been right. Not only were her defenses up, but she'd donned full body armor in the form of a gold pantsuit that would have been conservative on anyone else. On Charlotte, who, to his everlasting regret, wore the long-sleeved jacket with nothing beneath, the suit screamed come fuck me.

Imagination and a single button at her waist held the damned thing together, revealing provocative swells barely concealed behind wide lapels. Low-rise matching pants gave him a glimpse of the smooth skin of her belly and accentuated the slender length of her legs. Gold high-heeled sandals adorned perfect feet, and Marcus knew from experience they would bring her already five-foot ten-inch frame closer to his own six-foot-three.

He had often wondered if Charlotte's choice of clothing was her way of arming herself against his attentions. As if she knew her insufficient attire bothered him and she wore it specifically to deter him. Of course, that was his ego talking and he'd never allowed himself to believe it. But if that had been her goal, she had accomplished it with flying colors.

Until tonight.

Marcus let his gaze travel up her svelte frame, pausing once again at her breasts before moving on. Her sparkling blue eyes met his, and her glossy red lips, wet from champagne, parted in a sensual smile that sent a rush of heat to his groin. Again, not something he hadn't felt a thousand other times. But somehow the irritation he usually felt at the way she flaunted herself in seductive clothing failed to surface, leaving him to deal with his lust.

He tried to appear unaffected as he returned her sultry stare. What little blood remained above his waist roared in his ears, drowning out the music and chatter of the crowd. If he inhaled deeply, he imagined he could smell the scent of her trademark perfume. Exotic, spicy, mysterious. Enough to lure a man—

Hell, he was losing his mind. And his control.

Marcus dragged his gaze from her and caught sight of Nick in the crowd to his right, chatting with Natalie Weaver, their ranch foreman's daughter. He turned and headed that way.

His apology to Charlotte would have to wait for another time when the armor she wore served its purpose and deflected his interest as it had in the past. For a time when he'd mastered the desire to take what she so blatantly offered.

The thought of doing so had crossed his mind more than a few times over the years. It would have been so easy to act on his unexplainable and very much unwanted attraction to her, to finally have her and be done with her. But she'd made it clear she wasn't offering it to *him*.

Until that night in the mayor's garden.

Granted, he'd essentially caught her by surprise. By the same token, her strong and instantaneous reaction had surprised him. It had also been enough to convince him she wanted nothing more than sex. And he had admitted years ago, at least to himself, he wanted more than that from Charlotte.

For Marcus, it was all or nothing.

****

Charlotte's smile slipped as Marcus turned away to join his brother. What was she thinking, smiling at him that way? She had all but invited his approach. Thank God, he'd remained true to form and reacted exactly as she'd intended when she selected this outfit. One sure to draw male attention and an ardent group of admirers that would keep Marcus Preston away.

So why was she disappointed?

She had no right to be when she had purchased the pantsuit knowing Marcus would be here. In fact, she did a lot of things with Marcus in mind. More than half her reputation was based on moments when she clung to or flirted with the nearest available man for the sole purpose of keeping Marcus Fucking Preston at a safe distance.

From the moment Avery introduced them, Charlotte had known Marcus was different. The way his deep green eyes assessed her, certainly physically, but also with an astute sense of awareness. As if he knew the carefree persona she'd perfected over the years hid a vulnerability she tried to deny. Frightening her more than his insight was her own reaction to him, because she knew instinctively Marcus was the type who wanted more than she was willing to give.

She had sworn at an early age she wouldn't end up like her mother, loving a man who didn't return her affection and drinking her life away while he flaunted one mistress after another. Though Marcus sometimes looked at her with something other than lust, he was just a man. A man who, like every other, would grow bored and look elsewhere for entertainment once the challenge of taming a woman was met, once she'd fallen in love and become dependent on him.

An occasional one-night stand. That's all she needed. It took the edge off her constant loneliness as well as promoted her bad-girl image. An image that kept the commitment-seeking men—those she avoided at all costs—at bay.

Yet, while her self-imposed reputation had thus far put Marcus off, it hadn't stopped the longing she felt whenever he came around.

Charlotte shook off the depressing thoughts and turned a bright smile on the young man beside her. He couldn't have been more than seventeen, making her feel ancient at twenty-five. "Well, you've been very entertaining, but I really need to check on the auction proceedings."

Blowing a kiss to the group in general, she dismissed their long faces and strolled casually in Melody's direction. If only she could so easily dismiss the one face that stayed on her mind more often than not.

She tried to tell herself she wasn't keeping tabs on him. It was simply that Avery and Nick's arrival had signaled their family meeting over and the straw drawn. And by their relaxed expressions, it was clear they had dodged the bullet and Marcus would be the one up for grabs. She'd felt a moment of pity for him. Marcus was much too serious to let himself enjoy an opportunity like this. He would hate it. He would do it, but he'd hate it.

Then Melody and Spencer had appeared, and she knew Marcus wouldn't be far behind. She steeled herself for his entrance. Even so, she hadn't been prepared for the sight of him in his black tux that accentuated a sleek, muscular frame and dark good looks. The man was absolutely delicious.

And just like chocolate. Off limits.

A hard pinch on her ass cheek sent Charlotte into a near collision with one of the couples on the edge of the dance floor. She swung around to confront her assailant, clearly no gentleman, then let out a long breath as Harry Townsend, the biggest letch in three counties, winked and teetered toward the champagne fountain, obviously a return trip.

She cursed the male species all the way to the bidding tables and stopped beside Melody. "I swear that man has the manners of a goat."

"Who?"

Charlotte pointed toward Harry, who could barely stand to fill his glass.

Melody peered past her and blinked in disappointment. "Oh, and after he just got through promising he'd be nice to you."

"He doesn't know the meaning of the word." Charlotte rubbed her bruised flesh. "Do me a favor, will you, and don't invite him to the wedding?"

"That might be kind of hard to do, considering he's Spencer's brother."

Charlotte glanced quickly from Harry to the other end of the table where Marcus helped the lovely brunette Nick had been talking to fill her plate. It wasn't the first time she'd seen Marcus with another woman, and it wasn't the first time she'd felt the pangs of what she refused to admit was jealousy, an emotion she avoided. To be jealous would mean she cared, and to admit that…

She faced the dance floor and waved off Melody's misconception. "I can handle him. I'm talking about Harry Townsend. My ass is always black and blue after one of these gatherings."

"You shouldn't have made the mistake of flirting with him last year at Liz Melbourne's wedding. Now, he thinks you want him. *And* you shouldn't have worn that outfit."

She batted her lashes in mock innocence. "What's wrong with my outfit?"

"Why, Charlotte," Melody said in a voice that sounded much like Melanie Wilkes scolding Scarlett O'Hara. "It's simply disgraceful. What *were* you thinking?"

"I was thinking of all the bees I'd attract with its honey color."

Melody shook her head. "You were thinking Marcus would see you in that getup and steer clear."

She stilled in mid-motion of plucking an imaginary piece of lint from her jacket. "What do you mean by that?"

"Just that I used to think you were trying to find a man to replace your father, someone to love you because you felt he didn't. But then I figured it out."

Charlotte swallowed hard. "Oh, yeah. What did you figure out?"

"That you're afraid of commitment."

"You got that right," she said, trying not to panic as her friend's observations came a little too close to the truth. She waved a hand to indicate the crowd around them. "I'm afraid, with all there is to choose from, one man could never satisfy me."

"Don't."

Charlotte blinked at Melody's sharp tone. "Don't what?"

"Belittle yourself. You know how much I hate it when you cut yourself down."

"But Mel, I—"

"Don't 'but Mel' me. I know you're not what you try so hard to portray." Melody's brow unfurled as concern filled her eyes. "And I know there's more to it than just your fear of commitment. There's something going on between you and Marcus."

Charlotte felt the blood drain from her face. "Are you crazy? Don't you see the way he looks at me? He hates me."

"That's where you're wrong. I *have* seen the way he looks at you. That's not hatred in his eyes."

"So, there's a little lust going on," Charlotte said, fighting for composure. "I'm clearly not his type."

"Isn't that the kind of man you usually gravitate toward? The ones not looking for a particular type, who just want to have a good time?"

Charlotte shrugged. "Hey, I wouldn't mind sharing the sheets with Marcus, but…"

When Melody didn't say anything, she almost sighed in relief. She had been on the brink of blurting out the fact that she'd already given in to the attraction, had offered herself to him, opened herself to the pain of rejection. In that, Marcus hadn't disappointed.

She gazed across the dance floor and found the topic of their conversation, his attention still focused on the petite porcelain-skinned beauty at his side. He bent close to hear something she said, and a lock of jet-black hair fell across his brow. Snow White reached to brush it back, causing Charlotte's palm to itch. Whether to slap the other woman's hand away or to feel the cool strands of his hair slip through her fingers as they had that night in the mayor's garden, she wasn't sure.

She had known someday Marcus would find a woman who would live up to all he wanted, but for some unfathomable reason, watching it happen disturbed her more than it should.

"You're more his type than either of you think."

Charlotte shifted so that her view of the handsome couple was blocked and shook her head. "Marcus wants love and marriage and kids. He wants the girl next door, someone pure and sweet."

"Yes, he does, but he'd be bored with someone like that. He might not know it, but he would."

"My point exactly. And when he grows bored with someone devoted to him, what will he do? He'll do what all men do when tired of the toys they have. They get new ones."

"Marcus isn't like your father. He's a good man."

"Is he?"

"Yes, and if you'd spend some time with him, you'd know."

"Well, I don't see that happening."

Melody's brow lifted, and the corner of her mouth curled upward. "You could bid on him."

Charlotte almost spewed ginger ale all over herself and Melody but managed to choke it down instead. "Now, I know you're crazy."

"Think about it. What better way to show him what you're really like?"

"What makes you think I want to do that? All I said was I wouldn't mind having sex with him. He's an itch I'd like to scratch. It's not like I want to have his baby or anything."

"Okay, then think of it this way. Being confined with Marcus for a few days on a cruise ship or at a secluded ski lodge is a sure-fire chance to work your wiles on him. You could get him out of your system once and for all."

Charlotte groaned and searched her mind for a comeback. The last thing she wanted was for Melody, or anyone else, to know how much she wished she could do just that. She'd tried for years and sometimes even managed to convince herself she had. Only times like these reminded her how miserably she'd failed.

"Melody, honey." Mrs. Preston appeared at Melody's side, hugging her close. "How's the bidding going?"

Melody kissed her future mother-in-law's cheek and indicated the women standing in line to place their bids. "Fine, but could you imagine the chaos if the bidding was live?"

"I've been to live bachelor auctions before, and let me tell you, they're a lot more fun to watch. Hungry women can be pretty scary."

An ache Charlotte tried hard to ignore settled in her chest as it had earlier when she'd deduced Marcus would join the other bachelors on the auction block. She glanced over Melody's shoulder at the bidding tables. The lines were long for the other bachelors, but Elaine Richardson, a partner at the law firm that represented Preston Enterprises, stood alone in front of Marcus's bidding sheet and photo, poised to write her name. Elaine bit her lip, hesitating, then straightened, dropped the pen without signing her name, and walked away. The bidding for Marcus must have surpassed Elaine's budget.

Though curious as to who had jacked up the price, Charlotte wasn't the least bit surprised. No matter the cost, he would be worth every penny. For that very reason, she had avoided the bidding tables since placing the opening bids. And she'd done that before any of the guests arrived and before knowing which Preston had drawn the short straw. She'd been afraid she wouldn't be able to sign her name if Marcus won — or rather lost — the drawing, and others, namely

Melody, would see the omission and guess the reason why. It would be hard enough to explain her departure prior to the announcement of the winners, but no way she could watch one of these women claim Marcus.

"Listen," Mrs. Preston said to Melody, drawing Charlotte's attention. "I've talked your mother and father into staying at the ranch with us when they come for the wedding. There's no reason for them to go to a hotel. Besides, Christmas Eve is no time to be stuck in a hotel. They should be with family."

"Thank you. When we chose Christmas Eve to get married, I had no idea it would be so difficult for everyone. Especially the hotel reservations." Melody turned to Charlotte. "You know Spencer's mom, don't you?"

"Yes, how are you, Mrs. Preston?" She had met Marcus's mother on several occasions and always found her kind and generous. Yet there was something disconcerting in the way the older woman looked at her now. As if she could see straight to her soul, making Charlotte feel a nakedness that had nothing to do with scandalous attire.

"I'm wonderful now that one of my boys is finally settling down. I'm hoping another will soon follow."

Charlotte swallowed as Connie Preston's eyes bore into hers. She managed an airy laugh. "Well, I know dozens of Houston women who would gladly volunteer."

She was saved from further discussion on the prospects of wedded bliss for the Preston men as the oldest brother, Nick, joined them, placing a hand on his mother's shoulder. "Come dance with me, Mama."

"Of course, honey." She turned to Melody. "See

you tomorrow at the ranch." Then to Charlotte she said, "Why don't you come along with Melody? We'd love to have you."

Charlotte knew the entire family, including Marcus, planned to discuss the wedding over lunch. She wasn't about to subject herself to an entire afternoon of his company. "Thank you, but I have plans for the rest of the weekend."

"Perhaps another time then," Mrs. Preston said, smiling as if she knew perfectly well Charlotte had just lied.

Melody rounded on her the moment they were alone. "Why did you do that? You told me just an hour ago you had no plans. She was trying to be nice to you. She was letting you know she likes you for who you are, and she doesn't hold your father's actions against you."

"I know." She lifted a shoulder and let it drop, suddenly tired of trying to hide her feelings. "But you know me. I'd be bored stiff, talking wedding plans and all that mushy stuff."

"And I'm sure painting your toenails is so much more fun."

"Depends on who's painting them for me."

"Charlotte Reese, don't—" Melody's frown deepened. "It's Marcus, isn't it? He'll be there, and you don't want to see him. There *is* something going on between you two."

"For the last time, there isn't *now*, nor can there ever be, anything between Marcus and me." If she'd been confused about anything else that happened in the garden that night, he'd made that much perfectly clear. "Besides, I've got a paper due and finals to study for."

"Couldn't you put them off for a few hours? You need a break."

"I've taken too many breaks."

She hated to disappoint Melody, but keeping up with social commitments, like this auction, while trying to obtain her masters in psychology had been difficult. Keeping it a secret hadn't been any easier. Not that it was a secret, really. It just didn't fit the image she'd so carefully cultivated over the years. To her acquaintances she was a party girl and a career student, taking classes at the university for lack of anything better to do.

But after almost ten years, she was so close to her goal, she could taste it. She hated to deviate from her schedule whenever she could help it. Besides, after not seeing Marcus at all in the last two months, twice in twenty-four hours would be more than she could bear.

"Hello, ladies." Avery, the youngest Preston, filled the space between them, draping an arm over their shoulders. It seemed the Prestons were everywhere tonight. "You're both looking mighty lovely this evening."

With a raised brow, Charlotte let her gaze roam his slender yet well-toned frame. "You look pretty good yourself. But then you know that, don't you?"

He gave her a lopsided grin then turned to Melody. "Mind if I steal this hellion for a dance? This party needs shaking up, and I'm thinking she and I are the ones to do it."

"Be my guest."

Avery disentangled himself and held out his hand to Charlotte. "How about it, darlin'?"

Charlotte didn't feel much like shaking things up, but if it saved her from another of Melody's lectures, she was all for it. Besides, dancing with Avery would be another nail in her coffin since that one time she'd come on to him for Marcus to witness.

She'd done it, banking on two things—a rumor that Marcus never pursued women his brothers had dated and the hope that Avery wouldn't accept her offer because she was the daughter of his company's competitor. The gamble had paid off. Avery had declined, and Marcus had backed off.

She placed her hand in Avery's. "Let's show these people how to party."

Several songs later, Charlotte found herself actually having a good time. Avery had given her a run for her money twirling around the floor, then passed her off to Nick, who waltzed her in circles until the room tilted. She laughed at Avery's ridiculous sense of humor and Nick's dry cynicism. Both men seemed genuinely friendly as they took turns dancing with her.

Funny how only six months ago, the "Preston boys" had treated her with open disdain. It wasn't until her father's arrest and Melody's engagement to Spencer that they began to see her differently. All, except Marcus.

When she once more found herself passed off to Avery, she adjusted to his rhythm and let her gaze wander over those surrounding the dance floor. She wasn't looking for *him*. She really wasn't. But there he was, anyway, Snow White still clinging to his side as she had all evening, smiling at him with unmistakable adoration.

Charlotte looked away. If he was going to fall for that infant, she wasn't going to stick around and watch. It was time to make her exit.

As if on cue, the music reached a crescendo. Avery matched it, ending with a flourish of spins that left her dizzy and grasping his arm. She laughed despite her dejected state and, uncertain of her balance, let him lead her off the floor. When he came to a sudden halt, she stumbled past him and into a very masculine chest.

Her laughter died in her throat as strong fingers closed around her upper arms and the familiar scent of pine and musk surrounded her. She lifted her gaze from equally familiar shoulders to green eyes that grew as dark as the deepest recesses of the forest when they focused on her breasts, which were mashed solidly against his chest and threatening to spill from her jacket.

"Nice to—" He cleared his throat. "—see you again, Charlotte."

Chapter Two

Heat crept up Charlotte's neck to flood her cheeks as Marcus set her on her feet and stepped back. Geez, she hadn't blushed in…well, not in years. Not since she'd walked in on her father's chauffeur—the object of her thirteen-year-old infatuation—and the upstairs maid getting it on in the pool house.

She could barely pull two thoughts together much less form a sarcastic or witty reply, something her reputation demanded. Just when she thought her humiliation couldn't get any worse, she heard Avery say, "It's your turn to take Charlotte for a spin."

He made her sound like a sports car being test-driven. So much for thinking they were beginning to see her differently. Then again, it was probably for the best if she maintained the fast image she'd managed to build over the years.

She brushed her fingers through her hair and forced a laugh. "Now, Avery, you know as well as I do Marcus is too stuffy to drive in the fast lane."

"That's not true." Snow White's fingers curled possessively around Marcus's arm. "I can tell you from experience he knows exactly how it's done."

Charlotte met Marcus's preoccupied gaze, doubtful he'd even heard the girl's subtle insinuation. "Congratulations. I haven't had the pleasure myself."

Hearing the word *pleasure* in Charlotte's throaty voice jarred Marcus from his stupor and sent a rush of blood south, a direction it seemed to take whenever he saw her. Hell, who was he kidding? It happened at the mere thought of her.

He thought he'd pulled himself together since almost caving to her allure earlier. Natalie had been a good distraction, but when Charlotte collided with his chest and he'd been face to...breast?...with her, all coherent brain activity vanished.

He tore his gaze from her satiny blonde mane. "Nat, I'd like you to meet Charlotte Reese. Charlotte, this is Natalie Weaver."

Charlotte smiled. "It's nice to meet you, Natalie."

Natalie frowned. "Hmm, that name sounds so familiar."

"Charlotte's a popular gal." Avery draped an arm around her shoulders, hugging her close. "Aren't you, darlin'?"

Though Marcus had his own opinions on Charlotte's popularity, he appreciated Avery's attempt to spare her embarrassment. What he didn't appreciate was the familiarity with which his brother handled her. Not that she seemed to mind. Come to think of it, they'd been awfully cozy on the dance floor. His gut twisted at the idea of something going on between them.

Natalie gasped. "Isn't your father the one—"

"C'mon Nat." Avery released Charlotte and grabbed Natalie's free hand. "It's time for you and me to take a spin of our own."

"But—"

Natalie's protest was cut off as Marcus relinquished her to his brother's timely intervention. He frowned after them, still not certain whether he wanted to thank Avery or beat the hell out of him. A glance at Charlotte as she struggled to hold her smile in place told Marcus he would be thanking his not-so-subtle brother later.

"She's young, Charlotte. She doesn't know tact yet."

"It doesn't matter. I'm used to it." She lifted her chin and tossed her head, causing pale strands to cascade over her shoulders like a waterfall of moonlight. God, he loved her hair. "See you around, Marcus."

"Wait." He reached to stop her but pulled back short of touching her. He still hadn't apologized. "I thought we were going to dance?"

One corner of her lips curled upward. "Don't worry. You're off the hook."

"What's that supposed to mean?"

"Just that I know how hard it is for you to pretend and that there's no one around to tell on you if you're not nice to me."

Damn. Apologizing now would be futile if she thought he only did it to honor a promise to Melody. Yet somehow, he had to try. "That's not why I asked you to dance."

"I don't recall you actually asking."

"No. I didn't. But I am now." He forced himself to meet her confident blue eyes. "Would you dance with me, Charlotte?"

She seemed to consider his question, as if trying to guess his ulterior motive, then finally shrugged. "I guess we should. If only to make Melody happy."

Marcus supposed he deserved her indifference after the last time they'd been together, but it sure played havoc with his ego. Though by all accounts, he should be accustomed to it. She never failed to make him feel lame and uninteresting.

He took her by the elbow and led her onto the dimly lit dance floor before she changed her mind. A fast two-step played, a Texas swing, conducive to keeping intimacy at a minimum. However, as he swung her around the room it also made conversation impossible.

Then again, he needed a moment to get over the feel of having her close. He held one soft, slender hand. The other rested on his shoulder, her fingers near the collar of his shirt, within twining distance of his hair. Her silky blonde hair flew out behind her as they twirled the corners, then settled against her back during the straight-aways so the ends tickled his hand at her waist. Her spicy fragrance danced around him, reminding him of that night in the garden and how it had mingled with her unique feminine scent as she writhed under his touch.

Damn, now, he'd done it. Gone and worked himself up, with a hard-on to prove it.

He checked to see if she had any idea what she did to him and let out of long breath of relief. As usual, she seemed aware of everything but him. He glanced lower to make sure his embarrassing state wasn't as obvious as it felt, but his gaze stalled at the curve of her breasts at the opening of her jacket. He swallowed hard as the garment's only button pulled against the eyehole, and he wondered how much resistance it could withstand with all the twists and turns her body made before it popped open. If he were to—

The music stopped before his thoughts could lead

him into mischief or before he slammed into everyone in their path.

Charlotte stepped out of his arms and pushed her hair back. It fell forward again, one strand curling inside the vee of her jacket between her breasts. He envied that curl, wishing he could replace it with his lips.

"Snow White was right. You certainly know what you're doing. At least on the dance floor."

"Who?"

Her pink tongue slid out to wet full, red lips. "Your friend. Natalie, was it?"

"Oh, yeah, Nat." Marcus wanted to pound his head against a wall. How was he going to get through an apology when his thoughts strayed uncontrollably, misconstruing her every movement into something provocative and sensually erotic? More importantly, when he knew, if they were alone, he would probably repeat the mistake he'd made in the mayor's garden.

"Well, thanks for the dance. I'll see you later."

"Wait." He grabbed her hand as the band struck up another two-step, this one much slower. "You can't leave after half a song. You won't know for sure how light on my feet I am unless you dance an entire song with me."

Marcus didn't wait for Charlotte to refuse. He placed a hand at the small of her back and drew her closer, resisting the urge to crush her to him, to bury his face in her hair. Instead, he remained careful, keeping enough space between them so as not to reveal the bulge beneath his cummerbund.

"It must be hard."

Marcus almost choked on his next breath. "I beg

your pardon?"

"Being a bachelor on the auction block. I've always felt sorry for you guys, making yourself, or rather your time, available to the highest bidder, never knowing which woman"—she smiled that half smile again—"or man that will be."

This time he did choke.

Charlotte slapped him on the back and laughed, her blue eyes twinkling. "Hey, it could happen. Ralphy Jernigan would love to get his hands, not to mention other body parts, on a hot guy like you."

He shuddered. Not at the idea of spending time with a man, though he was team pussy all the way. But Ralph was old and smelled like moth balls. "Don't even joke about that."

"Oh, don't worry. There are so many salivating socialites ready to snap you up, Ralphy won't stand a chance."

"Does that mean you'd bid on me?" Now why the hell had he asked that? The last thing he needed was for Charlotte to purchase him, so he'd be forced to spend time with her. He'd never survive.

"I already have."

Marcus's jaw dropped. "You have?"

"Yes, as head of the silent auction, I place the first bid on each bachelor to get the ball rolling."

In other words, she had only bid on him because it was part of her job. It didn't bother her that he would end up with some other woman. He shouldn't be disappointed. He'd just admitted he couldn't handle time alone with her.

Then he remembered she'd passed on her duties as the benefit committee chair to Melody. "I thought Mel—"

A sudden nudge at Marcus's back knocked him

into Charlotte and together they stumbled. He quickly righted them and adjusted the space between them before she felt his swollen dick, then frowned at Spencer over his shoulder. His brother was so wrapped up in Melody he didn't realize what he'd done. Or simply didn't care enough to acknowledge it.

"Sorry about that," Marcus said as he moved them in another direction just to be on the safe side, then picked up the conversation. "You're not in charge of the auction this year, Melody is. Why would you open the bidding?"

She gave him a smirk that said he must have lost his mind. "And do you actually think Spencer would allow her to bid on another man?"

Marcus shrugged. "If it were for a good cause."

"Would you?"

He considered how he'd feel if the woman he loved wanted to put her name on a bidding sheet, leaving herself open to the possibility of spending time with another man. He thought, too, about Charlotte's admission that she always initiated the bidding. Neither sat well with him. "No, I wouldn't."

"I figured I owed it to Melody to step in since she took over the auction for me."

"I never realized you were even involved with the auction, much less in charge, until she told us she was taking it on for you."

Charlotte turned her attention toward the crowded edge of the dance floor as if bored with the conversation. "It's for the children at the hospital."

Marcus never thought she'd be one for thinking about kids. It was more her style to enter into a bidding war with a bunch of man-hungry debutantes. Yet he couldn't remember her ever having done that. She'd never bought a bachelor either.

"This can't be making Snow White very happy."

"Isn't she—"

Another shove from behind pushed him flush

against Charlotte. She clutched his shoulder this time to keep from falling, and he was certain she felt the jerk of his cock as it came in contact with her hip. He shifted to allow more space between them then turned to see who had bumped into him.

Nick gave him a sheepish grin and a mumbled apology over his dance partner's head, causing Marcus to suspect he'd become the target of a misguided matchmaking scheme. His brothers weren't clumsy.

Marcus ignored Nick and turned back to Charlotte. By the frown she wore, he figured her opinion of his coordination had dropped considerably. He muttered another feeble apology and steered her to an area near the open door, hoping the November air would cool both his irritation and his lust.

Once there, it took him a moment to remember what she'd said and who she'd dubbed Snow White. He failed to see what Natalie had to be unhappy about. In fact, she had seemed giddy all night just to attend one of society's big events. It wasn't often a ranch foreman's daughter found herself invited. He had tried to keep her company and introduce her to as many people as possible. Good connections never hurt.

Still, Charlotte may have seen something he hadn't, and Marcus was compelled to protect the girl who had dogged his steps as a child. "I thought Natalie was having a good time. Why would you think she's not?"

"Oh, I just figured she'd have something to say about you spending time with another woman even if it is for the kids."

He cocked his head, unable to comprehend her logic. "What's she got to say about what I do?"

She snorted. "It's just like a man to be oblivious to the world around him. That girl is over the moon for you."

"Nat? She's just a kid."

"Believe me, she's no kid, and she knows exactly

what she wants."

Her tone held just enough jealousy to give his ego a much-needed boost, though it was ridiculous to think he could possibly look at Natalie as more than a kid sister. Or to think the jealousy he heard was more than female insecurity talking.

Still, what could it hurt for Charlotte to think he might be interested in Natalie? He'd never seen her self-confidence threatened, and for some reason, it made her seem more human, almost vulnerable.

He glanced to where Natalie stood at the edge of the dance floor and pretended to study her. "Now, that you mention it, I guess she is pretty."

"Just your type."

Now, this was interesting. "What type is that?"

"Oh, you know. All small and meek and helpless with don't-touch-me-or-I'll-break porcelain skin. Sweet and innocent, round-as-saucer brown eyes. Pure to the bone."

Everything you're not. A pang of something he never expected to feel for Charlotte sliced through his chest. Regret. Regret that she wasn't his type, and that no matter how much he wished it, she never could be. Or at least, that's what he'd always believed.

So far tonight nothing in his reaction to her had been consistent with the past. Nothing except his rock-hard erection. "My type or not, there's nothing between Nat and me."

"Well, from the way she's been hanging all over you this evening and the way she's glaring at me right now, I'd say she thinks there is."

Surprise rippled through him. Not because Nat might have a crush on him, though until Charlotte mentioned it, he hadn't considered Nat's actions during the evening anything but friendly. No, what surprised him was Charlotte's slip. He doubted she even realized she had more or less just confessed she'd watched him throughout the evening.

A smile threatened, but he forced his lips into a thin line. If he was careful, maybe she would reveal something else. Besides, he didn't dare let her see how her interest affected him. Especially when he hated to admit it to himself. "I don't think—"

Someone slammed into Marcus, this time sandwiching Charlotte between him and the person behind her. The feel of her soft body pressed so firmly against his from chest to knees was too much to handle. He jerked away, his entire body rebelling against the restraint his brain was fast losing control of. Hell, he fairly shook with wanting to drag her out the door to someplace dark where he would be free to explore her soft curves and more.

He shoved his hands in his pockets to keep from doing just that, realizing too late how stupid that was since he couldn't very well dance with her without touching her. He withdrew them slowly and held one out. A long moment passed before he realized she hadn't moved and he was forced to look at her.

"You know, Marcus," she said, irritation flashing in her cat-like eyes. "I figure half of one song and half of another makes a whole. Why don't I deem you a competent dancer and put us both out of our misery?"

With that, she turned around and left him standing on the edge of the dance floor, feeling like the fool he was for lingering in her company longer than necessary.

"Sorry, man. That wasn't supposed to happen," Avery said beside him. "We were just trying to help you along. I mean, we all know you've got a thing for Charlotte, but you were dancing with her like you had a poker up your ass."

Marcus watched Charlotte's lithe figure disappear into the hallway before turning to his brother. "When and if I ever need your help with a woman, I'll let you know. Until then stay the hell out of my business."

He walked away from his meddling brother with

every intention of putting distance between himself and the woman he didn't need any help with. Instead, his feet carried him toward the same door she'd passed through. He'd almost made it when Natalie stepped in front of him.

"Marcus, I need to talk to you."

Her dark eyes flared with anger, and he remembered Charlotte's warning that Natalie fancied herself in love with him. He would have to set Nat straight, but the mood he was in at the moment, he wasn't inclined to do so easily.

"Not now." He patted her hand and ignored her protest as he brushed past her. Determination filled him with every step, though he couldn't say why he felt the need to rehash a history Charlotte obviously didn't remember.

One Marcus would never forget.

****

Charlotte paused in front of the country club's coat closet and read the sign "Back in 15 Minutes."

"To hell with that," she muttered as she slipped around the counter and through the open door of the closet. They would be announcing the winning bids by then, and she'd rather not live through that nightmare. The one she'd suffered moments ago was bad enough.

She must have been out of her mind to think she could dance with Marcus, be that close to him and not fall victim to her own longings or risk another rejection. But he had seemed sincere in wanting to dance with her. At least until the music slowed, forcing him to actually pay attention to his partner. That he was uncomfortable with her was an understatement.

She scanned the hundreds of coats that lined the walls on either side, but the faux sable mink she'd worn resembled dozens of others that were real. "Concentrate, Charlotte, so you can get the hell out of here."

"You're not going anywhere until I've had my

say."

Her heart plunged to her stomach at the sound of Marcus's hard-as-steel voice. She restrained herself from rubbing the goose bumps beneath her sleeves and, instead, shook her hair over her shoulder and continued her search. "What? You're not through insulting me?"

"I'm not the one who left you standing on the dance floor, looking like a fool."

"Well, it was obvious you couldn't stand touching me."

"That's not—"

A giggle from the hallway thwarted whatever reply he might have made, and relief swept over her when he turned to leave. Her relief was short lived when Marcus eased the door to within a couple of inches of being closed then returned to stand directly in front of her. He shoved his hands deep in his pockets, elbows grazing the coats on either side.

His nearness distracted her, as did his woodsy cologne and the jet-black hair that fell over his furrowed brow and emphasized the deep green eyes staring intently back at her. But she couldn't afford to get carried away by her attraction to him and end up hurt again. Her response to him in the mayor's garden had certainly proven her resistance was no match for his charm. Still, she had to keep the barriers up, to play her part.

Instead of waiting for him to finish what he'd started to say, she shrugged. "Hey, it's no big deal if you don't want to dance with me. To each his own, right?"

"You should know by now I never do anything I don't want to."

Charlotte sighed inwardly. She did know. Better than most. Marcus could be stubborn to a fault, a trait she often depended on. "I told you I know Melody asked you to be nice to me."

"Yes, but I wanted to talk to you. I'd been trying all night."

"You didn't try very hard. I've been here the entire evening."

"Surrounded by admirers," he mumbled and looked away for a moment, then once again steadied his dark gaze on her. "Look, I wanted to apologize."

Stunned, Charlotte could think of only one thing he would apologize for, and she'd be damned if she'd let him. Granted, she regretted how that brief episode had ended, but she wouldn't take it back or let him sully it with an apology.

"No need. It's already forgotten." With that lie, she turned away to resume her search. She thrust another black mink aside as silence filled what little space there was left in the narrow closet. Where was her stupid coat?

"I only meant to keep you from interrupting Spencer and Melody, but I shouldn't have let things go that far."

"Don't."

Her whispered plea went unheard.

"I shouldn't have used you."

She clutched the hounds-tooth overcoat in front of her as her heart lurched from her stomach to her throat. There it was, her suspicion put into words. She'd been nothing to him. Nothing but a means to an end, the pleasure he'd given her no more than a way of distracting her.

Swallowing the ache his words created, she somehow dredged up what little pride she still possessed, along with the carefree attitude she'd conveyed over the years, and turned to face him. This time with a practiced expression of sultry invitation.

The anger in his eyes faded to a wary glare. He obviously knew the game they'd played off and on over the years as well as she did. In fact, he could probably guess her next move. She certainly anticipated his.

"As I recall," she said, letting her gaze roam over his long, muscular, and sexy-as-hell frame before meeting his gaze again. "I was the one using you that night." She stepped close and ran her index finger down the center of his chest, her fingernail clicking over each onyx button. "I'd be more than willing to return the favor."

He caught her wrist as she reached his cummerbund. "I told you that night there could never be anything between us."

Charlotte knew rejection was imminent, but his nearness and his touch triggered a desire she had fought hard to deny, longings she couldn't control. For one brief moment, she questioned the sanity of her actions. Then she noticed the muscle of his jaw work as he clenched it tight. She wouldn't have to do much more. He was ready to bolt as always.

"I remember you telling me that." She moved closer, pressing against him, determined to drive him away, out of the closet, out of her life for good. "I remember everything about that night, Marcus. Especially, how good it felt when you kissed me." She curled her free arm around his neck and licked her lips. "Don't you want to kiss me now?"

"That's not why I'm here." His darkening gaze dropped to her mouth even as he denied it.

She smiled the lazy smile she'd used on so many men. One that reeled them in. One Marcus had always been immune to. "That's right. You came to apologize." She threaded her fingers through the hair at his nape and tilted her head. "I know the perfect way to say you're sorry."

Brushing her lips against his, slowly, softly, she felt the rush of his warm breath. His grip on her wrist loosened, and she readied herself for the moment he would break free.

In a move as quick as lightening, he fisted one

hand in her hair, startling a gasp from her. His mouth slanted across hers. His tongue surged forward, laying siege, seeking to do battle with hers. He tasted of champagne and one hundred percent pure lust.

As surprise gave way to the knowledge that she'd really screwed up, gone too far this time, Charlotte flattened a palm against his chest to push him away. But her fingers betrayed her, curling around his lapel, pulling him closer, and she surrendered to the assault on her senses, all resistance conquered.

Chapter Three

Marcus tasted the sweetness of her, drank in all that was Charlotte, and wanted more. He wanted to devour her, kiss every inch of her beautiful body, touch every curve and crevice, lose himself in the softness of her skin. He wanted to bury himself inside her heat, to fuck her here, now, in this cramped closet before common sense returned. He wanted everything she had to offer. And more. Always more.

He smoothed a hand down her back to palm her ass and lift her against his aching erection. Her soft moan washed over him, adding to his already burning need. She arched into him, and he felt the beaded tips of her breasts through their clothing.

One button. The thought resounded through his head. One golden button between him and the twin mounds of equally golden flesh that haunted his dreams. With a resigned groan, he reached for the button, desperate to know if she still tasted as good as he remembered. The button popped free, and he slid his hand inside her jacket at the base of her ribs just below her breast.

He started to move his hand upward then stilled when he heard voices just outside the closet.

"But Henry, they haven't closed the bidding."

"I'm ready to go home, Lilly. I've got a full day at the office tomorrow."

"But the coat-check girl's not here," Lilly wailed. "Can't you wait until she returns?"

"Who knows when she'll be back."

Marcus's first instinct was to spring away and pretend innocence, but one look into Charlotte's heavy-lidded, glazed blue eyes changed his mind. Even if she kept them lowered, there was still her flushed cheeks, swollen red lips, and tangled hair, not to mention his own irregular breathing. Anyone with half a brain would know what they'd been doing, and Lilly McAfee was no fool. She was one of the biggest gossips in Houston. She could write her own column.

Not that Charlotte's reputation hadn't endured worse, but he wouldn't add to its damage. And he'd be damned if he would be labeled as another of her conquests.

"Henry, you can't just—"

"I'm not waiting."

Marcus didn't hesitate. His hand still pressed to the bare flesh beneath her breast, he pushed Charlotte toward the far end of the narrow closet.

"Marcus, what—"

"Be quiet," he whispered as he shoved a multitude of coats aside and thrust her against the wall behind them, then ducked beneath the pole to join her. The shelf above barely grazed his head, and he had just enough room to flatten himself against her once he arranged the coats around them.

The door swung open, and Lilly's irritation rang clearly in the silence of the closet. "Why did we even come if you weren't going to stay to hear the results of the bidding?"

"I came to talk business." Henry moved closer, searching purposefully.

Marcus felt Charlotte tense as if only now aware of the invasion of their privacy. He pressed a finger against her lips, and she gazed up at him with startled eyes. Eyes a man could drown in, eyes that even now pulled him slowly under.

He closed his own and tried not to think about where his hand was. That with only the slightest move he would find the treasure he'd sought moments ago. Instead, he tried to concentrate on the conversation going on behind them and the whereabouts of the participants.

"So now that your business is concluded, you think I should drop my friends and hurry on home?"

Lilly remained in the doorway.

"They'll call you tomorrow, and you can gossip all day about the auction."

Henry was still some feet away.

Charlotte shifted, and Marcus stifled a groan. That she cradled his cock between her thighs wasn't an easy thing to ignore, but when she squirmed against him, his recognition of just how intimate their position was sprang to life again. Before he could relay his need for her to remain still, his thumb grazed the underside of her breast, and she froze.

He opened his eyes and, again, found himself looking into hers, wide with shock and just a hint of something else. That something else prompted him to disregard good sense, along with everything he knew and felt about Charlotte.

Holding her gaze, he slid his thumb up the underside of her breast, over its stiff crest, then back. Her eyelids fluttered down then up again, and even in the shadows, he saw the flame of desire ignite behind that veil of cool blue.

Like an addict needed his next fix, Marcus needed to see more of Charlotte's reaction to his touch. He repeated the action, adding to it a series of circles around the areola. When her eyelids lowered halfway, denying him his pleasure, his thumb came to a rest, cutting off her pleasure as well.

Lids lifting, she stared at him with the same fiery need as before, along with wary anticipation. He flicked his thumb over the tip of her beaded nipple, and she rewarded him with an indrawn breath.

His gaze fell to her wide full mouth. Still beneath his index finger, her lips were puffy and red, warm and inviting. He traced the seam of her lips, then gently tugged the lower one with the pad of his finger until they parted, revealing flawless white teeth. His dick stretched another half inch as he thought of those teeth grazing his flesh.

Lilly McAfee once more bemoaned the fact that her husband was forcing her to leave early, but Marcus blocked out Henry's reply. He lowered his head to catch the fullest part of Charlotte's bottom lip between his teeth and nibbled softly before sucking it gently into his mouth. At the same time, he rolled her nipple between thumb and forefinger, and her muffled cry filled the closet.

It was then he realized the McAfees had departed, and with their coats, they had taken his safety net. One kiss, he told himself as he removed his hand from Charlotte's breast and braced both forearms against the wall behind her. One kiss before he returned to sanity.

Even as he covered her mouth with his, tasted her sweetness, and inhaled the heady scent of her arousal, he wondered if one kiss would be enough to last a lifetime. With that thought came the knowledge it would have to be, and that he was a fool to have embarked on this impossible journey.

Marcus broke their kiss and rested his forehead against hers, trying to regain even breathing. "They're gone."

"Hmm?"

"The McAfees. They're gone."

"Mmm. We should go, too." Her husky voice oozed over him like warm honey, and Marcus barely suppressed a shudder. "I'll follow you to your place. Or will Avery mind?"

"No." Avery probably wouldn't return to the condo they shared for hours. Even if he did, they respected each other's privacy. But that wasn't the point. What was the point again?

"Do you want to follow me to my place, then?"

More than you'll ever know. "No."

"If you rode here with Avery, I could take you home later." Her hands were everywhere, driving him crazy. "Mmm, much later."

His body jerked as her fingers brushed the head of his cock on their way from around his waist to his chest. He lifted his head to put an end to this agony before he changed his mind. "I have my own car."

He watched her soft features—relaxed by their loving—harden with comprehension. She pressed the flat of her hand to his stomach as if to push him away, which left him totally unprepared when, with a swivel of her wrist, she palmed his dick. He didn't know who was more surprised, but by the widening of her eyes, he'd guess she hadn't expected to find him hard and throbbing. And damn, was he throbbing.

Charlotte felt the tremor that passed through Marcus, felt him twitch beneath her hand. She could have been any woman. He'd react the same way, but she had to continue as she had begun. She had to show him she wasn't hurt by his rejection, that it was what she'd wanted.

She slid her fingers from the tip of his dick to the root. "You want me, Marcus. It's more than obvious."

He clenched his jaw and stared at a point on the wall behind her. "I never said I didn't. Any man breathing would."

"Then why are you denying us both the pleasure of finishing what we started last summer?" She moved closer, rubbing her bare breasts against his crisp white shirt, then brushed her mouth across his jaw and whispered, "What are you afraid of?"

It took him a moment to reply. "Sometimes what we want isn't good for us."

She didn't know how much more she could take. If he didn't end this soon, she might just have to follow through on her actions. In a last ditch effort, she curled her fingers around his thick shaft and squeezed. "That's where you're wrong. I'd be very good."

"As I'm sure many would agree." He grabbed her hand, moving as far from her as the limited space would allow. "But I won't be just another notch on your bedpost."

Charlotte laughed to keep from crying as his hurtful words cut her to the quick. "Why Marcus, you sound almost virginal. But I know that can't be the case. Some of your old girlfriends think very highly of your...abilities."

"At least they were girlfriends and not picked out of a crowd for a one-night stand."

"Ouch. I guess the gloves are off." She sighed. "And to think Melody wanted me to bid on you."

His head jerked up, his gaze piercing. "Excuse me?"

"Don't worry. I wouldn't do that, at least not with the intention of purchasing you." She buttoned her jacket and pushed back the coats, ready to end this fiasco. "Not if you were the last man on earth."

"Thank God for small favors," he grumbled behind her as she stepped through the coats.

"Damn it, Lilly, if you knew the coat wasn't yours, why did you wait 'til we got to the car to tell me?"

Charlotte froze at the sound of Henry McAfee's voice. His shadowed form filled the gap of the partially closed door.

"I wanted to watch the end of the auction," Lilly replied.

Strong arms encircled Charlotte's waist, dragging her back into their safe haven, and once again she found herself flush against Marcus's solid frame, his chest to her back. The length of hardened flesh she had cradled in her hand moments ago pressed firmly against her ass. She squirmed to get away, but he held tight and stilled the motion of the coats as the closet door swung open.

Henry paused in the doorway, frowning at his wife. "Does it really mean that much to you?"

"Yes," Lilly said, following him into the closet. "I told you I wanted to see if anyone outbid the Reese girl."

Charlotte stiffened. Lilly McAfee had to be mistaken. She hadn't bid on anyone. Not really. Surely, the other bidders hadn't been cruel enough to leave one of the bachelors with only her opening bid. She racked her brain to come up with anyone who would have recently been added to society's blacklist.

Henry began his search for Lilly's mink. "I doubt anyone will challenge the ridiculous amount she bid."

Charlotte glanced over her shoulder at Marcus. He lifted a brow in question. She shook her head to indicate she had no idea what they meant, and he gave her a look that said, "Yeah, right."

"Fern thinks she's staking her claim, making a statement."

Charlotte whipped around to stare over the hangers at Lilly. What claim? What statement? And what was so ridiculous about five thousand dollars?

"Hell of a loud statement," Henry said. "I'd be more inclined to say she's picked out her next conquest."

Marcus snorted in Charlotte's ear. She would have planted an elbow in his ribs, but she didn't want to give him the satisfaction of knowing his opinion mattered. Not when she'd convinced him it didn't and that she would gladly live up to her reputation.

Lilly shook her head vigorously, obviously warming to the topic. "I told Fern that Charlotte's probably just protecting her interest. There must be a little hanky panky already going on between those two, and she doesn't want anyone else interfering."

"Five hundred grand buys a whole lot of hanky panky."

Marcus's grip on her waist tightened, but Charlotte was too stunned to care. Five hundred grand? Did he say *five hundred grand*? No, no way. It had to be a mistake. Or gossip. Yes, that's it.

She slumped against Marcus, relief flooding her. The chain reaction of the rumor mill could distort the most innocent circumstances. She knew that firsthand. It stood to reason her fifty-thousand-dollar bid for the poor schmuck who'd been blackballed could have been inflated to...*five hundred thousand*. Couldn't it?

Charlotte's small moment of relief gave way to doubt, and doubt to agitation. Not that she minded shelling out that much money. She'd donated significantly more than that in the past. Her father's imprisonment hadn't touched her financially. She thanked her lucky stars every day that she and her mother had their own money from her maternal grandmother's estate.

What niggled at her self-assurance was that she would end up with a bachelor she didn't want, a man who thought she'd bid an exorbitant amount for him and would now have an overblown ego as well as misplaced expectations.

Henry pulled a fur coat identical to the one draped over his arm from the rack and, at Lilly's nod, made the exchange. "Hope he's got the stamina."

"That man has 'go-the-distance' written all over him. If I was twenty years younger and fifty pounds lighter, I'd give Charlotte a run for her money."

Charlotte perked up, ignoring Marcus's fingers as they dug into her waist. She leaned forward to hear the name of this sex god. Damn, she wished she'd paid more attention to the names on the top of the bidding sheets. Of course, Lilly's idea of a real man could vary a great deal from hers. He could be anyone.

"Why, Lilly, I'm wounded."

"Oh, like you wouldn't gladly volunteer every year if you thought one of those young tarts would bid on you."

Henry chuckled. "I wouldn't mind walking in this particular bachelor's shoes. Charlotte is one fine woman."

Lilly took her coat from Henry and turned toward the door. "You used to say that about me."

"Still do, darlin'," he said and swatted Lilly's well-padded backside.

Charlotte rolled her eyes, wishing they would hurry and leave. She was eager to find out what was going on and if there was any possible way out of it.

"So," Lilly paused at the door, "will you give me five minutes to see if Charlotte gets her man? You know you're as curious as I am."

"All right," Henry grumbled as if trying to convince his wife he wasn't at all interested. Then he sighed. "Yep, that Marcus Preston is one hell of a lucky man."

****

Shock surged through Marcus, holding him motionless, speechless, as the McAfees exited the closet. It wasn't until Charlotte thrust the coats aside and rushed forward that he was propelled into action.

He snagged the sleeve of her jacket in a tight grip. She had some explaining to do. "Where the hell do you think you're going?"

She tried to pry his fingers loose. "Let go of me." When he held tighter, she tugged her arm. "I've…" *tug* "got to…" *tug – tug* "stop this."

She gave one final jerk, and the momentum yanked Marcus forward. His hold on her sleeve broke as his forehead collided with the cross pole, causing him to bounce backward and lose his balance. He grasped the coats nearest, but they only slipped from their hangers, and his descent continued. His right shoulder banged the wall, and he landed on his ass, momentarily stunned and covered in an array of wool, leather, fur, and hangers.

"Sonuvabitch." He slung expensive garments and wooden hangers this way and that and scrambled from under the ones left hanging above him to his feet. As he raced out the door to catch up with her, he couldn't help but wonder if her last statement had been a confession. Had she really bid five hundred thousand dollars on him? Why would she do that?

Then he remembered the inviting smile she'd given him when he first entered the ballroom. And hadn't she admitted she'd been watching him throughout the evening? Had she decided to take their relationship—if you could call it that—in another direction, then changed her mind after what had just happened between them?

He didn't have time to consider how he felt about that or why the possibility sent a rush of adrenaline charging through him as he rounded the corner and saw Charlotte plow into Henry McAfee a few feet ahead. Henry fell against Lilly, sandwiching her between his wide girth and the wall.

"I'm so sorry." Charlotte pushed off Henry's arm, whirled toward the direction of the ballroom, and kept running.

Marcus reached to steady Henry, and with his own mumbled apology to Lilly, sprinted after Charlotte. Henry's "harrumph" and Lilly's "Well, I never" were quickly forgotten as he gained ground on Charlotte, whose high heels impeded her escape.

"Charlotte," he called as she paused in front of the open door of the ballroom.

She whipped around, pale blonde hair flying around her. Wide blue eyes filled with distress stared at him for a fraction of a second before she ducked inside.

Still in a run, Marcus tried to put on the brakes but between his slick-soled shoes and the wax on the floors, slid past the doorway and only managed to maintain his balance by grabbing the frame. "Fuck."

Mrs. Gardner, one of his mother's cronies, gave him a sharp look from just inside the door where she stood watch, probably to guard against party crashers.

He pulled himself upright and entered with as much composure as he could muster. His gaze darted left then right.

Where the hell was she?

He caught sight of her arguing vehemently with one of the women at the bidding tables. The woman pointed across the room, and Charlotte looked that way. He followed her line of vision to where Melody stretched to hand a stack of papers to a man on the stage.

The bidding sheets.

His gaze flew back to Charlotte, but she had already disappeared. A flash of gold in the crowd spurred him forward, and only then did the voice of the emcee register.

"And the moment we've all been waiting for…"

Marcus cut directly across the dance floor, skirting the immobile dancers. Several men with sly grins slapped him on the back as he went. A few women tried to block his path, but he sidestepped them.

The stage and Melody were just ahead, Charlotte even closer, when Natalie appeared before him. "Where have you been?"

He tried to move around her. "Not now, Nat."

She clung to his arm. "But I need to talk to you."

"I'll talk to you later." He glanced over her head and watched Charlotte fend off Harry Townsend's drunken advances. Marcus took a step forward, intent on smashing the bastard's face.

"Wait." Natalie hauled him back. "Do you know Charlotte Reese bid five hundred thousand dollars on you? She's made a fool of you in front of all these people."

He heard the tears in her voice, and since Charlotte had succeeded on her own to get past Harry, he focused on Nat once more.

"I tried to tell you earlier, but you wouldn't listen," she accused. "You were like a hound hot on the trail of a bitch in heat." She let go of him, and swiping a tear from her cheek, she eyed him up and down. "Well, I guess you found her."

As she marched away, Marcus felt a little guilty that he might have given her the impression he was interested, but mostly, he felt relieved that she now understood he wasn't. He sighed and rubbed his hands over his face. He really didn't have time for this.

"And our next bachelor..." the emcee's voice resounded above the buzzing crowd.

Marcus shot forward again and didn't stop until he stood directly behind Charlotte.

"I know I've donated more than that before." She placed her hands on her hips and bent slightly toward Melody. "That's not the point. You've got to stop this. It isn't right."

Melody shrugged. "Sorry, I can't. The bidding has concluded, and the results are fi—" She swallowed as her gaze met his over Charlotte's shoulder. "—nal."

Charlotte turned sideways to glare at him. "Do something."

He opened his mouth to ask her what the hell she thought he could do; she was the one who had gotten them into this situation. But the hairs on the back of his neck suddenly stood on end, and he became aware of the hushed whispers around them.

"Marcus Preston goes to..." the emcee's voice echoed from the stage and silence fell over the crowd, "...Charlotte Reese for five hundred thousand dollars."

Marcus groaned. Too late.

"No, this can't be happening." Charlotte's words were drowned out by assembly's applause, whistling, and cheers.

"Where are they, ladies and gentlemen? We need them on stage."

"Here. Here, they are," someone close shouted.

"Get them on the stage. We have to have them up here."

Charlotte shook her head, her eyes narrowed on Marcus. "I'm not going up there."

"What? You think I want to? I'm not—"

His next words were cut off when a pack of well-meaning acquaintances waylaid him from behind and carted him toward the steps. He could demand his release or shake them off, but there didn't seem much point in either. The damage was done. The only thing to do now was figure a way to play this thing through without adding to it.

Released beside the podium, Marcus heard Charlotte screech and moved to take her from two overzealous teens. The scowl on his face must have scared them because they shoved her toward him and hightailed it off the stage. He caught her upper arms and steadied her. As angry as he was with her, he couldn't stand to see her manhandled.

"Geez," Charlotte whispered as she pushed her hair from her face. "How could this have happened?"

Marcus wondered the same thing as the emcee waved a hand toward them and began his speech. "Clearly, Charlotte was determined to get her hands on Marcus. Not only—"

"Looks like she already has," someone yelled from somewhere near the stage.

A roar of laughter followed, and Marcus looked at Charlotte's silvery blonde hair, matted from when his hands had made themselves at home. The absence of the bright red lipstick she had worn earlier only accentuated her still puffy lips.

"What happened to your cummerbund, Marcus?" shouted another heckler.

Marcus released Charlotte and stepped back to check out his cummerbund. Its metal hook caught on the gold button of her jacket then snapped free, popping him in the stomach. He bit back a curse as he rearranged his cummerbund, which had somehow—and he hated to think how—gotten turned around, facing backward.

He heard her gasp but was more concerned with the humiliation of his own dishabille to pay attention until she suddenly plastered herself against him, her arms wound tightly around his neck.

"What the hell?"

She shrugged and fingered his hair off his forehead. "I'm thinking our only alternative is to go along, play to the crowd."

A familiar voice boomed above the noise. "Where's your bow tie?"

"Bet Charlotte knows," someone answered.

Charlotte tilted her head back and toward their audience. With a lazy smile, she stuck her hand in his jacket pocket, pulled out his tie, and dangled it for all to see.

A multitude of bright lights flashed as picture after picture was taken, and the curse he'd held back earlier escaped. Not that anyone could have heard for all the whooping and hollering going on.

He grabbed the black ribbon and stuck it back in his pocket. He hadn't even known she'd removed the damn thing. How had she gotten it in his pocket without him knowing? Stupid question. She could have done anything to him, and he wouldn't have known it in that moment she'd played with his cock.

What the hell was her game? If she *had* bid on him, had she done it just to humiliate him? If so, it was sure as fuck working.

"As I was saying, not only did Charlotte break the record for the least number of bids on a bachelor, but Marcus now becomes the highest priced bachelor this auction has ever known. The children at…"

Marcus lost interest in the emcee when Charlotte nuzzled his neck. He jerked his head away and tried to step back, but she held on tight, causing him to stumble. His hands fell to her waist as they regained their balance. Damn, when had he become so clumsy?

"What's the matter Marcus? Can't you handle her?"

Marcus tried to locate the joker in the back of the room, but it was impossible with camera flashes going off. His anger once again rose to overshadow shock and embarrassment. He returned his attention to the cause of his humiliation. "Would you mind telling me what the hell you're doing?"

She smiled seductively, continuing to play to the crowd. "Paying you back."

His jaw clenched tighter. "For what?"

"Someone altered my bid." Her finger twirled around the hair at the back of his neck. "I think maybe it was you."

Of all the things she could be paying him back for, that wasn't one of them. "Why would I do that?"

She leaned in close, her angry whisper betraying the sultry expression she presented to the crowd. "You tell me. You're the one who chased me down. You're the one who had your hands all over me in the closet."

"I already told you I followed you to apologize, and I seem to remember an invitation."

She glanced at his mouth, and her smile widened. "And I seem to remember how quick you were to accept."

The fact that he couldn't deny her statement pissed him off. He'd been a fool to let lust rule his actions. "That doesn't mean I can't put a stop to this farce right now."

Her blue eyes clouded then hardened. "Yes, you could walk away. We both know you're damn good at that."

An invisible fist punched him right in the gut. He had hurt her. All night long, he had tried to find the right time, the right place to apologize, and yet with every word, with every action, he'd managed to inflict more pain. Still, he hated the position she'd put him in and couldn't find the forbearance to take it all back.

"But you won't walk away," she went on. "You can't. Not this time."

Her cocky self-assurance irritated Marcus enough to make him feel somewhat justified in his callous behavior. "What's to stop me?"

"Pride."

"Believe me, I've dealt with wounded pride before. I'll weather it a lot better than you."

"True." She bit her lip. "But there's another reason you can't leave me standing here."

"What's that?"

"My missing button."

Chapter Four

"There has to be something in here I can use." Charlotte held her jacket together with one hand as she searched the desk drawer in the country club manager's office.

"If you would wear clothes that actually cover you, you wouldn't be in this predicament," Marcus grumbled from where he leaned one hip against the other side of the desk.

"I was doing just fine until your stupid cummerbund caught on my button." She knew she should thank him for continuing the pretense she'd begun on stage, and not just because of her missing button. He could have rejected her again, this time humiliating her in front of Houston's elite, but he hadn't. Probably that innate sense of chivalry he clung to. Whatever his reasons, he'd played along until they were finally escorted off stage.

Oh, man had he ever. He had turned the table on her, kicking up the heat of their charade without ever laying a hand on her. Even now she could feel the hot imprint of his eyes as he'd looked at her while doing his best to remain a gentleman. Yet, despite the stoic performance he'd given the audience, the evidence of his desire had told her a different story as she pressed against him to keep her jacket closed.

"Things like that ought to come with a safety chain."

She grinned in spite of herself. "You didn't think so in the closet."

He peered over the copy of the bidding sheet he'd received from the emcee. For just a moment, his green eyes darkened, and Charlotte was certain he remembered how he'd taken advantage of that lone button.

Then his gaze cooled, and he thrust the sheet in front of her. "Is this your signature?"

She glanced at the handwriting before turning her attention back to the contents of the lap drawer. "Yes, but that's not what I bid."

"So you say," he muttered under his breath.

"What's that supposed to mean?" She grabbed a gator clip and used it to clasp the edges of her jacket.

"You said yourself you were paying me back."

"That was before I realized you weren't responsible for this fiasco." She stretched her arms back to test the reliability of the temporary solution. The metal clip slipped off one side of the slick material, and she barely managed to keep from exposing herself to Marcus. Again.

She glanced to see if he'd noticed and sighed with relief. He was lost in thought, still frowning at the bid sheet.

"I'm not talking about responsibility for the auction or what happened in the closet," he said, his voice somber. He looked up, his serious gaze locking with hers. "I'm talking about what happened the night of the mayor's party. All of this could have been set up by you to get back at me."

Charlotte stared open-mouthed for a moment, amazed at his oversized ego, then she shook her head and tossed the clip in the drawer. "You certainly think a lot of yourself."

Or very little of me.

As the thought skittered through her mind, she recognized its truth. She'd known it, of course, and many times used his low opinion to her benefit. Still, the surge of hurt caught her unaware, as did the burning sensation behind her eyes.

Needing to get away before she did something

stupid, like cry in front of him, Charlotte slammed the drawer and strode around the desk on her way to the door.

Marcus stepped in front of her, grasping her arm. "What am I supposed to think? I said a lot of things I shouldn't have that night, things you'd probably want to get back at me for. I'd say the humiliation I just endured in front of half of Houston's society is one hell of a payback."

"Sounds like a good plan; wish I'd thought of it. But I assure you, I had nothing to do with it."

"Who else would gain from doing something like this?"

"I would."

Charlotte and Marcus turned as one to face Melody who stood just inside the door, Spencer, Nick and Avery behind her. Charlotte wondered how long they'd been there and if they heard Marcus's mention of the incident at the mayor's party. She hadn't been able to confide that particular event to Melody. Hell, she tried to pretend it never happened.

Marcus released her and shifted slightly away as the foursome moved into the room.

Charlotte focused on her friend's guilty expression. "Geez, Mel, tell me you didn't have anything to do with this."

"Here, pull yourself together," Melody said, handing Charlotte a safety pin. She waved a tissue at Marcus. "Clean the lipstick off your face."

Marcus dabbed at his mouth and cursed when the tissue came away stained with red. He glared at Charlotte. "You could have said something."

She dangled the safety pin at him. "I had my own problems."

He pulled a handkerchief from his pocket and moved aside to finish wiping away the evidence of their passionate interlude. If only she could wipe away the memory as easily.

"I had to do something," Melody said, drawing Charlotte's attention. "It's obvious you two are made for each other, but at the rate you were going, you'd never have gotten together. I thought you needed a little help."

"More like a miracle," Charlotte mumbled as she pinned her jacket together.

She had hoped it was all just a big mistake, better yet a nightmare she would soon wake from. But she should have known better. Especially when Melody had become such a romantic since her engagement to Spencer, crooning on and on about love and marriage and happily ever after. Charlotte didn't believe in those things but humored her friend by pretending to understand.

"I don't get it," Marcus said, the rasp of his voice indicating the restraint he tried to preserve. "Are you saying *you* did this?"

Melody gave him a crooked grin. "Yes, and I'm not sorry. You two were beyond hopeless."

The vein on Marcus's neck bulged, and Charlotte readied herself for an explosion, yet his voice remained deceptively calm. "How could you do this?"

Melody swept a hand down the back of her gown and settled into one of the wingback chairs near the fireplace before she met Marcus's gaze. "I simply added a couple of zeros to Charlotte's opening bid."

"I meant why?" Marcus asked through clenched teeth, then held up his hand. "No, don't answer that."

Charlotte inhaled deeply, relieved he'd changed his mind about wanting to know the *whys* of the situation. Melody probably wouldn't hesitate to offer her theories on Charlotte's feelings for him.

"Just tell me this," Marcus said. "What gave you the right to play with my life?"

Spencer moved to stand between Melody and Marcus. "If you want to take your anger out on someone, take it out on me. I had as much to do with it as Melody. We all did."

"What are you saying?"

"We fixed it so that no matter which straw you drew, you'd get the short one."

Avery stepped forward from where he'd been leaning against the glass trophy case. He pulled his hands out of his pockets, revealing a straw in each hand. He held up the shortest. "We all drew the same size." He indicated the other. "We had longer ones in our pockets. You were so busy checking out yours, you didn't see us switch."

"You set me up?" Marcus asked, looking from one brother to the other, each admitting their part with a nod.

The stunned disbelief in his voice echoed Charlotte's thoughts. It was bad enough to know she'd been the target of Melody's misguided matchmaking, but to know Marcus's brothers were in on it as well was beyond belief. She cringed inwardly at the thought that they believed as Melody did. That she had feelings for Marcus.

"How could you do that to me?" Marcus slapped the bidding sheet with the back of his hand. "And in such a way that would draw the attention of everyone we know." He began to pace, his voice rising with each step. "I mean five hundred thousand dollars. You might as well hang a sign around my neck that says, 'Stud Service' because everyone now thinks I'm Charlotte's next fuck."

Four pairs of sympathetic eyes glanced her way, but Charlotte refused to let them see how much his crude words hurt, that with each syllable he opened a new wound.

With a stiff shrug and a forced smile, she said, "I'm sure you all meant well, but you can see we don't exactly get along."

"And you." Marcus turned to point a finger at her before continuing his rampage. "Climbing all over me in front of everyone when I've gone out of my way to keep any contact between us discreet. If I'd wanted my name added to your list of conquests, I'd have stood in line a long time ago."

Charlotte flinched.

Melody gasped.

Spencer and Avery both took a step toward Marcus.

Nick even straightened from his casual pose against the mantle. "Apologize to Charlotte."

Charlotte tightened her grip on the chair as Marcus swung stiffly to face her. His dark green eyes bore into hers. She arched a brow, and it took every ounce of strength she possessed not to look away, to show him she was indifferent to his hateful words.

Then his features softened, his anger replaced by chagrin, and she knew she hadn't pulled it off. He'd seen right through her. Damn, she hated revealing her weaknesses, especially to him.

"Sorry. No matter what's happened, I shouldn't have said that."

She waved a hand and circled the chair. She could have argued that he didn't know as much about her as he thought, but what would be the point when he believed exactly what she wanted him to. "Don't apologize for how you feel."

To avoid looking at him, or anyone else, and before her knees gave out from under her, she eased into the chair, making a show of getting comfortable. "At least with you, I know where I stand. That's more than I can say for most of the men I know."

An uncomfortable silence fell over the room until Melody leaned forward, placing a hand on Charlotte's knee. "You have to believe we only did what we thought best."

"Best for whom?" Marcus grumbled.

Melody sat back in her chair. "For the two of you."

"Hmph." Marcus wadded the bidding sheet in his

hand and tossed it into the wastebasket beside the desk. "Well, you can count me out. The fact that the bid was altered nullifies any agreement I might have made," he looked pointedly at Spencer, "had I been selected fairly."

Spencer nodded. "You're right. You don't have to follow through."

"No, he doesn't," Nick said. "But one of us will. Preston Enterprises can't afford any negative publicity."

Melody turned to face him. "But Marcus was the bachelor on the block."

Nick shrugged. "We could always make up a story about an emergency business trip that prevents him from fulfilling his promise."

Marcus muttered a curse and rubbed the back of his neck. Charlotte also understood what Nick meant and wondered if Marcus would cave to the pressure or if he would take advantage of the opportunity and bow out, leaving her to spend time with one of his brothers. Part of her hoped he'd cling to righteous indignation, while another part longed for the opportunity of revenge for the things he'd said and done tonight.

"Hey," Avery nodded. "I'll do it."

When Marcus remained silent, she assumed he'd made his decision. She waited for relief to set in, but an ache lodged itself so deep in her chest that she found it hard to breathe.

"It'll be fun," Avery continued, his enthusiasm growing. "We'll have a great time. Won't we, darlin'?"

She attempted a saucy grin to match his but knew she fell short. "I'm sure we'll find something to occupy our time."

He slapped his hands, rubbing them together as he started toward her. "It's settled then—"

"No." Marcus caught his brother's arm. "You won't."

Avery's grin widened. "Change your mind?"

Marcus ignored the taunt. "I don't like being manipulated like this, but I was the bachelor auctioned. If I don't follow through, someone might find out the truth."

"That's true," Nick said. "If word of how we fixed the auction reached the press, funds could be withdrawn and the children would be the ones to suffer. Preston Enterprises would also find itself involved in another scandal."

Marcus looked pointedly at Charlotte. "The company's been dragged through enough mud in the last few months."

The reference to her father's attempt to sabotage Preston Enterprises wasn't lost on Charlotte. As he intended, she was flooded with guilt. Still, she did her best to pretend otherwise and pasted a bright smile on her face. "Hey, it's no big deal. We can arrange to have our picture taken while we have dinner. Surely, we can manage that. Two hours together tops, and we can go our separate ways."

Spencer cleared his throat. She looked at Melody, who shifted her gaze toward the empty fireplace.

Dread lodged in Charlotte's chest. "What?"

"We figured this was exactly the reaction we'd get from you two," Spencer explained. "So we brought in extra sponsors, promising them a high-profile couple on a weekend trip to Aspen."

The band around Charlotte's chest grew tighter. "And you guaranteed Marcus and I would be that couple with the five-hundred-thousand-dollar bid."

Melody nodded.

Charlotte slumped against the chair and closed her eyes, suddenly weary. If she was this tired after only one evening of trying to keep up her guard in Marcus's company, how would she ever make it through an entire weekend? Just thinking about it exhausted her. "How many sponsors are we talking, Mel?"

"Five, possibly six."

Charlotte sensed Marcus's presence near her chair, felt him draw near before she heard his voice. "Excuse me, but would someone mind telling me what the hell all this means?"

"It means," Charlotte opened her eyes and locked gazes with him, "that each sponsor will want their own photos. It means we'll be forced together on at least five different occasions throughout the weekend."

He turned to the others. "Is this true?"

Melody nodded. "They won't want to run the same publicity shot as everyone else. They'll want theirs to be unique, down to the slightest article of clothing. They'll be hoping for something better than everyone else's."

Charlotte flinched at the string of curses Marcus let fly as he stalked past her. A second later, the door slammed. Like she'd said, he was damn good at walking away, getting better with all the practice she was giving him. Good thing this time would probably be the last.

She tilted a glance toward Avery and smiled. "Well, it looks like we'll be having that good time after all."

He laughed. "Charlotte, darlin', as much as I'd like to spend a weekend painting the town with you, it'll never happen."

"But you said—"

"Yes, but you heard Marcus. He said he'd do it."

Charlotte snorted. "I don't think so."

"Believe me, he'll do it," Avery said. "Whether he admits it or not, you're under his skin, and he can't stand the idea of anyone else near you."

A glance at the rest of the conspirators showed they agreed, and Charlotte had to wonder if Marcus was really that angry about having to spend time with her. Or if perhaps he was afraid. Afraid of what might happen between them if he did. After all, every time they'd been alone, which had only been twice, they ended up hot and heavy.

She thought about those moments in the closet. He had condemned her in one breath. In the next, he had stolen hers with a kiss that melted any resistance she might have offered. He had pushed the limits, taken what he could in the limited privacy allotted, then stopped the minute they were alone again, prepared to walk away. Just as he had before.

Charlotte released a long, pent-up breath and shook her head. "I'm sorry to disappoint your efforts at matchmaking, but I just don't think it's going to work."

"Avery's right. Marcus will do it," Melody said. She scooted to the edge of her chair. "I want you to remember what we discussed earlier this evening about using this opportunity to—"

"Yes, Mel, I remember." Charlotte glanced pointedly at the others who looked on with interest. She was sure Melody would tell them exactly what she meant later if she hadn't already, but for now, Charlotte could pretend otherwise and retain some semblance of dignity.

Sighing, she closed her eyes and recalled Melody's words.

What better way to show him what you're really like?

No. Hell no. She didn't want that.

Okay, then think of it this way. Being confined with Marcus for a few days on a cruise ship or at a secluded ski lodge is a sure-fire chance to work your wiles on him. You could get him out of your system once and for all.

Melody was right about one thing. She needed to get Marcus out of her system. Until she did, she would never be happy with the solitary life she'd chosen.

What better way to do it than to actually have him in a position guaranteed to keep him constantly within reach? For all that he tried to be different, he was only a man, and when it came down to it, lust overpowered the strongest will, given the opportunity.

Charlotte felt the corners of her lips tilt upward. She could do it. She could seduce Marcus, have a wild weekend full of hot and steamy sex, and finally get him out of her system.

And once she did, *she* would be the one to walk away.

Chapter Five

On Thursday morning, almost a week after the bachelor auction, Marcus entered St. Anne's Hospital for the first of many embarrassingly difficult publicity appearances as Charlotte's bought-and-paid-for bachelor. He still hadn't gotten past the fact that he'd been backed into a corner—trapped no less—by those he trusted. They'd known just which buttons to push to ensure his cooperation.

Using the threat to Preston Enterprises and the children's benefit had been irritating but understandable. He had always considered himself an honorable man. But knowing they'd guessed his secret, an unwanted attraction to Charlotte, was humiliating. More so, they'd known he would never stand for one of them assuming the role of auctioned bachelor and spending a weekend with her. For a moment, he'd almost let pride overrule honor.

He cringed every time he thought how close he'd come to calling their bluff. God knew he'd wanted to. But there was no way in hell he could let Avery take his place. His younger brother got along with Charlotte too damn well. No telling what kind of trouble they'd get into.

Marcus had almost insisted Nick step up to the plate since he'd recently sworn off women but reconsidered after a brief glance at Charlotte. If she had an entire weekend to work her wiles, even Nick might succumb to temptation. The only brother he figured she couldn't and wouldn't try to seduce was Spencer. Somehow, Marcus didn't think Melody would agree to that solution.

Pausing in front of the swinging doors that led to the game room for the children of the burn unit, Marcus tried to collect himself. He hated that he even gave a damn who Charlotte seduced. But it had bothered him over the years, watching her flirt and flaunt and literally fall into men's laps. He'd tried not to imagine what she did with them in private.

Then things had changed. He had changed. Since the night of July fourth at the mayor's party when she'd come apart in his arms, he hadn't been able to think about much else. Just the idea of her with another man made him crazy. And that pissed him off more than anything.

Over the last few days, he had dealt with this realization—or tried to—and had come to the conclusion that the only way to survive the weekend with Charlotte was to avoid her. He would do no more and no less than necessary to fulfill his obligation as bachelor. She was on her own, and he would tell her exactly that given the first opportunity.

Dragging in a deep breath, he pushed the doors open and stepped inside, prepared to face yet another humiliation. The scene that greeted him caused all frustration with Charlotte and anger at himself to dissipate. Whatever his problems, they paled in comparison to ones faced by the innocents staring back at him with curious but wary eyes.

In one quick glance, he took in the group of bachelors and their buyers who hovered in one corner while the children stood stiffly in another next to a massive artificial Christmas tree. The only sound in the room came from a photographer as he busied himself setting up equipment beneath large silver umbrellas. It seemed Melody had yet to arrive with the gifts from the children's foundation, and if he knew Charlotte, she'd be late for no other reason than to make a grand entrance.

Marcus started to join his acquaintances, but the

smug look on Daphne Cohen's face made him hesitate. Peter Dawson stood beside her, grinning like an idiot as he waved Marcus over. Marcus knew damned well they couldn't wait to offer their two cents on the subject of him and Charlotte.

It was all he'd heard since the bachelor auction. Everyone wanted to know what was going on between them, if he thought he could tame her, some even suggesting ways to go about it. Dawson had a loudmouth and wouldn't care what he said or whether the children across the room heard.

Marcus dismissed Houston's elite in favor of more interesting company and strolled slowly toward the children. They perked as he neared, their eyes round with cautious anticipation. He stopped to linger in front of the fake pine.

"Pretty tree," he said, fingering a paper snowman covered with silver glitter. "You guys make these ornaments?"

"I made that one," a tiny voice answered.

Marcus looked down to the elfin figure beside him and couldn't stop the raw emotion that raged through him. Tight blonde curls haloed one half of her head, enhancing angelic blue eyes that peered up at him with timid curiosity. He fought the anger and revulsion he hoped was only natural when faced with such tragically marred beauty.

Squatting beside her, he braced his forearms on knees and grinned. "I sure like snowmen. Especially this one."

That garnered a smile, so he asked, "What's your name?"

"Amy."

"Well, now, Amy. My name is Marcus, and do you know the only thing I like better than snowmen?"

Amy shook her head.

He reached to tuck a lock of gold behind the nub of scarred tissue that should have been a shell of soft flesh, and her eyes flared wider than he thought possible. His heart wrenched, and he swallowed the lump in his throat. "Guess."

She tilted her head to one side, lips pinched in avid concentration. Then, her eyes brightened, and she whispered, her voice filled with awe, "Charlotte."

Marcus had been so intent on her reaction to his touch that, at first, her answer didn't register. He frowned and, for a second, wondered if his brothers had set him up again. "Uh—"

"Charlotte!"

Amy skittered around him and almost fell when one of the other kids bumped against her in his rush to get by. Marcus caught her, but she wriggled loose, determined to follow the rest of the children as they swarmed past him, all squealing and yelling Charlotte's name.

Marcus swiveled on booted heels and nearly fell on his ass.

The forlorn waifs he'd thought to make comfortable had become a bunch of excited, jabbering jumping beans, each clamoring for Charlotte's attention. As if she were their pagan goddess and her very touch would somehow make them whole again. The similarity between himself and these children suddenly struck him. The only times he had ever felt complete were when he'd held Charlotte in his arms.

Rejecting the idea, Marcus rose to his feet and brushed glitter from his jeans. As the little nymphs tugged Charlotte toward him, he got his first really good glimpse of the woman who enthralled them.

He had never seen her look anything but provocative, yet there she stood, a vision of refined loveliness in black wool slacks and a red cashmere sweater with pearl buttons done up to her throat. She wore her long silvery-blonde hair swept into some kind of twist, held in place with a clip made of pearls that matched the ones on her ears. Damn, even dressed in sophisticated elegance she exuded a sensual air.

"Close your mouth, Marcus."

Melody's whisper behind him came just in time to save him from total embarrassment. Still, he couldn't pry his gaze from Charlotte and her escorts.

"What are you doing here today?" one of the older girls asked Charlotte as they drew near.

Today? Marcus frowned, still trying to figure out how these kids knew her.

She smiled and took the girl's hand. "I'm here for the promotion, Sarah. Just like you guys." Her soft voice held only a hint of her usual sultry drawl and none of the sarcasm.

"Are you going to read us a story?" asked a freckled face boy with bandages on both hands.

A story? Marcus figured the only stories Charlotte knew were the dirty limericks he'd heard her recite at one of Avery's frat parties.

She reached to ruffle the boy's hair. "Oh, baby, I'm sorry. I didn't bring a book today."

Amy tugged on Charlotte's sweater. "I want you to meet somebody."

Charlotte let go of Sarah's hand and stooped to lift Amy in her arms, kissing her on the rosy cheek untouched by scars. "Sure, sweetie. Who is it?"

Amy's gaze landed on Marcus as she pointed a stubby finger toward him. "He's my new friend."

Marcus waited for Charlotte's cutting remark and was surprised when she said, "Then you're a lucky girl. Marcus is a good friend to have."

"You know him?" Sarah asked, eyeing him a bit more favorably than she had when he first entered the room. It seemed their goddess held a lot of sway over whom they accepted and didn't. He probably ought to feel honored that she deigned to grant him approval. Funny thing was, he did.

Charlotte turned her attention to Sarah. "Mmmhmm. We're here to have our picture made together."

"Not everyone's here, Char," Melody said behind him. "You've got time for a story."

Charlotte's smooth composure was at odds with the blush that crept up her neck and cheeks. "Oh, I'm sure whoever's late will be here shortly."

The little boy who wanted her to read pounced on the opportunity, determined to have his way. "Please, Charlotte, tell us a story, please."

The group erupted into loud pleas, and when Charlotte's flustered gaze met his, Marcus added his own. "Yes, Charlotte, tell us a story. Please."

She lifted a finely arched brow, and her full red lips thinned into a smirk that said she'd pay him back in spades. "All right, let's get settled."

He chuckled at the squeals of delight and turned to leave the little pagans to their goddess of storytelling.

"Not so fast buster." Melody grabbed his arm. "I need help putting gifts around the tree and hanging ornaments."

Marcus started to tell her she hadn't yet gained his forgiveness when a small hand slipped into his.

"Don't go." Amy's little voice reached up to seize his heart, and there was no way in the world he could have walked away from those huge needful blue eyes.

Again, he had to swallow the rise of emotion in his throat. "No, darlin', I won't leave. I'll be right here, helping Melody."

She smiled a crooked smile, all that the scarred half of her face would allow, before returning to the group gathered on the floor not six feet away. She tiptoed her way over the others and crawled into Charlotte's lap.

Charlotte wrapped her arms around the little girl and lifted a misty gaze to his. Then she cleared her throat and smiled at the children. "So how about *Jack and the Beanstalk*?"

Amy squirmed in her lap to look up at her. "No, tell the one about the beast."

"Sweetie, that one's kind of long."

"That's okay," Sarah said. "I know it by heart. What you don't get to I'll finish later."

Charlotte bit her lip, and Marcus wondered at her obvious reluctance to tell this particular tale.

"Very well," Charlotte glared past him at Melody, then softened her expression. "The beast it is."

"Are you going to stand there all day?"

He turned back to Melody, who, by the smug expression on her face, had no doubt noticed him held spellbound by the entire scene. She thrust an ornament at him. "Here, make yourself useful. I can't reach the top."

He took the ornament, a clear glass globe with shredded strips of silver and gold stuffed inside and the name "Sarah Talbert" written on the outside. He stretched to place the glittering ball near the top of the tree, then paused to look at it.

Would Sarah spend the holidays at the hospital or at home with her family? He hated the idea of any of these children here and alone at Christmas.

"Once long ago," Charlotte began her story, "there was a handsome prince who was very spoiled and self-centered. His name was...Phillip. One—"

"No, no, Charlotte," Amy chirped. "His name wasn't Phillip."

"I-it wasn't?"

"It never has been before. The prince's name has always been Marcocius, kind of like Marcus."

Marcus jerked his head around and caught Charlotte's jittery gaze. She smiled nervously. "Isn't that amazing?"

"Here." Melody handed him another ornament. "Get busy. You're much too slow."

Recognizing her attempt to keep him occupied, Marcus stifled his suspicions and took the ornament.

He read the name, not one he could put to a face but one who no doubt had his own story.

"One day, an ugly witch came to the castle, begging for food and a place to stay for the night."

"And her name was Charliss," Amy inserted.

Marcus paused in mid stretch. He tilted a look over his shoulder, but this time, Charlotte refused to glance his way.

"When the prince selfishly refused to let the witch—"

"Charliss."

"—stay in his castle," she paused, then with a pained expression, continued, "Charliss...put a curse on him."

She had his full attention now.

"She turned him into a horrible beast, saying that since he was so ugly on the inside, everyone would see his true nature until he learned to be kind and considerate to others. After everyone ran from him, frightened by his beastly appearance and ferocious roar—" She snarled and growled. "—the witch transformed into a beautiful lady."

"To show him what she was on the inside," Sarah supplied. "Then she left him, and he was all alone for a long time."

Melody poked him in the ribs. "Are you going to help me or what?"

He realized he was scowling and tried to smooth his features, afraid the similarities between him and Charlotte's prince would suddenly dawn on the kids. He didn't think he could bear for little Amy to look at him as if he were a beast.

"It's just a story, Marcus," Melody said. "The kids like it because it helps them focus on what's inside instead of worrying about their outward appearance."

He grunted. "I suppose Charlotte supplied the names."

Melody smiled, giving him his answer.

He rubbed a hand over his jaw, then through his hair as if he might have suddenly grown a shaggy beard and mane. "Do I really act like a beast?"

"When I first met you, I thought you were a teddy bear."

"But?"

"Well, to be honest, the last few months, since the party at the mayor's house, you've been a real grouch. That's why—"

"Don't go there, Mel," he warned. "I haven't forgiven you for your part in all this."

She sighed, then shrugged and turned back to the tree. "You will when you finally get your head out of your ass and see the truth. You might have been the prince in that story, but Charlotte assigned herself the role of the witch."

"What's that supposed to mean?" When she only shrugged again, he pressed for an answer. "Are you telling me Charlotte isn't what she seems?"

Not that it was the first time he wondered if he'd been right all those years ago when he first met Charlotte. He was at one of Avery's frat parties, and he'd watched her all night. He'd seen her mask slip when she thought no one was looking. She'd seemed almost tired, as if it took every ounce of energy to keep up the façade. He'd been certain there was more to her than she allowed everyone to see, more than the flamboyant personality and outrageous clothing. That beneath her flirtatious manner and sultry smile lay a frightened and vulnerable soul.

In the next moment, he'd been sure he was mistaken when she began to dance on the coffee table, drawing the attention of every male in the room as she writhed to the music in the skimpiest dress he'd ever seen. He'd written his assumption off as a trick of the lights.

"If you really want to know," Melody said. "You'll use your time together to figure it out."

She left him to ponder that bit of advice, and Marcus wanted to growl like the beast he'd been compared to as he turned to hang the rest of the ornaments. He should have known he wouldn't get a straight answer from Charlotte's best friend and loyal protector.

He slanted a peek at the woman who had become an enigma to him. Sitting on the floor amongst children the other high society women in the room hadn't known how to deal with, she appeared the epitome of a true and compassionate lady. Exactly the kind of woman he had always intended to choose as a wife.

Yet, not for one moment did he believe she had changed just because she hid her feelings from the children. Her praise of him to Amy hadn't been real. Nor did he think she'd forgiven him for the things he'd said to her the night of the auction. He winced, remembering some of them. While he *had* apologized, hell, he hadn't meant it. Only at Nick's insistence had Marcus realized she too had been deceived and was paying the consequences. And that his manners bordered on atrocious.

Still, if Melody's implication and his own gut instinct could be counted on, then the things he had learned about Charlotte today might be worth exploring. Of course, he had his work cut out for him. It would take some digging. But he intended to peel away her exterior layers one by one, stripping her bare if need be, until certain he had completely exposed the woman beneath, leaving her nothing to hide behind.

Marcus caught himself smiling and shook his head. What the hell did he have to be so happy about? He could only accomplish the task *if* he could get past her anger over the way he'd treated her. And *if* he could control his libido when she reverted to her usual relentless aggression and her naturally sensual behavior.

He groaned at the prospect of going up against

Charlotte again. It was the hardest thing he'd ever done; he almost hadn't survived. But by God, he had, and he'd proven he could be selfless. Hell, he deserved a fucking medal for his sacrifice in the garden. If he could do that, he could manage anything. He could resist temptation—heaven help him—and show her once and for all, she didn't have to flaunt her charms to gain a man's attention, that she had more to offer than her body.

And if only for the sake of his injured pride, he would prove to Charliss that Marcocious wasn't so beastly after all.

Chapter Six

He'd invaded her territory.

In one afternoon, Marcus had wedged himself between her and these children, the closest she would have to her own. He had infiltrated the hospital—her refuge—the only place she felt safe enough to let down her guard. He had invaded it, the same as he had her every waking thought. Geez, he had even taken control of her dreams.

His deep, throaty laughter rose above the children's giggles and shrieks, making Charlotte resent him all the more. She glanced over her shoulder to where he sat in her designated neon-green beanbag chair, sharing in the excitement of a new video game with *her* children.

Amy, imp that she was, leaned over his back, her tiny arms wrapped around his neck. With his freckled face turned toward Marcus, Dylan's eyes were glued to the man, rather than the television screen, with something akin to hero worship. And Sarah, bless her heart, tried her best not to reveal a quickly developing crush.

Charlotte frowned. She could see the attachments forming and knew the children would end up hurt if he stayed much longer. They didn't know this was a one-time visit for Marcus, that once he left, he would never return. She hadn't been able to save herself from the sting of his rejection, but she refused to let them experience it.

"He's waiting for you."

Charlotte spun to find Melody studying her over the promotional contracts and liability release forms the other bidders and bachelors had signed before they left. "Why do you say that?"

"He's intrigued. He's seen a side of you today you don't allow many to see."

Another reason to resent him. "Yeah, well, I didn't have much choice."

The past three hours she'd been trapped in a web of her own making. Because of the children, she hadn't had the luxury of hiding behind witty sarcasm or sexual banter. To become someone else, especially a slutty flirt, would confuse them and damage their faith in themselves to judge who they could accept at face value. She'd had no choice but to remain open, her defenses down, and could only hope most of those assembled here today were too self-involved to notice.

She rubbed her temples to relieve some of the pressure and tugged at the neck of her sweater. After an hour of smiling on demand then posing in way too close a proximity to Marcus for the publicity photos, her nerves were frayed to a fine, strained thread. All she wanted was to get the hell out of Dodge while the getting was good, while he was occupied.

Charlotte handed Melody her own contract, which she had signed against her better judgment. She wished she could tear it up and forget the whole thing. Especially her plan to seduce Marcus. Only the thought of the children and what this promotion meant to them kept her from doing so. "If you don't need me anymore, I'm out of here. I've got a killer headache, a paper to write, and a ton of packing to do."

"I'll see you in the morning. Bright and early," Melody said, then surprised Charlotte by grabbing her hand. "Give Marcus a chance. Get to know him."

Charlotte laughed and picked up her black leather purse and matching calf-length overcoat. "Why Melody, that's what this weekend is all about. And believe me, I plan to get to know him very well."

Before Melody could admonish her, Charlotte

turned away and headed across the room. As much as she wanted to hit the door running, she couldn't leave without telling the kids good-bye. She'd be damned if she would allow Marcus to cause her to be the one to bring them more pain.

As she drew closer, he glanced in her direction almost as if he'd been aware of her the entire time. His smile was genuine, similar to the ones he'd bestowed on the children. The warmth of it poured over her like hot fudge on soft-serve ice cream. She'd always been a sucker for chocolate. "I'm sorry to interrupt, but I wanted to say good-bye to the children."

"That's my cue." He passed Dylan the controls to the video game and stood, gently lowering Amy from his back to the deep indentation he'd left in the beanbag chair. "Can't have a pretty lady walking to her car alone in the dark. Can we, kids?"

Amy squealed in delight. Sarah sighed dreamily and held out the brown leather jacket she had been hugging to her chest while the rest agreed heartily with their new knight in shining armor.

Charlotte refrained from rolling her eyes and managed a smile. "That's really not necessary. It's not dark yet."

"Close enough."

His expression made it clear his mind was made up so instead of arguing in front of the children, she hugged each one and promised to see them next week. At least in accepting his escort, she'd get him away from the kids before they were sucked in further by his charm.

He fell into place beside her, and Charlotte tried to keep her pace casual and unhurried. But when his hand settled at the small of her back, branding her, she felt as if time slowed to a crawl and the door lurked a hundred miles away. The same heat that rushed through her veins earlier when the photographer had draped Marcus's arm around her seeped slowly over her skin, giving rise to hundreds of goose bumps.

As they neared the exit to the unit, the glass door swung open. Spencer smiled in greeting as he stepped inside, holding the door ajar with one hand. "Hey, Charlotte. Ready for your trip?"

With Marcus behind her, hovering close, the scent of his cologne enveloping her, the urge to run overwhelmed her. "Um, no. As a matter of fact, I've got a lot of packing to do. Better get a move on." She ducked under Spencer's arm and twisted to wave good-bye. "See you later."

Marcus started to follow, but Spencer caught his arm. "Avery tried calling you on your cell phone."

"I turned it off during the shoot. What's up?"

Charlotte didn't stay to hear Spencer's reply. Hurrying down the corridor, she didn't stop until she turned the corner and came to the elevators. She pushed the call button and plucked at her sweater, suddenly hot. Blowing out a long breath, she unbuttoned the top two buttons, then a third.

She'd never felt so off balance. Marcus had a way of doing that to her. And though she had dealt with it many times in the past, today had been especially difficult. She had known it would be, had prepared for the inevitability of the children revealing her as a regular visitor.

What she hadn't been prepared for was the moment she had first entered the game room to find Marcus already present, hunkered down in front of Amy, tenderly brushing the hair from her face. She had been both touched and surprised but mostly just plain scared. She didn't like thinking of him as gentle and caring. It was much easier to believe his behavior was all an act. Problem was, those kids could smell insincerity a mile away, yet they had taken to him like bees to honey.

She was a coward, pure and simple. Instead of running, she should have stayed to take advantage of his attention and set her plan of seduction in motion. Why wait for tomorrow?

The elevator doors parted, and she hesitated for a mere second before entering. She couldn't do it. Not now. Not when her head pounded as if it would explode at any minute. Not when she felt so out of sorts at the lingering image of Marcus with Amy clinging to his neck.

"Coward," she muttered as she pressed the button for the lobby then retreated to the far corner of the empty compartment and closed her eyes. She released the clip from her hair and shook it loose, hoping to ease the pain.

"Are you going to undress right here in the elevator?"

Charlotte didn't have to open her eyes to know Marcus wore a frown. She heard it in his voice, the same as she had so many other times. She opened them anyway and found him standing in the doorway, one hand braced to keep the door from closing. She hoped that meant he hadn't made up his mind to ride with her.

She let her gaze travel from his tense chiseled features past broad shoulders encased in a black long-sleeved pullover that fit snug across his chest and brought out the green of his eyes. His faded jeans emphasized narrow hips, the length of his muscular legs, not to mention the curve of his ass.

She licked her lips and looked at him from beneath her lashes. In her most sultry voice, she asked, "Would you like me to?"

He straightened but remained where he was, as if still undecided as to which way to go. Hoping to give him the extra push he needed to fully retreat, she flicked the fourth button, exposing the lacey edge of her red bra. "I've never done it in an elevator, but I've heard it can be…uplifting."

The doors began to close, but instead of backing

out as she'd hoped, Marcus slid forward, his frown intensifying. "I'm sorry, I shouldn't have said that."

"You know, Marcus. You spend a lot of time apologizing to me for some infraction or another. You should try to relax, loosen up." She gripped the silver bar behind her, knowing the position thrust her breasts forward. "You should just accept me as I am."

"You're right." He took a step toward her. "If we're going to make it through the weekend without getting into it every five minutes, we'll have to accept each other as we are."

He moved closer until he stood inches away, his unreadable gaze locked with hers. She forced herself to remain still when inside she trembled with anticipation. She wanted so desperately for him to touch her, to kiss her. And yet, she feared it. "Every five minutes, huh? Sure, you can manage that?"

"The question is," he reached for the buttons of her sweater, "will you let me?"

His calloused fingers grazed the swells of her breasts, and Charlotte shivered as heat spread through her belly. Her gaze fell to his lips. It didn't take much to imagine them replacing his fingers. She knew firsthand the pleasure both could bring. "I—uh, I…"

Then suddenly he stepped to the far side of the small space, his hands clasped behind his back. "Will you?"

"Huh?"

"Let me accept you as you are?" He smiled knowingly. "As you truly are?"

Charlotte glanced to where his fingers had been and felt as if the floor had dropped out from under her. The pearl buttons she had freed moments ago were now tucked safely in place.

The elevator doors opened, and with a smug grin, he gestured for her to precede him. She lifted her chin and strode forward, angry at herself for letting him have the upper hand. She had to get herself together, and to do that, she had to put some distance between them. Which went in direct opposition to her plan. Geez, the weekend could prove more difficult than she thought.

At the front door of the hospital, she paused. December in Texas could be warm during the day, but the sun had set and the chilling wind at night sometimes carried a mean bite. Marcus took her coat before she could protest and held it out. She reluctantly accepted his assistance and murmured a wary thanks before passing through the door he held open and heading for the parking lot.

This was getting way too weird. Seeing his kindness to Amy was one thing, but being on the receiving end of it was another. It made him too human, too…not like the other men in her life. Not like her father.

But he was. All men were. She had to remind herself of that, could never forget it.

Charlotte stopped beside her car, a little red convertible—just one more detail of her well cultivated façade—and dug in her purse for the keys.

"I thought we could go to dinner and discuss the promotional part of our trip."

She glanced up, only now realizing Marcus had followed her. He had remained silent, keeping his distance. Probably had some ulterior motive, though she couldn't begin to guess what. It didn't matter. It was there, and she refused to be taken in or to let down her guard. If he thought otherwise, he was sadly mistaken.

Opening the car door, she forced him to stand aside, then slid behind the wheel. "Sorry, I can't. Sam's waiting for me."

Marcus moved between her and the door, leaning forward, one arm on the roof. "Sam, huh? Is he your latest plaything?"

She smiled, knowing by his frown she'd struck a

nerve. Might as well play it for all it was worth. "I have to admit, he does like to play."

"How does he feel about you coming on this trip with me?"

"He really doesn't have any say in what I do, but to answer your question, he won't like it." Though Sam hated it when she left him alone, he didn't have a jealous bone in his body. But then the over-indulged feline thought he was the only male in her life. "Of course, I'll have to do my best to make it up to him tonight."

Charlotte almost laughed as Marcus's frown turned into a full-fledged scowl. She took advantage of his shocked outrage and reached for the door handle. He moved out of the way, and she quickly shut the door. As she backed out of the parking space, he didn't say a thing, just stood there, feet braced apart, arms folded over his chest. It was rather exhilarating to think she'd shaken him up.

Of course, she'd seen that look on his face before and knew it wasn't jealousy. He, like most men, simply didn't like the idea of sharing a woman, even if he didn't want her.

Unable to resist, Charlotte lowered her window halfway and gave him a grin and a wink. "Oh, don't let it concern you, Marcus. I'll still have enough energy to make this weekend one you'll never forget."

And she would, too. She would keep him so rattled, he wouldn't know what hit him. She would tease and taunt, entice and enchant, lure him in until he didn't know which end was up. He'd be putty in her hands.

Same as you were in the elevator.

Charlotte groaned. She had practically melted under his touch. If she wanted to succeed in her plans to seduce Marcus and leave him high and dry, she needed to think of a way to fortify herself against his charm.

****

The sun barely up, Marcus knocked at the front door of Charlotte's condo and rubbed a hand over his face, not quite awake at such an early hour. He glanced back at Spencer, busy rearranging luggage at the rear of Melody's white sedan. Melody looked up from supervising Spencer and smiled, urging him to try again. He sighed and knocked a second time, trying not to think about what might be going on inside that kept her from answering.

He'd been up half the night, fighting off images of Charlotte, her hair and skin damp with sweat, tangled in satin sheets with her lover, the unknown Sam. Marcus had tossed and turned, his gut twisting as helpless desperation seized him until he finally jumped out of bed and grabbed his keys, ready to race to her condo to interrupt their liaison. He'd come to his senses, remembering she owed him nothing and that the trip to Aspen was a promotional gimmick, not a lover's rendezvous.

Luckily, he'd recalled that fact before he reached his front door and before Avery—or his latest bed partner—caught him bare-assed naked in the middle of the living room. He'd given up on sleep after that, something he regretted now as he stifled another yawn. He would need his wit and all the stamina he could muster to deal with Charlotte Reese this early in the morning.

Marcus raised his fist to knock a third time as the door opened. Charlotte eyed him lazily. Her blonde hair fell around her shoulders in a disheveled yet provocative mess. If not for the formfitting black dress she wore, he could, without difficulty, picture her reluctantly easing from her lover's embrace to answer the door.

He banished the image to the back of his mind, since he couldn't fully erase it, and forced a smile. "Morning. You ready to go?"

She blinked her confusion. "Well, um, thanks, but actually you should go on ahead. Melody is picking me up."

Marcus hooked a thumb over his shoulder, pointing to Spencer and Melody. "I didn't want to leave my car at the airport, so Spencer offered me a ride."

"Oh."

That single syllable, though barely audible, rang with disappointment, its echo in his ears nearly drowning out the clickety-clack of her high heels as she started across the white marble foyer. Marcus ground his teeth to keep from telling her he didn't like the situation any more than she did. That she was the last woman he would spend time with if given the choice. But he *didn't* have a choice, and arguing wasn't the best way to start the weekend.

Without waiting for an invitation—he'd probably see hell freeze over before he got one—he moved through the door and closed it behind him. With each step his irritation gave way to curiosity. He'd often wondered what comforts a creature like Charlotte surrounded herself with.

He paused at the doorway of a spacious living area. At first glance, he found the room as sleek and lush as its owner, a setting obviously designed for seduction. Velvet, the color of fine claret, draped the windows to create a dark and secluded atmosphere. Overstuffed chairs and a sofa upholstered in burgundy and vanilla, with huge throw pillows, flanked a fireplace made from the same crème marble he stood on. Wine-red candles of assorted widths and heights lined the mantle, and the hearth blended smoothly into carpet so thick and plush it made him think of quicksand.

If he'd seen the room a week ago, he would have wondered how many men had been sucked under. He would have thought it mirrored the sultry personality of the Charlotte Reese he'd known these last five years. Now, he questioned why the room held none of the personality of the woman he'd glimpsed yesterday at the hospital.

The tapping of Charlotte's heels fell silent, drawing his attention across the entryway where the hard flooring ended and more of the soft, crème carpeting began, a direct contrast to the clingy dark fabric that curved across swaying hips. Stirred to action and definitely interested in seeing the rest of her home, he took the steps two at a time to catch up.

He reached her side on the landing halfway up the stairs. "You have a nice place."

"Thanks," she muttered absently.

"Doesn't seem to really fit you though."

She jerked to a stop and looked at him as if he were a big hairy spider and she suffered from arachnophobia.

"Sorry, didn't mean to offend. It's just—"

"What are you doing here?"

"I thought we'd already established I'm here with Spencer and Melody to take you to the airport."

She shook her head and pointed to the spot where he stood. "No, what are you doing *here*? Why aren't you waiting outside?"

"I'm helping you with your suitcases."

He placed a foot on the next step. She stayed him with a hand on his arm. "Thank you, but you don't have to do that."

"It's no problem."

She darted a quick glance toward the room at the top of the stairs, then climbed to the step above him and placed a hand on his chest. "I can manage. Really."

For one who hid her feelings well, this show of apprehension—surely not due to modesty—surprised him. His curiosity spiked. She obviously didn't want him entering her bedroom. The question was, why? He smiled at the possibility of underwear on the floor, candy wrappers on the bedside table, an unmade bed?

An unmade bed with red silk sheets.

And a gilded mirror on the ceiling.

He groaned inwardly, and his smile slipped. Maybe it wasn't a good idea for him to see where Charlotte slept. Or sometimes didn't sleep but rather found her pleasure. He wasn't certain he could survive his already vivid imagination were it to become more explicit in detail.

Yet her reluctance to admit him nudged his curiosity to the forefront and self-preservation took a backseat with common sense. "If you've packed as much as most women, you'll need my help. Even if you are too stubborn to admit it."

Marcus started around her, but she moved to block his way and he crashed into her. She tumbled backward, but he caught her quickly, yanking her tightly against him.

A silent moment passed as he held her, and his body grew increasingly attentive to her slender frame and how it fit so perfectly to his. The angle of her head left her throat bare, inviting his lips to explore its length. The deep neckline of her dress stretched taut, revealing a fraction of a black lace bra. Did she have one in every color?

Lust pooled low in his gut, and the semi-aroused state he stayed in whenever he was around Charlotte stretched to full length. The shock in her almond-shaped eyes quickly faded to a questioning awareness his body begged to answer. She licked her lips, and he almost lost the battle his conscience waged to keep his vow to honor her this weekend. To show her she deserved to have a man treat her with respect and not expect sex as payment for his attention.

Granted, a kiss wasn't sex, and Melody and Spencer waited just outside to take them to the airport, yet every kiss he'd shared with Charlotte had taken on a life of its own. Up to now, he had kept a tight rein on his control, but after a night of explicit imaginings and dreams, it wouldn't take much to sever his grip on reality. Especially when he wanted so damn much to lay her down on the stairs and slide deep inside her wet heat.

Marcus released her, shoved his hands in his pockets, and cleared his throat. "I've seen my fair share of women's underwear, you know."

She stopped smoothing her dress and gave him a blank look.

"If that's what you're afraid of." Though the state he was in, he wasn't at all sure he could handle seeing Charlotte's flimsy lingerie.

She smiled and placed her hands on her hips. "Now, Marcus. Why would I be afraid for you to see my panties? You've seen them before."

His erection pressed painfully against the button fly of his jeans, reminding him to steer the conversation in another direction if he wanted any relief. He should have known better than to engage in sexual banter with Charlotte Reese.

He sighed and rubbed a hand over his jaw. "Then is there a particular reason you don't want me in your bedroom?"

"Other than I didn't invite you?"

The truth of her statement hit him like a sucker punch to the stomach, and his desire waned as the visions he'd had earlier of an unmade bed came rolling back with an unwanted addition. Along with red silk sheets and a ceiling mirror, he conjured images of a satisfied lover still slumbering in the heated aftermath of early morning sex.

He had almost forgotten about Sam in his eagerness to see more of her home and hated to entertain the possibility that while he had fantasized about having his own sexual adventure with Charlotte on the stairs, the man could still be in her bed.

He backed up a step. "You're right. I should have

realized."

She swallowed, clearly uncomfortable now that he understood. "It's just that—"

"You don't have to explain, but you could have told me sooner that Sam was still here. I'd have waited outside." He turned to go.

"Marcus, wait."

He stopped on the landing but couldn't bring himself to look at her. If he moved one inch in her direction, he wasn't certain he could restrain himself from physically removing her from his path so he could see who this Sam was. More than that, he wanted to rip the guy to apart.

"Um, actually, Sam's asleep, and he's really grumpy if I wake him. But I don't think I can carry the largest suitcase down the stairs. Do you think if I brought it to the edge the stairway, you could take it to the car?"

He thought his jawbone would crack from the pressure of holding back what he thought of that idea. She could wake lover boy and have him fetch and carry. But then, essentially, their relationship was none of Marcus's business, and to have a face to go with the name would only drive him nuts later, make his imaginings too vivid, real. "Sure, no problem."

Marcus waited for her to leave before he sank to the top step of the landing. It was crazy, this compunction he felt to punish himself, as well as the fierce need to pummel a man he didn't know for taking advantage of Charlotte's promiscuity. He refused to believe there was more to it than his protective nature, or that a possessive streak—at least where she was concerned—lay buried somewhere inside him.

"Are you two going to take all day?" Melody asked from the bottom of the stairs. "You've got a flight to catch."

Spencer joined her. "Where's the mountain of luggage?"

Marcus couldn't manage more than a shrug.

"I'll go see what's taking so long." Melody started to climb the steps, Spencer on her heels.

"I wouldn't go in there if I were you."

She stopped in front of him. "Why not?"

He stared at the carpet between his feet, afraid if Melody didn't read the jumble of fiery emotion boiling inside him, ready to erupt, his brother would. "Sam's still asleep."

She brushed off his concern. "Sam's always asleep."

"Big slug's asleep every time I'm here. Lazy good for nothing—hey, that hurt." Spencer rubbed his side where Melody poked him.

"Just because you don't like Sam," she said, massaging his injured ribs in silent apology, "doesn't mean you have to be nasty. I think he's adorable."

Spencer's obvious dislike of Sam should have made Marcus feel better. Instead, his concern for Charlotte grew. His brothers usually judged men fairly, and if Spencer held a low opinion of Sam, he had good reason. Melody might think she knew the guy better, but she trusted far too easily and like most women, could be swayed by a man's charm.

"Besides," Melody added, smiling as she moved to the step above Marcus, "you'd need your sleep too if you stayed up all night."

Marcus clenched his fists. "Look, she said she'd bring her suitcases out when she's ready."

"Yes, but if I know Charlotte, she's not finishing packing." She started up the stairs, adding over her shoulder, "She's curled up on the bed beside Sam, scratching that hairy belly, trying to make up for leaving him."

Marcus lurched to his feet, his entire body shaking with the violence her words produced. He started down the steps. "I'll be outside."

"Oh, no you don't," Spencer said, catching his

arm. "I can't carry all her shi—stuff by myself."

Marcus jerked out of his brother's grasp. "Then get lover boy to help you."

Spencer gave him a strange look. "Who?"

"Sam," Marcus hissed, too angry now to care what his brother made of his behavior. He pointed at Melody as she entered Charlotte's room. "Doesn't it bother you, Melody going in there?"

Amusement filled Spencer's eyes and the corner of his mouth quirked up. "Why should it?"

"Sam's in Charlotte's bed?"

"That's nothing new."

After all the times he and Avery had teased Spencer about his hair-trigger jealousy over Melody, Marcus couldn't believe he would stand by while she entered a room where another man lay possibly wrapped in nothing but satin sheets. Yet Spencer didn't seem at all disturbed. Something wasn't right.

Marcus ran his hand over the back of his neck. "And you don't care if Melody sees him?"

Spencer laughed. "Nah. I don't like the big fella, but he's pretty harmless. Come on, let's get this show on the road."

Suspicious and intrigued, Marcus followed. Entering Charlotte's bedroom, he stopped in his tracks and gaped at the scene before him. Charlotte was nowhere in sight, but Melody sat on the bed across the room, her fingers caressing the exposed belly of an enormous, orange tabby.

"Marcus," Spencer said with barely controlled laughter. "Meet lover boy."

Heat crawled slowly up Marcus's neck and face. He started to tell Spencer where to get off, but the room's decor gave him pause. He snapped his mouth shut and took a closer look. What he saw surprised and fascinated him beyond anything he could have imagined when pondering Charlotte and her private domain.

The furniture, definitely designer quality, wasn't what captured his attention. It was the clutter. Knickknacks of every variety scattered across almost every flat surface. Books were stacked in the corners and beside the unmade bed. And the bed, where he'd thought to see a satisfied lover and not the furry feline stretched out on his back, was small with frilly ruffles and flowery sheets. A homemade quilt stuck out from under a giant black suitcase and dangled off the end where several stuffed animals lay discarded. Not at all what he'd envisioned.

He shook his head as he considered the extreme differences in this busy but cozy room as compared to the lavish living area below. Yet another contradiction in the woman he knew as Charlotte. Though what it meant he hadn't a clue and didn't have time to contemplate since she walked out the connecting door he assumed was the bathroom.

She stopped, apparently startled to see the three of them in her room. Or was it just his presence that bothered her. Had she lied about the cat because she didn't want him here?

"We introduced Marcus to Sam," Spencer said.

"Did you?" Charlotte's nervous green eyes flickered over Marcus before she moved to the bed and drew the sheet over several large books and a stack of papers he hadn't noticed before. Then she placed a small bag into her suitcase and zipped it closed. Were her hands trembling?

"Yep," Spencer said. "And it's funny, because I'm almost positive he thought Sam was your—"

"Spence." Marcus folded his arms across his chest. "Why don't you start loading Charlotte's luggage?"

His brother laughed again but refrained from further comment and hefted the suitcase off the bed. The cat sprang to his feet, back arched, teeth bared as he hissed at Spencer for intruding on his nap.

"Damn fleabag," Spencer muttered and headed

toward the door. "Come on, Mel. Three's company, five's a crowd."

Melody glanced from Marcus to Charlotte, as if trying to figure out what she'd missed, then bounced off the bed. "I'll see you downstairs."

Charlotte gathered the temperamental tabby in her arms and stroked him as if he were the lover Marcus had pictured her with all night. The thought made him smile. He knew he should be angry. She'd played him for a fool, purposely allowed him to believe the worst of her again. She knew perfectly well he had thought she planned to spend the night before their trip in the arms of another man. Why had she done that?

Hell. Why did Charlotte do anything?

At the moment, he didn't care. All he felt was relieved.

Marcus walked slowly toward her, stopping inches away. She looked up at him with defiant eyes and lifted her chin, as if daring him to criticize her. He cocked his head to one side, letting his smile broaden. "So this is Sam, the reason you couldn't have dinner with me last night?"

Her frown faded and a smug smile took its place. "Sam takes precedence over certain things. Dinner the night before I leave him for the weekend is one of them."

"You know what I thought."

Her shoulder lifted and dropped, drawing his attention, not for the first time this morning, to the plunging neckline of her shape-hugging dress. The ruffled collar with its drawstring effect ensured his gaze lingered on the soft swells it showcased. The fire that had simmered in his gut earlier flared hot in his veins.

The flames jumped higher when Sam's whiskered nose intruded, rubbing against one peak. Her long, slender fingers automatically moved from where they stroked the lucky furball's back to scratch its chin.

Massive front paws—devoid of claws—began to knead the spot his nose had nuzzled, and Marcus could swear the cat blinked at him with a hint of triumph.

"The rest of my things are there," she said, pointing to a garment bag draped over the large wingback chair and a smaller suitcase his mom would call an overnight bag. She moved to wait by the door, clearly anxious for him to leave.

Gathering the luggage, he motioned her forward. "After you."

She hesitated, then, carrying Sam with her, hurried from the room. Marcus took one last look around before following. If she'd had her way, he might never have seen the place in which she lowered her guard. Might never have seen a side of Charlotte that thoroughly shook his fast and easy image of her.

His steps grew lighter as he thought of the trip ahead and wondered what else he would discover about Charlotte Reese before the weekend was over.

Chapter Seven

Charlotte clutched the arms of her aisle seat and stared at the *Fasten Seatbelt* sign overhead as the aircraft vibrated around her. She hated to fly. Had always hated it. Fretted for days beforehand, preparing for the inevitable. She understood that her phobia boiled down to a fear of heights she'd had since childhood. However, rationalization never stopped the panic that seized her once she was more than three feet off the ground.

Strangely enough, she hadn't given this flight a second and chalked it up to the last few days' events along with her failure to come up with a plan to seduce Marcus. Sure, she could come on strong during the sponsor promos when they were forced together, but the photo shoots wouldn't last long enough to hook him, much less reel him in. And they were far too public.

Besides, with his tendency to walk away when pushed too far, he would hightail it the moment one shoot ended. Likely, she wouldn't see him again until the next one began.

The solution to her problem had come early this morning. The head of public relations at the children's hospital, Rita Guerrera, phoned with a last-minute change in their trip's itinerary. Having worked with her on other campaigns and dodged several of the woman's attempts to matchmake, Charlotte shouldn't have been surprised to hear Rita exclaim over her perceived romantic involvement with Marcus.

The doorbell rang just as she started to deny it, and Rita rushed on to say rumors abounded all over town, everyone speculating on the outcome of their relationship. When she added how pleased the sponsors were to have a real couple for the Valentine's seasonal promotion, an idea had begun to develop. Before the doorbell rang a second time, Charlotte's plan was clear.

Though confident she could carry it off, she remained unconvinced she'd make it out of their weekend affair unscathed. Their past encounters had proven that already.

From the corner of her eye, she could see him watching her as he had from the time she found him in her bedroom, taking in every detail and no doubt dissecting it. She had to believe he hadn't seen the psychology books on the bed or noticed the difference in her bedroom's decor compared to that of the living room since he hadn't called her on it.

Not like he had about Sam. But even then, his calm acceptance of her little prank, when she'd expected anger, had amazed and disturbed her.

More disturbing was the remorse she felt for misleading him. She didn't understand its sudden manifestation. Everything she'd ever said or done in Marcus's presence was meant to mislead him. But while her deception had niggled at her conscience over the years, this was full-fledged, no-holds-barred guilt.

"You know," he said, drawing her attention. "I've been thinking about this whole situation."

She blinked, trying to recall their conversation since boarding the plane. "What situation?"

"The bachelor auction in relation to the children's hospital benefit."

"What about it?"

"I'm wondering if the integrity of the benefit isn't somewhat slurred because of its association with the bachelor auction. Isn't there a moral issue here?"

Her mouth dropped open, and she had to mentally nudge herself to shut it. "Are you serious?

Did you know that when the league first convened, they barely scraped together enough to cover medical supplies? There was nothing left for the kids or their families. Some of those people don't have insurance and have to depend on charities like ours to help them."

"I'm sure—"

"And not just with medical bills. There's the cost of a place to stay while their child is hospitalized. Food, transportation, counseling. Until I got involved, I had no idea."

"I don't doubt—"

"And that's the problem. So many of our acquaintances turn a blind eye to those in need, when as a privileged society, it's our duty to help in whatever way we can. We tend to be stingy with our treasures, only giving enough to satisfy our consciences. That's why the league instituted the bachelor auction. What better way to squeeze a few extra dollars out of the rich than to let them think they're having fun?"

"Yes, but—"

"I'll have you know that since implementing the auction, donations have quadrupled. And furthermore, nowhere is it mentioned or intended that anything unsavory or out of line take place between the participants. Nor should the auction be held responsible if they choose to test the waters when the urge strikes." She paused for a breath and caught Marcus's amused expression. "What? Do I have lipstick on my teeth or something?"

He laughed. "No."

"Then what?"

"Nothing."

"You're laughing at me."

"I'm not laughing at you. It's obvious you're dedicated to your cause. I admire that."

"The children aren't a cause. They're human

beings and as such—" She snapped her mouth shut. His grin widened, and she knew she'd just fallen into his trap again. "You're purposely trying to get a rise out of me."

"Why would I do that?"

"You tell me."

"I'm not trying to make you mad, though it worked like a charm as a distraction. Since you began your defense of the auction, you haven't noticed the turbulence. You know, there's nothing to be ashamed of. A lot of people are afraid of flying."

"What makes you think I'm afraid?"

"Well, for starters, you asked for the aisle seat."

She shrugged. "That doesn't mean anything."

"No, but then you wanted me to close the window."

"The sun was in my eyes."

"It was raining."

"Still doesn't mean anything. Rainy weather depresses me."

"Maybe." He lifted a brow. "But there's also the fact that every time it gets a little bumpy you cut off the circulation in my arm."

Her gaze followed his to where her hand grasped the armrest between them. Only it wasn't the armrest.

His muscled forearm flexed beneath her palm. She jerked her hand away and rubbed it along her thigh to erase the tingling his scratchy wool sweater caused. She refused to acknowledge the true origin of the sensation.

"Now, how about a drink. What would you like?"

"I don't drink," she said and instantly cursed her slip. Not many people knew how much she feared following in her mother's footsteps and becoming a prisoner to the bottle. It wasn't an easy secret to keep when everyone expected the life of the party to imbibe.

"I've seen you drink before."

"Have you?"

"You drank like a fish at all those frat parties. And at the benefit you had champagne."

Charlotte was saved from replying as the airplane suddenly skidded through an air pocket. She let out a strangled yelp then clamped her teeth on her lower lip and pinched her eyes shut. She'd almost forgotten she sat thousands of feet in the air in a contraption that weighed tons and that a wing and a prayer wouldn't save her if the engines failed.

"I think we should discuss our itinerary."

She peeled one eye open to look at him. "What about it?"

"Melody gave me a schedule of our promotional obligations. I think we should skip some of them. Do you think they'd mind? They could probably get anyone off the street to pose for these things."

"Are you nuts? These people expect—You're trying to distract me again, aren't you?"

He grinned. "Is it working?"

She laughed and felt the muscles in her shoulders relax. "You had me going there for a minute. It's just that this weekend is so important to the benefit."

"So, do you think we can call a truce? Maybe try to get along while we're there?"

"Well, actually, I've been giving this a lot of thought, and I think we need to do more than just get along."

"What did you have in mind?"

"Geez, I hate this." She faced him squarely. "Look, I know this will be difficult for you, but because of the publicity we—you and I—received at the auction, rumors are circulating that we're an item. The sponsors are ecstatic. They expect us to be a real couple."

"Hmm."

"Lovers even."

He frowned. "I see."

She hoped not. "We need to appear as if we're madly in love."

"Madly? In public?" He forced the words out as if he found them distasteful.

"Yes." Anticipation bubbled inside Charlotte, and she fought the urge to squirm under his steady gaze. His agreement was not only important for the sake of the bachelor auction's reputation, but it was also imperative to her plan of seduction. If he guessed she intended to rake him over the coals of desire in order to achieve that end, he'd never agree.

"I wouldn't want the children, or Preston Enterprises, to suffer because of our inability to get along." He cocked his head to one side. "I don't see why we can't put aside our differences for one weekend."

Charlotte caught her smile as it started to slip. The airy excitement she'd felt moments ago vanished, as if he'd taken a pin and popped all the tiny bubbles and kept on going until he struck her heart. It didn't matter that his reasons for cooperating were the same she'd used to ensure his participation. The reminder of his initial reluctance still hurt. "Great. You don't know how much—Oh!"

The plane dipped to one side, slinging her against him. If not for her seatbelt, she'd have been in his lap. As it was, she clutched his sweater and buried her face in the crook of his neck. His arm came around her as the aircraft evened out, and his heat seeped through the thin material of her dress to warm her.

His whispered breath fanned the hair at her temple. "Are you okay?"

"Yes, I think so." Even as she said the words, she couldn't stop the tremor of fear that shook her body. His arm tightened, joined by the other to encircle her, and she knew he'd felt it and probably guessed its cause.

As much as she loved the feel of his embrace, she hated his knowing her weakness. Granted, he considered her completely flawed, but the defects he'd seen before were only the ones she'd purposely shown him.

She sighed inwardly. She could play the situation two ways. Pull away and let him continue to feel sorry for her. Or turn his suspicion around.

Pushing upright, she braced one hand on his thigh, the other on his chest, and looked at him with heavy-lidded eyes and a sultry smile. "Mmm, I think I'm beginning to like this ride. It's producing some rather unexpected results."

His gaze, as dark green as the forest on a cloudy day, slid to her mouth then downward to linger on her breasts before returning to lock with hers.

"While we're on the subject of unexpected results..." She eased her hand up the heavy denim covering his thigh. "And since you agreed so easily to our pretending to be lovers, what say we slip into the restroom and make it real. Let's join the mile high club?"

Chapter Eight

"Mr. Preston, could you place your right hand on Ms. Reese's thigh?"

Straddling a bale of hay draped with a wool horse blanket, Marcus had one foot in heaven, the other in hell. And both hands on Charlotte's hips to still her wriggling ass.

Her thighs, spread wide, pressed against the inside of his. Her familiar scent, mingled with her spicy perfume, and her small shell-like ear, so near his lips, teased him. Almost as much as the view over her shoulder. Twin mounds of satiny flesh—peaks budded from the cold—swelled above her low-cut sleeveless blouse and quivered as she searched for a comfortable position.

He welcomed the discomfort of the scratchy blanket and straw beneath, hoping it would distill the same predicament he had struggled with on the flight to Denver. Somehow, he had managed to decline her offer to initiate him into the mile high club, but only barely. He counted himself lucky she'd taken his refusal well and napped during the rest of the flight, even if she had snuggled against him as close as the seatbelt and armrest would allow.

He couldn't deny he'd been tempted. If the seatbelt sign hadn't remained lit, he might have whisked her to the nearest unoccupied restroom to get his membership card stamped, punched, and validated.

But he'd seen the spark of terror in her troubled blue eyes, felt the shudder that shook her body, just seconds before her invitation. She couldn't have recovered from her fear so quickly. Which led him to doubt the sincerity of her invitation. He wondered if her seductive behavior in the past was her way of dealing with and hiding insecurities. Up to now he hadn't considered she had any. He'd pay closer attention in the future.

"Mr. Preston, your right hand?"

Marcus stared at the photographer he'd come to think of as Slick Rick, then down at the tanned appendage he wanted to touch more than he wanted to breathe. But he couldn't move his hand from her hip, afraid Charlotte would start that infernal squirming again and discover the exact nature of his condition.

She twisted to look at him over her shoulder. "Marcus?" Her worried, green eyes met his then flared with recognition which was followed by amusement.

"If I had a beautiful woman like Ms. Reese in my arms," the photographer said from behind the camera, "I wouldn't have any problem cozying up to her."

"Here, let me help you," Charlotte whispered, seeming not to notice the guy's flirtation or the warning glance Marcus gave him.

She pried his fingers from her hip and placed his hand on her thigh just below the edge of the ruffled, skirt that had climbed several inches higher than its already short hem. The smooth skin beneath his palm was as soft as he remembered.

But, instead of the searing heat he'd stroked last summer, he felt the icy chill of winter. And no wonder when the outfit she wore barely covered her. "Are you cold?"

"A little."

Without thinking, he wrapped his arms around her and began rubbing her bare arms. She snuggled closer, reminding him why he'd avoided touching her.

"Mmm," she murmured. "I'm getting warmer."

"Now, there's the couple I expected to see." The owner of the stable and adjoining western wear boutique, a statuesque woman in her mid to late fifties with overly dyed black hair and thick makeup, pushed away from the stall door she'd been leaning against. "I was beginning to wonder if all the rumors about you two were false. I'd heard you were a hot new item."

Marcus frowned, taking in the woman's jeans, boots, and thick sweater. "I just don't see the need for Charlotte to advertise her body along with your stable and in clothing not fit for the climate."

The woman laughed. "Spoken like a jealous lover."

He bit his tongue to keep from correcting her. He'd promised, though he must have been insane at the time, and he wouldn't go back on his word.

"But the fact is," she continued, "sex sells. And I don't have the luxury of waiting 'til it's warmer. This layout is going in the January issue of the resort's promotional packet for February reservations."

"You'll have to forgive Marcus," Charlotte said, tilting her head against his shoulder to smile up at him. "He just doesn't like to share me with anyone else. Do you, baby?"

He grunted as she shifted again and dug her elbow into an area of his belly way too close to something else. "No, darlin', I don't."

The photographer released a dramatic sigh. "If you two are finished playing around, I'd like to finish this sitting. Now, Mr. Preston, do you think you could show us a little sex appeal instead of that scowl?"

Marcus tried his best to smooth his frown into something resembling a smile. Pretending to pretend. That was a new one. And it took a lot more concentration than he'd thought.

"Why don't you kiss her?" the shop owner asked.

"Mmm, I like that idea." Charlotte turned to offer her glossy red lips.

He looked at her mouth and felt his body jerk to attention. She smiled, telling him she'd felt it, too. God, he wanted to kiss her if only to wipe that smile off her face.

"Hold it right there. Don't move." The camera began to click and whir. The photographer had obviously gotten the look he wanted. "Now inch closer."

Kissing Charlotte was out of the question. It would be like pouring gasoline on a match. And he would be the one going up in flames.

He improvised by burying his face in the crook of her neck and nuzzling the back of her ear. He tried not to think about the familiarity of his actions or the possessiveness behind them. He had a part to play. And a point to make. "You're enjoying this aren't you?"

"Immensely." She arched against him, pressing her ass against his crotch. "I'd enjoy *it* even more if we were alone."

Marcus released Charlotte and jumped up so quickly both the shop owner and the cameraman blinked in confusion.

He rubbed his butt. "Piece of hay stuck me."

The woman looked at him as if she didn't believe him but nodded. "Okay, next outfit."

He offered Charlotte a hand up and watched her disappear behind a curtained area set up in one of the stalls. The drape hung to her knees, giving him full view of her slender calves. She stood on one foot then the other to remove red ankle boots. A second later, the denim skirt pooled at her feet.

Disgusted with himself, he turned away, only to discover he wasn't the only one ogling her legs. Slick Rick was getting an eyeful. No wonder Charlotte thought sex was the only way to get a man's attention when every male between the age of thirteen and ninety-nine stopped whatever they were doing and stared as soon as she entered a room.

A rusty chuckle from boutique owner and the

knowing look on her face kept him from suggesting to the photographer that he keep his eyes in his head and his mind on business.

"This just gets better and better," she said.

Snorting, Marcus headed to his own designated dressing area, determined to get *his* mind off Charlotte and back on safe territory. Digging in the jeans he'd worn on the flight, he pulled out his cell phone and powered it up to check his messages. Both Avery and Spencer had called—Avery to yank his chain about Charlotte and Spencer to make sure his flight went all right since the storm hadn't let up.

Knowing his family would worry, he speed-dialed Spencer's cell number only to get his voice mail. "The flight was fine, a little bumpy. I'll have my phone on except during the photo shoots. Call if you need anything."

Against his better judgment, he called Avery. He lucked out and got his voice mail as well. "Don't call me again unless you have something of interest to say. Later."

Marcus tossed the phone next to the clothing he had yet to change into. Two other shirts, one red flannel plaid, the other similar to the one he had on, hung on a nail along with a fleece-lined denim jacket. Another pair of jeans and a pair of corduroys sat on a stool. Snake-skin boots stood on the floor beside it, brown calfskins next to them.

With a shake of his head, he pulled the curtain back to ask which outfit he was supposed to wear next. Instead, he caught another glimpse of Charlotte's legs, and his mouth went dry. Then the saliva flowed as she used the top of her foot to rub the back of her other leg.

He slammed his eyes shut, but it was too late. Images of her foot sliding up the back of his leg then locking with its mate at the base of his spine played against the back of his eyelids. He shuddered.

Two more sessions. He didn't know if he could

make it.

"Oh, Mr. Preston," the shop owner said, drawing his attention. "I'd like to offer you and Ms. Reese a couple of my horses. There's a nice trail that leads to a clearing beside the mountain. It's lovely there."

"That sounds wonderful," Charlotte said from behind the curtain, her voice full of excitement. "I haven't ridden in long while."

A ride alone with Charlotte? No way in hell.

He opened his mouth to decline when she swept the curtain aside and stepped out wearing a red leather skirt slung low on her hips and no longer than mid thigh. Her white blouse had long, puffy sleeves, but they were sheer, and he'd swear the bodice covered only enough to keep her from getting arrested.

She looked at him, a slight smile on her face. "Unless you'd rather go back to the hotel and get some...rest."

"A ride sounds good," he said and pulled the drape into place.

As much as he enjoyed the way Charlotte had snuggled against him on the plane and during the promo shoot, holding her had to be the dumbest thing he'd ever done. But being alone with her in a hotel room bordered on the height of idiocy. On second thought, that prize belonged to his actions the night of July Fourth. A night that would forever haunt him. Long after this weekend had come and gone and she had forgotten he existed, he would remember it.

And like that night, this weekend would take its toll. Hell, it already had. There would be no peace for him these next forty-eight hours. Not when he could — would be forced to — expected to — hold her soft body against his. Not when his fingers could dive, of their own free will, into her silky moon-kissed mane.

Marcus snorted. And not when his dick stuck out like a diving rod, searching for hot, wet pussy.

****

Marcus pulled his horse to a skidding stop behind Charlotte's, his heart beating a mile a minute in his chest. She turned the mare with ease, and his breath caught in his throat. He might have fared better at the hotel.

"I win. You lose," she said, her voice full of triumph.

He could have beaten her, won the race by several lengths. It would have saved him the agony of watching her writhe in the saddle, hugging the horse's sides with her thighs while he imagined her doing the same to him. He wouldn't have had to see her long blonde hair whipping at her back.

She'd been a vision to behold, racing with wild abandon across the snow-covered meadow, a veil of white spraying behind her. The laughter in her voice as she urged her horse onward had held him back and the smile on her lovely face now made all his suffering worthwhile.

"Geez, I haven't ridden like that in years. I'd forgotten how exhilarating it can be."

"I didn't realize you rode."

Leaning forward, she rubbed the mare's neck. "I wanted to barrel race when I was little. But it wasn't dignified enough for my father. He bought me a jumper instead."

She murmured something to the horse then straightened and smiled again. It was a dazzling smile, like that of a child, completely unguarded, totally without guile. He'd never seen her this way before.

"I got pretty good at it, too. Even won a few ribbons." She closed her eyes and breathed in deeply. His gaze delved between the edges of her red goose-down vest to the open collar of her flannel shirt designed to match his. The curve of her breasts peeked over the top of lace-edged long johns. The shop owner had gifted them with all three ensembles, and they had opted to remain in the ones worn during the last session of the promo.

He'd been relieved to see almost every inch of Charlotte's body covered, even if the tight fit of the scarlet jeans did nothing to hide her figure or curb his hunger.

"But I don't get to ride much anymore. And when I do, it's a much more sedate ride. The kids aren't used to riding, but they like it when they get to visit the stables. Sarah's taking lessons and actually coming along nicely. Amy's a little timid around the horses, but she's starting to get used to them."

He wanted to ask questions, to know more about her relationship with the children at the hospital. But she'd never offered this much information about herself, and he was afraid to break the spell. Then he remembered something Amy had asked him to do.

Leather creaked as he shifted to rest a forearm on the saddle horn. He held the reins loosely in his fingers. "What the hell is a snow angel?"

She gave him a look of disbelief. "You don't know what a snow angel is?"

"Am I supposed to?"

"I guess not. After all we don't get enough snow in Houston to fill a bucket. Why do you ask?"

"Amy asked me where we were going. When I described Aspen, she asked if I'd make her a snow angel."

"In that case, I'll have to show you." She threw a leg over the saddle and slid to the ground. A few paces away, she lay on the ground and began to flap her arms and legs. After a few swipes the pattern of an angel evolved.

He smiled at the spectacle she made. Never in a million years had he pictured Charlotte, in all her wild ways, doing what amounted to horizontal jumping jacks in the snow. Jumping Jack or Dick or Harry horizontally, yes, but not this.

"Come on, try it."

"That's all right. You're doing fine."

She moved to another spot to make a second angel. "Don't be such a fuddy-duddy."

Was he? He had never thought of himself that way. He and Avery always cut up. *Good time* was their motto. But let Charlotte walk in the room and his mind went rigid.

He snorted. His mind wasn't the only thing that stiffened.

"You promised Amy."

She had him there. And he suspected she knew it by the grin on her face. He *had* promised Amy he'd make a snow angel for her.

Resigned, he dismounted and wrapped the reins around the saddle horn then settled his Stetson over it. He did the same to the straps of leather she'd left dangling in the snow. His boots and the hem of his jeans grew wet as he trudged to a spot of untouched powder. Lying down, he felt the cold seep through the his jeans and was glad he at least had the protection of the thick coat against his back.

His awkward movements made him feel uncoordinated and stupid, but her laughter was infectious, and he found himself smiling despite the chill working its way to his bones.

"See, that wasn't so hard, was it?" She stood over him, hands behind her back, rocking on her heels.

He grunted.

"Of course, it's not as easy as this." Grinning, she bent low and, before he could react, shoved a handful of snow in his face, half of it in his mouth.

"Why you little—" He jerked upright, slapping ice from his neck, trying unsuccessfully to keep it from going down his shirt. Her laughter carried across the meadow, bouncing off the nearby trees to echo around him. He grabbed for her leg, intent on retaliation.

Squealing, she dodged him and ducked behind the horses. She scooped up another handful of snow.

"What's the matter, Marcus? Can't take the heat?" She let it fly, hitting him in the chest. "Oops, should I say cold?"

"Get out from behind there."

"And give up my cover? Not on your life."

"You'll spook the horses. They'll run off and leave us here."

"You afraid to be alone with me?"

Hell, yes. Not that the four-legged creatures were any kind of chaperone, but he'd just as soon not lose his means of escape. "My jeans are wet, and I don't want to freeze my ass off if we get stuck out here."

"I'd warm you up."

"I'll bet," he muttered beneath his breath and dragged himself to his feet. He wasn't sure if she was trying to truly seduce him this time or push him away, but he was determined to keep her playful mood alive and headed in the right direction. He started toward her. "Let's see how you like the taste of snow."

She darted toward the trees, calling over her shoulder. "Stuffed shirt."

He chased after her, giving her just enough room to think she was safe. Gathering snow in his palm as he went, he packed it tight and aimed. It hit her smack in the middle of her back just as she started around the wide base of a tree. He heard her shocked cry, followed by a giggle.

He stopped in his tracks. Had she just giggled? Surely not.

A hard ball of snow landed high on his upper thigh, much too close for comfort. He glanced up to find her peeking from behind the tree in wide-eyed innocence.

"I'm sorry," she said then giggled again. "Really, I was aiming much higher."

"Oh, you were, were you?" He took off after her, sliding around the tree.

She screamed and ran, laughing, into the open,

and the chase was on again. Snowballs whizzed through the air, her aim hitting its target more often than his, though he did land a few strategically placed shots, making her squeal with cold and delight. After a particularly successful assault on her part, she darted past him. He dove, catching her foot, and she went down in the thick snow.

"I've got you now."

"Marcus—I—wait—no, don't—" Shrieks of laughter and gulps for air fractured her words. She tried to break free, but he held tight and crawled his way up her wriggling body. He wedged his legs between her thighs before her knee found its mark— intended or otherwise—and settled his weight on her upper body. Her arms flailed as she pushed at his shoulders, his neck, anywhere she could reach. More snow found its way down his shirt.

Marcus captured and pinned her hands above her head in his left hand, then shifted his weight to that side so he could use his right hand to scoop snow.

"All right, hellion," he said between heavy breaths. "Your turn to eat snow."

His hand was inches from shoving ice in her mouth when she dug her heels into the snow and bucked beneath him. Thrown off balance, he missed, and his hand landed elsewhere. Her sharp gasp and abrupt stillness made him pause.

He stared at his hand palming her breast, rising and falling with her ragged breath. Her goose down vest lay open, and the flannel shirt had come unbuttoned during their play. Only a thin layer of thermal underwear and her bra separated him from her silky skin.

She shivered. Her nipple puckered.

The snow began to melt beneath his palm. Moisture soaked through the thin material and trickled from his fingers over the soft swell of her breast. It puddled in the hollow of her collarbone, and he wanted to drink from it, to taste her.

Her breath shuddered against his cheek and drew his gaze to her mouth, her full pink lips slightly open and a little dry from the thin mountain air. Her tongue darted out to wet them, and his cock hardened. He looked away, only to drown in the steamy depths of her tempting blue eyes.

God, she was beautiful.

And he was in trouble.

Big trouble.

Chapter Nine

Charlotte watched as Marcus warred with indecision, his dark green eyes focused on her mouth. He wanted to kiss her, wanted to do more than kiss her if the bulge pressed against her thigh was any indication. But he wouldn't. He hated his attraction to her and fought it to the death, his distaste for her winning out over desire every time.

But she was here this weekend to change that. Now was as good a time as any to get the ball rolling. Especially when it felt so good to have the weight and warmth of his hard body bearing down on hers and his hand on her breast.

He lowered his head to lightly touch his lips to hers. He drew back and looked at her as if trying to figure out why he'd done it. She held her breath, afraid to blink, to do anything to remind him whose lips he kissed.

With a low groan, he slanted his mouth over hers, his kiss hot and urgent as he pressed her deeper into the snow. She registered the cold, but it paled in comparison to the fire his tongue built with each stroke against hers.

His fingers flexed, squeezed her breast, then abandoned their claim to yank both shirts from the waistband of her jeans. He spread the flannel wide and shoved the thermal underwear up and over her bra. That obstacle went the way of her long johns.

Finally, flesh met flesh.

Charlotte sucked in a sharp breath at his icy touch yet arched into his palm, needing what he offered. He obliged, rubbing the pad of his thumb across her nipple. Like a fuse to dynamite, tiny sparks of fire sizzled their way from her breast to her core. She hooked one leg around his and strained to fit herself against the hard ridge beneath his jeans.

He adjusted his weight, his hips surging forward to grind against her. Heat speared down her thighs. A small whimper escaped her. His tongue plunged deeper as he repeated the action until the need inside her built to a fevered pitch.

His breath grew faster, heavier with each thrust. He was close. And so was she. But she wanted him inside her. Now.

As if reading her mind, he released her hands to grip her shoulder and keep her from sliding when he rocked against her. She reached for his belt buckle. He shifted to allow her access. Loosening the notch, she popped the top button of his jeans and started on the next.

He groaned and pressed himself against her hand. She went for the last button then paused when he…vibrated?

He tore his lips from hers and looked at her. The vibration came once more. He muttered a curse and shoved to his knees. She stared up at him, not quite certain what happened as he dug in his front pocket and pulled out his cell phone.

She pushed up on one elbow, still yearning, unfulfilled, goose bumps prickling her skin. "Don't answer it."

He punched a button and raised the phone to his ear. "Yeah?" He hugged the phone between his ear and shoulder to fasten his jeans. "No, you didn't interrupt anything. In fact, your timing is perfect." His gaze swept over her once more before he stood and turned away, dismissing her. "What's up?"

Tears threatened as Charlotte pulled her bra and thermal shirt into place and sat up. Despite her plan to keep an emotional distance during physical contact with Marcus, his rejection hit her like a bucket of ice water. The heat they'd generated moments ago vanished.

It wasn't supposed to be this way again. He wasn't supposed to walk away; she was. Yet while she couldn't have stopped had the mountains announced an avalanche, the mere ringing of the phone had cooled his ardor.

She'd been so certain of his response, that victory was within her grasp, so close she could almost taste it. Hadn't he been as lost to passion as she, as eager to finish what they'd started? Geez, what *he* had started. *He* had kissed her, after all. Come to think of it, he had kissed her first all those months ago and in the closet last week.

Anger and determination, fueled by feelings she didn't care to examine, flamed to life inside her as she stood and brushed the snow from her clothes. He might have won this round, if only by default, but she'd never given up easily. He wouldn't break her. And she absolutely refused to let him win.

She glared at his back before turning to trudge through the snow toward her horse. For one brief second, she thought of taking his mount with her. Leaving him stranded would be just what he deserved. But returning to the stable alone would be hard enough to explain. She couldn't take the chance of ruining the appearance they'd created. Revenge would have to wait.

But not long. Then Marcus would pay.

And boy would he ever.

****

A boy still young enough to have peach fuzz on his mottled cheeks and strongly favoring the owner of the boutique-slash-stable ran out to greet Marcus. "Name's Lenny. Let me know if I can do anything for you."

Marcus handed the reins to the eager stablehand

and scanned the corral for the little mare Charlotte had ridden. He found it already amongst the others, still slightly wet after a rub down. She must have ridden hard. He'd started back within minutes of her departure not so eager to catch up but to make sure she made it back safely.

Stupid. Damned stupid. He followed Lenny inside the barn, cursing himself again for almost losing control. Hell, he had lost control. If not for Avery's interruption, he would have made love to her on the cold, wet ground and destroyed any chance of convincing her that sex wasn't the only way to attract a man.

That fact had been established during their snowball fight. Her natural exuberance for the moment had done more to draw him in than any sexual byplay she could have used. Her laughter had been genuine, not forced or designed to seduce. Feline blue eyes had sparkled with excitement and mischief instead of sultry invitation. Her body had writhed to escape retribution, not with desire. She had been perfect in her innocence, as pristine as the snow surrounding them.

Then he'd gone and screwed up. He'd kissed her. Awakened the side of Charlotte he condemned and tried to avoid. And kissing her hadn't been nearly enough. Didn't come close to what he'd desperately wanted to do.

He'd let her down, and she didn't even know it.

The large blue sack with gold letters scribbled on the side and containing his old clothes and the rest of the new ones he'd been gifted sat where he'd left them. The bag with Charlotte's things was gone. No doubt she had already changed clothes and was waiting in the limo.

Marcus thought about changing out of his wet clothing, almost stiff from the cold, into something dry. His thighs and ass stung where the air from the barn's heating system seeped through his jeans; his feet were like blocks of ice. But the two other times he'd lost control with her had proven difficult to face her afterward. Best to get it over with if they were to get past the situation he'd caused and continue the pretense they'd agreed upon. For the sake of the children and Preston Enterprises.

"Mr. Preston?" The boy stood in the doorway. "I almost forgot. Mom wanted me to let you know Miss Reese caught a ride to the hotel. She left you the limo."

So she was mad enough she didn't want to be within breathing distance of him. Not that he blamed her. Some women couldn't achieve a high level of desire easily, and to bring one to the brink of climax then suddenly stop was cruel not to mention inconsiderate.

Charlotte seemed able to attain that level more easily than any woman he'd known. Her reaction to his touch had been explosive. Likely her temper would be, too.

Maybe he would change clothes after all.

He handed Lenny a tip. "Thanks for relaying the message. Mind if I use the tack room to change clothes? I hate to track mud into your mother's shop."

The boy looked at the money, smiled a mouth-full of braces, and stuffed it in his front pocket. "Go ahead. And I'll make sure no one walks in on you."

Marcus dug in the sack as Lenny started to close the door. "Thank your mother for me, would you? For taking Ms. Reese to the hotel."

"Mom didn't take her. She was too busy," the boy said through the crack. "Miss Reese left with some dude."

Marcus dropped his sweater back in the sack and grabbed the door just before it shut. He yanked it wide. "What du—?" He shook his head. "Who did she leave with?"

Lenny's eyes rounded, and both his bony shoulders lifted. "I don't know, but he had a cool car."

Marcus's first thought was the photographer. He'd given Charlotte the once over—more than once. Had he hung around, hoping for a chance to pick her up? The guy had unloaded his equipment from the back of a silver BMW. Did that qualify as a cool car to a boy Lenny's age? "What kind of car?"

"Ah, man, it was awesome. A black Porsche with custom…"

Marcus didn't hear anything after "black Porsche." He reached for the sack, crumpling its decorative handle in his fist, and stalked past Lenny. He stepped outside into the cold, too worried to care about its bite or feel any relief that she hadn't left with the photographer.

If not him, then who? A complete stranger?

He chucked the bag across the backseat of the limo and climbed inside, knowing that, in her current state of mind and body, she would be easy prey.

And he had no one to blame but himself.

****

Wet, cold, and a bit calmer than he'd been when he left the stables, Marcus tossed his key card on the side table in the entryway of the hotel suite he would share with Charlotte. He searched the living room, his gut clenched with dread that he would find her in another man's embrace. He took in the hot tub, the sofa and fur rug in front of the gas fireplace, and the pool table near the wet bar—all hot spots for an illicit interlude—and came up empty.

Stepping farther into the room, he set his bag aside and shrugged out of his coat. The bedroom door to his left stood open. His luggage had been delivered and sat near the foot of the bed.

He turned slowly toward the door on his right. It was closed. Were they in there? Would she really bring someone here? If only to punish him?

Marcus rubbed a hand over his face and once more cursed his stupidity. He should have called her bluff instead of going riding. None of this would have happened.

But he'd been a coward.

Since coming to terms with this trip, just the idea of her sleeping in the room across from his got him hard. Then he'd read the hotel brochure. The suite's features had inspired forbidden fantasies, and he'd figured the less time spent alone with her here the less temptation he would have to overcome. He hadn't wanted to test his resolve against Charlotte in such intimate surroundings.

He went to stand in front of her door. Should he knock or just walk right in and proceed to beat the hell out the guy? Or should he mind his own fucking business? He leaned forward to listen. Nothing. He pressed his ear to the wood panel.

The door swung open, and he barely caught himself from falling forward. Blue eyes met his and flared with surprise. Heat rushed up his neck and burned his ears. He backed up and couldn't resist darting a glance over her shoulder. The bed was rumpled but still made. And vacant. The tightly coiled knot in his belly began to unwind.

Until he looked at her again and realized she had followed his gaze and no doubt guessed what he suspected.

He waited for her to face him, gearing himself for her anger. He could handle that. Hell, he welcomed it, preferred it over the alternative—the provocative performance he now suspected she would use to distract him.

Instead, she looked at him with that familiar mask of indifference he'd come to resent, and asked, "Did you need something?"

He cleared his throat and tried to shove his hands in his pockets, but the damp denim made it difficult, so he let them hang limp at his sides. "They said you caught a ride."

"Mmm." She cocked her head to one side to fiddle with her earring as if bored and eager to get on her way. Obviously, the information he desired wasn't forthcoming.

Feeling clumsy, he hooked his thumbs in his belt loops. "Just wanted to make sure you got back okay."

Brushing past him, she stopped in front of the mirror in the entryway to fluff the wisps of hair dangling free around her face. "As you can see, I'm fine."

He'd have to be blind not to notice how *fine* she was. Black velvet emphasized her slender frame from mid thigh to the base of her throat and every curve in between. From the front, the dress stated modesty and elegance. It was the dress's back—or lack thereof—that caused a reaction so primitive it startled him.

He stared at the smooth skin between her shoulder blades and the dimple at the base of her spine and tried to convince himself his response was one of protection, not possession. But there was nothing protective in what the sight of her bare back encouraged him to do.

She gave her upswept hair one last pat, then turned, cutting off his view, and picked up the small black purse beside the key he'd thrown down. Had it been there earlier, or had she carried it with her from her room? He hadn't noticed.

"I'll be in the hotel bar when you're ready."

"Ready?" God, he sounded like a moron. But then, she did that to him.

"The restaurant promotion," she said over her shoulder as she sashayed to the door, her hips enticing him to follow.

He stopped and folded his arms across his chest, tucking his hands under his armpits, afraid they'd reach for her without his permission. Then her words registered. "That's not for another hour."

She paused in the threshold, and her eyes locked with his for the first time since she opened her door.

Her blood-red lips tilted upward. "That gives me plenty of time."

Marcus didn't have to ask what for. The woman disappearing behind the closing door was a woman clearly bent on seduction.

He closed his eyes against the rising number of emotions that thought caused. So many he couldn't sort them. She'd sought pleasure with other men before, and he couldn't deny it had bothered him. But for some reason, this time was different. Maybe it was the guilt he felt for turning her on and leaving her wanting that had him tied in knots. Or perhaps he just didn't like the idea of another man finishing what he'd started.

The question was, what man would have that pleasure? The guy who had given her a ride to the hotel? Someone else she'd met along the way? Or would anyone do? Would he?

He groaned and turned toward his bedroom. He couldn't believe he was even considering the possibility of initiating sex with Charlotte. He'd come on this trip with altogether different plans. Noble plans.

He emptied his pockets on the dresser and glared at his reflection in the mirror. "Not feeling so noble now, are you?"

And he'd feel worse if he gave in. Not just for taking advantage of her unfulfilled needs. Doing so would let her within reach of that part of him he guarded so closely. He'd always known making love to Charlotte meant relinquishing his soul.

He straightened. Who said he had to make love to her? He'd given her pleasure before without taking his own. If he had to, he could do it again. Couldn't he? Maybe. Maybe not. But wasn't he a better option than someone who wouldn't at least try to resist?

Marcus rubbed a hand over his face, scratching the stubble on his jaw. He didn't know what he was worried about or what difference anything he decided might make?

Judging by the way she'd looked right through him, he was the last man she wanted.

****

Damn Marcus Preston for making her want him.

Double damn him for *not* wanting her.

And damn me for wanting him to.

Charlotte stared at the milky liqueur she had no intention of drinking, disgusted with herself for letting him get to her and for losing sight of her goals and control of the situation.

"Does Marcus know the truth about us?"

She looked at the sleek, sophisticated man leaning against the bar beside her. In a navy Armani suit that brought out the blue in his eyes and the blond streaks in his golden-brown hair, Grant Wylie could have stepped off the pages of GQ. He was by far the most beautiful man she'd ever seen. She'd forgotten that about him.

Yet not once in the history of their acquaintance had he made her yearn for the things she'd vowed to forgo. Love. Marriage. Family. They came at too high a price.

Marcus was the only man to make her consider paying it.

She set her glass down with a thunk, sloshing a good bit of its contents onto the counter, some dribbling over her fingers. The bartender handed her a napkin and began mopping her spill.

She sighed and wiped her hand. "No, he doesn't."

"Are you going to tell him?"

"It would only complicate matters."

"I told Robyn."

Charlotte handed the soiled napkin to the bartender and waited for him to move on before facing Grant. "Why?"

"She asked."

"And just like that you told her?"

His cheeks glowed beneath the tan he'd probably gotten from too many hours on the slopes. "When Avery called, I got a little wound up about seeing you again and she wanted to know if she should be worried. She's about to become my wife. I couldn't lie to her."

"Really?" Charlotte laughed. More to cover her surprise than because of his discomfort. She didn't understand that concept of honesty in a marriage. Her father had built—and eventually destroyed—his life and her mother's with lies.

"I won't start my marriage with secrets." He lifted a hand to caress her cheek with the back of his knuckles. "And if you want this relationship with Marcus to work out, you shouldn't keep secrets from him."

From the corner of her eye Charlotte saw Marcus watching them across the bar. His posture was ridged, his fists clenched, and his eyes held the same look she'd seen earlier when he searched her bedroom for signs of a lover.

At the time she'd been too angry to question the gleam in his eyes. She'd figured it was the same as always. He'd heard she'd gotten a ride to the hotel, assumed the worst, and was passing judgment.

But now she understood. The conceited jerk was jealous. He didn't want her, but he didn't want anyone else to have her either.

She bristled at his audacity. He'd awakened her appetite for his touch, made her ache with a need no other could arouse, then declined to satisfy that hunger. He had no right to object if she sought to ease her craving with another man.

After all, she didn't know who had been on the other end of the call that interrupted their lovemaking. It could have been a woman. It could have been Natalie what's-her-name, the girl he'd spent most of the evening with at the bachelor auction.

She pushed that disturbing thought aside but couldn't resist one last jab at his super-sized ego before letting go of her anger. It would serve no purpose to let her feelings interfere with her goals for the children's benefit, not to mention the ones she had for Marcus this weekend.

Sliding off the stool, she stood in what little space there was between it and Grant's tall muscular frame. She fingered his lapel. "You're sweet to be concerned, but things haven't progressed quite that far yet. If they ever do, I promise to tell him the truth."

She rose on tiptoes and placed a kiss on his cheek.

****

Fifteen minutes. That's all the time it had taken for Marcus to shower, dress, and find Charlotte. But he was fifteen minutes too late. She'd found her quarry.

His chest constricted as she stretched to kiss the man, her soft body pressed against his entire length. Her actions were familiar, both to Marcus and to the guy who bent to return her kiss. Grant Wylie, one of Avery's fraternity buddies from college. One of her former lovers.

Unclenching his fists, Marcus started toward them and tried to quell the fury rising inside him. He wanted to smash his fist into the guy's perfect white smile. Instead, he would offer his hand, knowing Wylie had to release her to return the gesture. He would then step between them. As plans went, it sucked, but then so did everything about this situation.

To Marcus's surprise he didn't have to put his strategy to work. The minute she saw him, Charlotte stepped out of Wylie's arms and into his. They automatically slipped around her, his palms flattening at the base of her spine. Before he could correct them, her full red lips met and lingered on his. He wondered briefly if Wylie's body had reacted the same as his.

"You remember Grant, don't you, baby?" She

rubbed lipstick from his bottom lip with her thumb in a manner that suggested familiarity.

He couldn't decide if she was playing her part for the other man's benefit or his—to throw him off track from whatever plans she had with her ex-lover. By the daggers she sent him, she expected him to play along.

He nodded and stuck one hand out behind her while keeping her firmly tucked to his side with the other. "Wylie."

"Marcus." Grant shook his hand easily. If he was at all perturbed for having his time with Charlotte interrupted, he didn't show it. "Sorry I missed you at Lucky's."

Marcus frowned. "Lucky's?"

"The stable," Charlotte said, wriggling out of his grasp to perch on the bar stool. Her knees grazed Wylie's thighs when she twisted to beckon the bartender. "I told Grant we'd buy him a drink since he was nice enough to give me a lift to the hotel. I didn't want to be late for our next promo, and I wasn't sure how long you'd be with your business call."

So, Wylie had been the man in the Porsche. And she'd explained their separation as a matter of business. She hadn't used their altercation as an excuse to cry on Wylie's shoulder in order to seduce him. At least not yet.

She picked up her drink and stabbed the ice at the bottom of the glass then smiled, all daggers sheathed for the time being. Tugging Wylie's tie, she brought him closer and whispered, "Marcus works too much, but I'm trying to break him of that bad habit."

"Well, if anyone can do it, you can." Wylie gave her a soft smile. "You sure broke me of mine."

The moment reeked of intimacy, and Marcus ground his teeth against the feeling of being on the outside looking in. Again, he couldn't stop himself when he moved behind her and laid a hand on the back of her neck. The move was possessive, pathetic really. Wylie would think he felt threatened. He didn't. He just couldn't let the guy believe he would step aside so easily.

She let go of Wylie's tie and straightened. Marcus pretended her movement caused his fingers to trail down her spine to just between her shoulder blades and then slid them back up to reclaim his original hold. God, her skin felt good. Smooth and silky. Cool yet burning his fingertips. It certainly started a fire in his blood.

"What can I get you?" the bartender asked.

Wylie pushed his glass forward. "Scotch, neat."

Charlotte shifted, crossing her legs, and held up her glass. Ice tinkled as she jiggled it. "I'll have another, please."

"And you, sir?"

Marcus glanced at the half empty tumbler in Charlotte's hand and remembered she'd told him she didn't drink. He hadn't believed her at first but later decided, out of courtesy, to refrain from alcohol in her presence. "Give me a beer. Whatever you have in a bottle will do." He turned to Wylie. "I'm curious. How exactly did you get mixed up in this dog and pony show?"

"Grant runs the resort," Charlotte answered for him. "He's also engaged to the owner's daughter, lucky girl."

Marcus wondered where the lucky girl was and if she had any idea her fiancée might have more interest in one of the auction's participants than the resort's promotion.

Wylie hooked the heel of his shoe on the rung of his stool and propped himself against it. "I couldn't believe it when Avery called last week to tell me you were the ones coming. I told Robyn all about you, and she was just as excited as I was to meet you at the airport, but something came up and neither of us could get away."

Marcus doubted Wylie told his fiancé everything. Or maybe he had and that's what had come up.

"Anyway," the other man continued. "I feel like I've fallen down on the job."

"We managed." Marcus hugged Charlotte close. "Didn't we darlin'?"

"Mmm, yes, I'd say the shoot went very well." She uncrossed her legs and recrossed them, shifting slightly away from him. Either she was uncomfortable with the conversation, or she wasn't as immune to his touch as she'd like him to believe.

"That's what Rick said."

"Rick?" Forced to give up his hold on her, Marcus ran his hand down the length of her velvet-covered arm and tried to link his fingers with hers. She dodged him by reaching to brush an imaginary speck of lint from his sleeve.

"Rick was the photographer," she said with a teasing smile. "Didn't you pay attention to anything today?"

He caught her fingers and brought them to his lips for a quick kiss, and he reveled in seeing her eyes widen. He grinned. "You know I can't concentrate whenever you're around."

It was the absolute truth. She never failed to turn his brain to mush.

"She has that effect on a lot of people."

Wylie's words wiped the smile off Marcus's face, and he searched the man's expression for hidden meaning but found nothing except friendly observation. Had he been wrong to assume the guy had illicit intentions toward Charlotte? Or was he a total player and wanted her to read between the lines? It was hard to tell.

The bartender placed Wylie's drink in front of him. "One Scotch, neat." He handed Marcus a longneck. "One beer."

"Thanks." Marcus raised the bottle to his lips and

let the cold brew cascade over his dry throat. She had that effect on him, too. When she wasn't making him salivate.

Holding Charlotte's glass out of reach, the bartender winked. "Promise not to spill this one?"

Marcus glared at the guy over the bottom of his beer bottle, but it didn't faze him. Especially when she winked back and nodded then held out her hand and waited for him to deliver her drink. He did so with flare. "Then here you go. One Buttery Nipple."

Beer lodged in Marcus's windpipe then shot up his nose, and for just a moment, he thought he wouldn't mind at all if he choked to death. At least he'd die with an image of Charlotte's golden breasts slathered with melted butter, pink nipples beaded and glistening.

Not a bad way to die.

Chapter Ten

Marcus suffered the pounding Wylie administered to his back, along with the smug look on Charlotte's face.

There was no doubt in his mind she'd ordered that drink for shock value. Probably with him in mind. She had done no more than stir it while he drained the rest of his beer and half another. Oh, she had closed her full sensuous lips around the little red straw now and then, but she never drank from it. Only an industrial strength vacuum cleaner could get liquid through those useless holes.

In retribution, he'd made her squirm while he perfected his act as her lover, displaying intimate yet respectful affection. He didn't want to embarrass her or himself. Just get even. And get his point across to Wylie. *Back the fuck off.*

So far, he couldn't tell if it was working.

Marcus checked his watch and interrupted another damnable stroll down memory lane. "We should probably go."

"Already?" Her disappointment pricked his nerves like bamboo shoots under his fingernails.

"Yep," he said, setting his beer on the bar to lift her off the stool. He left his hands on her waist after she had her balance for Wylie's sake, though it was all he could do not to drag her against him. "And you better freshen up. Your hair's a mess."

Cocking her head to one side, she tilted her chin up at him provocatively and jabbed him in the chest with her finger. "If my hair is a mess, it's only because you can't keep your hands out of it."

He ignored her playful reprimand—mostly because it was true—and reached to finger a long lock that had fallen from the neat twist at the back of her head. It was satiny smooth, and even in the dim light it shimmered like moonlight off water. "I've always loved your hair."

The moment he said the words, he wished he could take them back. Damn, but what else was new? He let the tendril slip from his fingers and forced himself to meet her confused gaze. She was probably trying to decide whether he really meant it, or if it, too, was part of their game.

Grabbing her purse, he handed it to her and lowered his voice so only she could hear. "And you might want to touch up your lipstick. You left most of it on Wylie."

That earned him a frown. She took the little black bag and turned to Wylie, who sat observing them quietly. "Don't go anywhere."

Wylie nodded. "I'll be right here."

"Not if I can help it," Marcus muttered under his breath as he snatched up his beer and parked himself on the stool she had vacated.

Resisting the urge to follow her departure in the mirror, he took a long draw and studied his nemesis. He might not be able to save Charlotte from herself, but he could damn well save her from Grant Wylie. "I never pegged you as stupid."

Wylie jerked his gaze from Charlotte's rearview to Marcus. "I beg your pardon?"

Marcus leaned both elbows on the bar. "You've got a pretty good setup here. Executive position at a major hotel resort, conveniently engaged to the boss's daughter—"

"There's nothing convenient about it. I love Robyn."

"How long do you think she'd believe that if she saw you watching Charlotte's ass or her lipstick on your face?"

Wylie withdrew a handkerchief from the inner pocket of his suit coat and eyed Marcus cautiously as he erased the annoying red smear. "I'd thank you for the heads up, but somehow, I don't think you meant to be helpful."

Marcus lifted his beer to toast the man's brilliance. "See? I knew you were smart."

"What's on your mind, Preston?"

He angled his head and pinned the man with a hard stare. "Don't think you're going to use this weekend to pick up where you left off with her, because you'll have to go through me first."

"Ah," Wylie said, tension visibly draining from his face, amusement taking its place. Cocky bastard. "And where is it you think we left off?"

Marcus gripped the bottle in his hands to keep from encircling the man's neck and forced out the words that twisted his gut. "I know you were lovers."

"Did Charlotte tell you that?"

"She didn't have to. Everyone on campus knew."

All humor left Wylie's face as he shifted to study his empty glass, rolling it around in his hands. It wasn't so much guilt Marcus saw, though there was some, but mostly frustration, as if he wanted to say something and had to bite his tongue to keep from it.

Then he shrugged. "What happened between me and Charlotte is ancient history. We're different people now. Besides, the Charlotte I remember wouldn't have bid on you. She wouldn't have put herself in that position. The fact that she did says a lot."

Marcus bit back his own reply. He couldn't very well admit Charlotte hadn't bid on him—at least not with the intention of buying him—or that his relationship with her was a lie. And his pride balked at telling one of her ex-lovers she didn't want more from him than she could get from any man.

"And even if I'm wrong," Wylie continued, "I'm

engaged."

Marcus snorted and pushed away from the bar. "That little detail hasn't stopped others." He dug out his wallet and covered their tab. "Thanks for giving Charlotte a ride earlier, but from here out I'll give her whatever she needs."

"You know, I'm beginning to think you don't know her very well if you think she'd pick up with me or anyone else."

"It's not her I'm worried about." The lie gnawed at his gut as he turned to leave. She would probably jump at the chance to reunite with Wylie if only for the weekend, regardless of his affianced status, were it not for the consequences of getting caught.

"Marcus, wait." Again, Wylie seemed to struggle with his words. "What I had with Charlotte wasn't what you think."

"What do you mean?"

"That's for you to ask her."

"I'm asking you."

"If she wants you to know, she'll tell you."

Wylie indicated Charlotte's approach with a nod, and Marcus was left to speculate the meaning behind the man's vague statement. Had they not been lovers? He had a hard time swallowing that. No matter the things he'd recently learned about her.

But the alternative tortured his very soul. What if they'd been more than lovers? What if their feelings had run deeper than anyone thought? What if they still did?

****

"Well, I'm off," Grant said as the photographer headed toward the exit with the last of his equipment and the restaurant manager shooed the hovering waiter from their partially secluded table in the corner of the candlelit dining room. "You two did a great job for Max. He'll make sure you're taken care of for the rest of the evening. Enjoy your meal."

Charlotte clasped Grant's hand with mixed emotions. "I wish you wouldn't go."

He cast a cursory glance at Marcus in the chair across from her then extricated his hand from hers and bent to kiss her forehead. "As much as I'd like to stay and catch up some more, you don't need a third wheel and Robyn's waiting for me. I'll see you in the morning for the hotel shoot."

She stared after him, somewhat relieved since he might have accidentally let something slip, but mostly amazed at how much she had allowed herself to trust him not to. They'd made a pact in college, and he hadn't betrayed her. Not then and not tonight.

He paused at the door and waved. She smiled at his boyish grin and waggled her fingers back at him. She'd never had a male friend. Or at least not that she'd realized. Turns out, she'd had one all along in Grant Wylie. Too bad his kisses had never made her lips burn, her breasts tighten, and her belly quiver. Not like—

"How long has it been since you've seen Wylie?"

Charlotte flushed to find Marcus studying her over a silver vase of red roses, his dark eyes void of all emotion. She scooped a forkful of steak from her plate, glad he couldn't read minds. "Geez, it's been years. Not since college."

At the first taste of the succulent beef topped with sautéed mushrooms, onions, and melted cheese, she closed her eyes and moaned. Cardboard would have tasted good after skipping breakfast and lunch, but this was heavenly. Like an orgasm for her taste buds.

When she opened her eyes to go for another bite of bliss, Marcus was still watching her. More specifically her mouth. His gaze dropped to the untouched food on his plate. But not before she noticed his eyes weren't as blank as they had been throughout the shoot.

Feeling once more self-assured and a little more in control, she pointed with her fork and asked, "Aren't you going to eat? It's really wonderful."

He picked up his wine glass and sat back. "I ate too much at lunch."

She scrunched her nose. "Lucky provided a nice spread, but something about eating in the same area where animals eat, sleep, and do other unmentionable things just didn't appeal."

His lips quirked as she'd intended but thinned again just before he drank the last of his wine. He'd been quiet—more so than usual if that was possible—and somewhat distracted during the promo for the restaurant.

Not that he hadn't played his part. He'd done and said all the right things. But his hands hadn't lingered on hers between poses. He'd pulled them back to his side of the table. He hadn't glared or growled at Rick, not even when the photographer put his clammy fingers on her back to adjust her position.

Still a bit off balance because of the admission he'd made at the bar about her hair, she hadn't noticed his withdrawal until after they arrived at the restaurant. She had tried to take everyone's attention off him by chattering incessantly—something she never did—with Grant and the restaurant manager. Rick hadn't complained so she must have succeeded.

"Did you know he'd be here?"

She nodded then swallowed and raised the napkin to wipe the corner of her mouth. Once again Marcus's gaze followed her actions, and she couldn't resist licking her lips. "He told me on the way to the hotel this afternoon that he'd be at all the sponsor promos."

"No, I mean in Aspen."

"Oh." So, the reason for his irritation hadn't changed. Grant remained his concern. "Yes, I knew."

"So, you've kept in touch?"

"No, Melody told me when she gave me the itinerary." Charlotte took a sip of water, then added, "He looks good, don't you think? I'd forgotten how gorgeous he was. Still is."

His answer came in the form of a grunt as he glanced out over the room and seemed to draw inward. The waiter approached to freshen their wine glasses, though hers remained full, and Charlotte let Marcus deliberate in peace. She took the opportunity to study him as he had her.

The minute the shoot ended, he had removed his charcoal suit coat, loosened his multi-colored tie and rolled up the sleeves of his crisp white dress shirt. If she thought him breathtakingly handsome before, his casual appearance only enhanced the raw sensuality she'd always responded to.

Jet-black hair fell over his brow to one side, casting a shadow of mystery over brooding emerald eyes. He'd shaved before meeting her in the bar, but the smooth skin along his jaw revealed a hint of new growth every time he clenched and unclenched his jaw. The corded muscles of his bronzed forearms bunched and relaxed as he gripped and released the stem of his glass.

Maybe it wasn't a good idea to keep prodding his jealousy over Grant. If he continued to withdraw to the extent he wouldn't interact with her, she'd never succeed in her plan. She needed to bring him back around. But how? Nothing she'd done so far had worked so far.

Right now, she'd settle for a smile. And if she were honest, she'd admit how much she needed one. Like the kind he'd given her this afternoon during their snowball fight prior to…

Her lips curled upward. Maybe that was it. They had both been so caught up in the fun and excitement of the moment, their natural attraction had snuck up on them before either could deny it. Getting Marcus to drop his guard without dropping her own would be difficult. She would have to let go a little to draw him in, be more herself and less the woman he expected.

But as long as she was careful, she'd be safe.

Taking a deep breath, Charlotte turned a deaf ear to the little voice in her head that said she'd lost her mind and reached across the table to close her fingers around his wrist. "Marcus, what is it you want to know? Just ask."

He looked at her hand then up to pierce her with his gaze. She almost changed her mind but held firm. "Do you still have feelings for Wylie?"

"Would you be jealous if I did?"

He tried to pull away, but she tightened her grip. "Wait." Letting herself go wasn't as easy as she'd thought. "I'm sorry. You asked a serious question, and I…well, it took me by surprise. Old habits are hard to break."

"Are you going to answer it?"

She released him and slid her hand back but didn't allow her gaze to waver. "My relationship with Grant ended years ago. We parted as friends."

"That doesn't answer my question."

His persistence both amused and confused her. He was like a dog with a bone. Did he really care? Did she want him to? "Why do you want to know?"

"I don't want to see you get hurt."

Okay, so he cared, but not in the way she'd hoped—no, feared. She meant feared. She picked up her fork and poked at the steamed vegetables on her plate. "That's very sweet, but there's no need for you to worry. Grant's a lot of fun, but he's off the market."

"What if he wasn't engaged?"

"He is."

"But what if—"

"I would never jeopardize the charade we've built. The reputation of the bachelor auction and the children's benefit means too much to me."

"Dammit, Charlotte." His hand snaked out to grasp her chin. His elbow knocked the flower arrangement to one side. It clanked against her wine glass, sloshing the burgundy liquid onto the pristine white tablecloth. "Stop hiding behind the auction and the children. Answer the question. If you had the chance to resurrect your relationship with Wylie, would you?"

Startled by his actions and how close he'd come to the truth, she almost missed the stares from the occupants of the surrounding tables. Once again, she'd pushed him too far at the risk of all that was dear to her. Yet she didn't know what to say short of the truth.

But then, why not tell him the truth? Part of it anyway? It wouldn't make any difference. He wouldn't believe her. And as long as his ego felt threatened by the possibility of her hooking up with Grant, his damned honor and pride would stand between her and her goal. He'd never give in to her seduction.

Cupping a hand around his, she pressed her lips to his palm. Then with a repentant smile she hoped appeared sincere, she said, "I'm sorry, baby. But I couldn't resist pushing your buttons. You know how much your jealousy turns me on."

His frown deepened, and she waited for him to understand her words were meant for the audience his behavior had garnered. When she had his complete attention, she spoke in a soft tone. "I've answered your questions. You're just not listening."

When he started to interrupt, she turned his hand over and brushed her lips over the soft hair dusting the back of his fingers. His fingers curled around hers. "I'll tell you once more, though I don't expect you to believe me this time either. I didn't come here intending to resurrect my past with Grant. We both got what we wanted out of the relationship we had in college. We don't need the same things anymore. And if I felt the need to pursue anyone this weekend, it would be the bachelor whose services I've already bought and paid for." She slid her tongue between his fingers.

Frissons of heat shot up Marcus's arm to ricochet through his body and converge full strength in a growing erection that strained against his zipper. How did she do it? Make him go from insanely furious to sexually charged in seconds flat?

He couldn't think when she looked at him like that, her eyes full of invitation. Touching him, she was a force unto herself. He eased his hand from hers and sat back to study the hem of the tablecloth, glad the table hid his more than evident response.

A sigh across the table signaled her acceptance of his silent refusal. He glanced up and wished he hadn't when he saw the fork glide from her closed mouth. Watching her eat had been almost as difficult as watching her with Wylie.

Frowning, he lifted his glass to swallow its contents. He was no closer to discovering the truth about Charlotte's past relationship with Grant Wylie than he had been an hour ago. And he was more confused than ever. He'd seen her gaze follow Wylie all the way to the door when he left and watched her face soften. That, along with the man's cryptic comment, had Marcus going in circles. Probably their intent. And she'd reverted to seduction to ensure he backed off, a dead giveaway that she was hiding something.

Well, he would back off. For now. But no way would he give up.

Clearing his throat, he broached a topic that had weighed on his conscience for days. "I've been meaning to talk to you about my bachelor fee."

The little half smile she was famous for appeared. "What? You think you're worth more than I paid?"

"Hardly," he said, unable to keep from returning the smile.

She lifted a brow. "That's not what I heard."

"So you've said. But we won't go there now."

"Does that mean we will later?"

"Charlotte," he warned.

She leaned forward and wiggled her delicate brows in a suggestive manner. "When? Tonight?"

He laughed and shook his head, for the first time enjoying her sexual but playful banter. "I want to pay you back."

She cocked her head to one side. "Why?"

"My brothers are partially responsible for this mess, and you shouldn't be expected to clean up after them."

"And neither should you. Why not make them pay?"

"Believe me, they'll pay."

She sat back in her chair. "Actually, Melody and Spencer offered to pay your fee the night of the auction. Nick tried the next morning, and Avery the night before the hospital promo."

"And?"

She leaned forward again and winked. "I came out ahead by two hundred percent. Think they'll catch on?"

Marcus knew she was teasing, but her comment stirred the gnawing guilt that had been festering in the back of his mind for months. "Are you...having financial trouble? Because if you are—"

"Geez, Marcus, I'm kidding." Her blue eyes ignited as she tossed her napkin on the table and folded her arms under her breasts. "I can't believe you think I'd really do that. I'm not my father."

"I never meant to insinuate you were." Though, at one time, he'd suspected her of helping her father steal information from Preston Enterprises. Those unfounded suspicions had caused him even more remorse. "But it's occurred to me that things might have been difficult after his arrest. I'm sorry for that, and if I can help in any way, I will."

"If you're feeling responsible for my father's

incarceration, don't. He deserves everything he got. I'm sure yours isn't the only company he stole from. He probably had spies everywhere."

The bitterness in her voice only added to his guilt. "Have you been to visit him?"

She shook her head, and a wisp of pale hair escaped from behind her ear to meander down her throat. "He was never interested in being a father unless it could get him another business deal or into one of my friends' beds. I was just another pawn to be used in his games."

Marcus thought of his own father. William Preston expected those around him, especially his sons, to work hard, but no harder than he worked himself. He demanded honesty, loyalty, and integrity. Yet his wife and sons never doubted his love. "How is your mother?"

"She's in rehab. Admitted herself the day after he was sentenced."

She unfurled her arms and bent to one side. He leaned to watch her remove one of her heels and twirl her foot at the ankle. The jerk behind his fly reminded him he wasn't doing himself any favors by staring.

He straightened in his chair and wondered if she knew what she was doing to him. Odd, but he didn't think so. He suspected her gestures were more a means to hide her nervousness. The way his stillness was meant to conceal his.

Marcus cleared his throat again. "Rehab?"

Slipping her shoe back on, she sat up. "Yes, an alcohol treatment center. And she filed for divorce. Took her twenty-seven years to figure out he wasn't worth it."

He'd heard rumors but never paid much attention. Knowing the difficulty Charlotte had faced in the past, he could see where she might feel bitter.

"Do you mind if we change the subject?" she asked as she placed the napkin she'd tossed aside on her lap again.

"After we agree that I'll pay my bachelor fee. I know your father's assets were frozen and the board of trustees relieved him of his stocks."

Her laugh had a hard edge to it. "They were very nice to mom and even apologized to me for the condo."

"Condo?"

"That's what my mother said. Geez, I can still see the look on her face when Leo—you know Leo don't you?"

He did. The new C.E.O. of what used to be Reese's company.

At his nod, she continued. "Anyway, when Leo explained how my father had recently purchased a condo in my name with company funds, I couldn't let her find out it was where he kept his flavor of the month. I told her that Daddy had bought the condo for me for my birthday. She believed it because I'd been hinting about moving out for a while. I assured Leo's silence by reimbursing the company. Unfortunately, I had to follow through and move into the damned thing."

A light bulb went off in Marcus's head and energy zinged through his veins. Her condo wasn't a reflection of her taste but her father's. "You haven't redecorated."

"Only my bedroom. I—" She blinked then waved a hand in the air. "Anyway, the money I received from my father every month was just icing on the cake. The majority of my money comes from a trust fund established by my maternal grandmother. She created one for my mother, too. My father couldn't get his hands on either. Seems Nana didn't trust her son-in-law. As for your fee, I give twice that amount every year so don't worry about it."

Her eyes took on a gleam that hadn't been there since he'd asked about her father. "However, if you feel so strongly about it, you could match the fee with a donation of your own. The hospital needs every penny they can get."

"Perhaps I will." He wanted to ask why she hadn't wanted him to see the part of her home that would alter his perception of her. For now, it would have to be enough to know she hadn't. He didn't want her to shut down completely. She didn't seem to realize everything she said gave a little of herself away, and in trying to avoid one subject, she enlightened him in another.

Content to listen, learn, and hopefully peel away another layer of her well-constructed façade, he said, "So tell me how you got involved with the auction."

The light in her eyes faded, and her gaze fell to her lap. For a moment, he thought she wouldn't answer, but then she said, "My father wanted an 'in' with someone he was trying to land an account with. I don't remember who, but the guy was into charitable events big time. My father convinced my mother she should become involved. She did. Shortly after that, he took off with his latest mistress, and she dove into a bottle of bourbon. I stepped in to pick up the pieces. Once I met the children, I was hooked. They're such innocents. I couldn't let them suffer because of my dysfunctional family."

She looked up, blinking back the moisture in her eyes, and smiled a little too brightly. "That's why I asked Melody to take over as head of the auction this year. I didn't want the benefit to suffer from its association with my family. I should probably give up my place on the committee altogether, but..."

As much as he had wanted to break down the barriers of defense she hid behind, witnessing her anguish and vulnerability as they crumbled knocked a few dents in his own. With every detail she revealed, he wanted to know more—a warning signal if ever there was one. She was sucking him in. Still, he couldn't retreat. Not yet.

He slid his hand across the table to squeeze hers. "I think you should do whatever it is you want to do. Everyone else be damned."

She stared at him for a moment in silence. Then her thumb grazed the back of his knuckles, once, twice, and a mischievous glint replaced the bleak despair in her eyes. "Is that an invitation?"

Marcus heard the provocative purr in her voice and knew he'd gotten all he was going to get out of her. She'd gone seductive again. Giving her hand another squeeze, he tugged his free and shook his head. "Ah, Charlotte, what am I going to do with you?"

"Anything you want, Marcus. Anything you want."

Want? God, if she only knew how much he wanted. In fact, the *want* beneath the table still stood at full attention, saluting smartly as if reveille played. Ready and eager, it waited for him to yell charge. He bit his tongue to hold back the war cry.

It was time to retreat.

Chapter Eleven

Pausing in front of the restaurant doors, Charlotte shivered. The bitter cold from outside hissed through the cracks, chilling her to the bone. An old-fashioned lamppost with a triangle of globes cast a faint glow on the thick blanket of white that covered the street they had crossed only a few hours ago. Snow whipped in circles, swirling like a Texas twister.

Appropriate, since she felt like she'd been caught in one. Geez, she needed to be fitted for a muzzle. Marcus had made her so nervous she'd rambled, saying more to him tonight than she had in all the years she'd known him. She could only hope he would forget half the things she said.

"Hmm, fresh powder," he said, catching up to her. He leaned close to peer out the window over her shoulder. "Good for skiing."

Heat radiated from him, warming her bare back, and another tremor shook her. She would be an icicle by the time they got back to their room. Served her right for wearing the stupid dress without at least a wrap. But she hadn't thought past trying to invoke both his jealousy and desire.

"Here." He placed his suit coat around her and rubbed his hands up and down her arms.

She pulled the coat tighter and closed her eyes for a moment, reveling in his touch and the piney-musk scent that emanated from him and the jacket. Though unspoken, they had reached a plateau in their relationship, an understanding of sorts that scared her at the same time it beckoned. It was almost comfortable. Perhaps a little too comfortable.

"You want to take the chance?" His breath whispered against her temple.

She knew he meant against the weather, but his words expressed what her brain tried to warn her heart against. She might be lulling him into dropping his guard, but by lowering her own, she had grown vulnerable. "It's too late to turn back now."

His hands ceased their ministrations but stayed where they were, slightly above her elbows. "Hmm?"

She opened her eyes and flashed a grin over her shoulder. "I said it's now or never."

Smiling, he pushed the door open and grabbed her hand. Together, they hurried down the sidewalk in the direction of the hotel, the icy wind at their backs, pushing them along. He stopped to check traffic at the intersection, pulling her in front of him to block the brunt of the gale's force even though, in just a shirt, he had to be as cold as she was.

"C'mon," he said when the coast was clear and hustled her across the street, his arms around her. When they reached the curb, he slowed and held her tighter for support. "Careful, it looks icy."

At the hotel entrance, he urged her into one of the revolving door's little pie-shaped compartments and wedged in behind her, an arm around her waist, then pushed them through. Whether his caring actions were just part of the performance they'd agreed on or Marcus being himself, she didn't argue because of the cold. It had nothing to do with how good it felt, how right, or that while his actions warmed her body, they also warmed her heart.

Geez, this *wasn't* right. She wasn't supposed to feel all mushy inside just because he treated her as if she were something special, someone he cared for. She certainly couldn't proceed with her plan feeling the way she did at this moment. As if she lived for his touch.

She had mistakenly believed he was falling into

her trap when just the opposite was true. Somewhere along the way, control had shifted to Marcus, and she couldn't afford to set foot in that hotel room until she had it back.

A little distance was required. That's all. Then she would be okay.

The blast of hot air that hit them on the other side was a welcome relief from the biting cold outside and the excuse she needed to put some space between them. In her haste, she twisted out of his embrace and attempted to step past him only to stumble over his feet. He caught her and swung her around, trying to dodge the door's next panel, but it struck her left foot and took her shoe with it.

"It'll come back around," he said as he righted her.

She watched the black stiletto tumble with the door's circular motion and promptly roll out the other side to land on its side in the snow. Without a word Marcus released her and entered the next opening of the slowing door. On the outside turn, he bent and grabbed the shoe in one hand without having to exit or break stride.

Once he was back inside, she reached for her shoe, but he ignored her and dropped to one knee. He lifted her foot and placed it on his thigh. Her toes curled into the hard muscle beneath his trouser, seeking warmth while he dumped ice crystals from the shoe's interior onto the marble floor.

The gesture made her that much more aware of his thoughtful actions over the last half hour. Not to mention her fluttery reaction to them. Irritation bubbled inside her. She didn't ask him to retrieve the damned shoe. She could have gotten it herself. She didn't need him playing the hero.

She slid her foot from his thigh onto the icy floor and grabbed her shoe. "Thanks, but I don't require the Cinderella treatment."

He looked up at her with a knowing half smile.

"You have a thing about fairy tales, don't you?"

She blushed, remembering that he'd heard her version of *Beauty and the Beast*. "That doesn't mean I believe in them."

He rose to his feet, his sympathetic smile suggesting he understood all too well why. Before she could stick her foot any deeper in her mouth, she slipped the shoe back on and removed his suit coat. "Thanks," she said, thrusting it at him. "You can go on up to the room. I need to pick up a few things in the gift shop."

"What do you need that you can't call room service for?"

Her first instinct was to tell him feminine protection, but that didn't exactly fit into her plans. "I wanted to try out the hot tub tonight but forgot to pack a swimsuit."

His gaze swept down her body.

She pointed to the gift shop. "I saw a bikini in the window earlier."

His Adam's apple rose and fell. He literally took a step back. Charlotte was certain she had him on his way to the room when loud boisterous laughter filled the lobby. Three men spilled from the bar and zigzagged toward the elevators not far from the gift shop.

Marcus arranged his coat over her shoulders again but not before the drunken louts aimed bloodshot eyes and a few wolfish remarks at her. When they were gone, he sighed. "Maybe I'd better go with you."

Great. She needed five minutes to herself, and he was determined to play Prince Charming. "That's not necessary," she said and started across the lobby.

He fell into step beside her, his hand at her back. "I don't mind. We probably won't have time to shop tomorrow, and I promised Mom and Mel a souvenir."

The shop clerk greeted them when they entered the shop. "Are you looking for anything in particular?"

"A muzzle," she muttered under her breath then smiled at the gray-haired woman. "I'm looking for a swimsuit." She tilted a glance at Marcus and added, "A two-piece, preferably a thong bikini."

The strained look on his face made her feel somewhat better. Maybe it wouldn't be so difficult to get the space she needed. She gave his tie a light yank when the clerk indicated a rack of suits in the back of the store. "Come help me pick one out."

As she'd hoped, he pried her fingers loose and shook his head. "I'm sure you can manage without me, and I've got some shopping of my own to do."

A half hour later, Charlotte had managed to regain control of her body's betrayal and the silly notion that Marcus could be different from the rest of the male species. She was ready to proceed with her plan. Though three swimsuits lay nestled in her luggage upstairs, she had gone through the motion of trying on several.

That alone had gone a long way in her recovery, especially when she'd asked for his assistance with a tricky hook to one of the bikini tops. He'd fumbled for what seemed like hours and finally given up, blaming his ineptitude on cold fingers. A lie since his hands had been warm against her skin. He'd since kept his distance.

That particular suit along with gifts for her mother, Melody and some of the children at the hospital waited in a monogrammed bag at the register while she searched for him.

She grinned when she found him with a collection of scarves around his neck and draped over each arm. "Thinking of doing a veil dance for me later?"

He smiled. Good. He'd lost some of the discomfort she'd caused. "I need some advice."

"Hmm, the green one goes with your eyes."

Pulling the emerald scarf from around his neck, he handed it to her. "Then that one is for Mom. We have the same color eyes."

She ran the scarf through her fingers, enjoying its silky texture. It reminded her of the lingerie she'd packed with Marcus in mind—black satin with slits in all the right places. She couldn't wait to see his expression when he saw her in it.

He cleared his throat. "How about Mel?"

"She likes yellow."

He passed her the lemon chiffon. It wasn't as soft as the silk, but it was nice against her skin. Sifting through the rest, he set aside one after the other until he was down to two. She wondered why he didn't ask her opinion for this selection, and why he glanced at her every few seconds then grew flushed. Was he buying it for her?

The thought warmed her. More than it should have. Still, she could make it easy on him. "The orange one is pretty."

"Would it clash with brown hair? Maybe I should get the purple?"

Brown? Her fists tightened around the material in her hands. "Melody doesn't look good in orange, but I don't think she'd like the tie-dyed purple either."

"It's not for Mel. But you're right. The purple one is more appropriate for a younger woman." He tossed the orange scarf back in the pile and reached for the ones she clutched. "Let me have those before you wrinkle them."

She stared after him as he strode to the front counter and added them to an assortment of items to be rung up. Picking up a glass globe with a wooden pedestal from the shelf near the register, he shook it and grinned at the fake snow that drifted through the watery sky to engulf the miniature town at the base of a mountain. "She'll love this."

Behind him, Charlotte fought the streak of hurt and disappointment that ripped through her at his barely audible words, obviously not meant for her to hear. Instead, she concentrated on keeping her pride intact. He wasn't going to tell her who *she* was. Well, that was fine. He didn't have to. Natalie Weaver was both brunette and young.

So much for her Prince Charming theory.

It was time to snare the Beast.

****

She's willing.

Or at least that's what it seemed like when they'd returned to the suite and Marcus had pleaded exhaustion then hightailed it to his room. He'd heard the frustration in her voice, seen it in those goddamned blue eyes of hers.

He yanked a towel off the ring with enough force to bring down the wall, stepped out of the cold shower and began a brisk rubdown, hoping to dispel some of his own frustration along with his goose bumps.

He sure as hell didn't look forward to spending a night between cold sheets. Alone. And with visions of Charlotte tied to his bed with the same silk scarves she'd run through her fingers, her naked body writhing and moist from where his mouth…

"Hell, go tell her you want her," he grumbled as he leaned against the sink to glare at the mirror. "Just do it and get it over with."

But the image staring back at him didn't budge. He couldn't. Not if he wanted to live with himself after this godforsaken weekend finally ended. Regardless of what Charlotte thought, he cared about her.

With a disgusted sigh, he left the bathroom and sat on the edge of the wide bed to towel dry his hair. A light tapping sound filtered through the brisk rubbing. He lowered the towel to his neck and waited, not sure if wishful thinking had affected his hearing. The knock came again, but not at his door. It came from the suite's main entry.

The door to Charlotte's room opened with a squeak, followed a few seconds later by the sound of a deadbolt being unlocked at the main door. The murmur of a male voice and Charlotte's husky laughter brought him off the bed.

He seized a pair of jeans from his suitcase, jammed one leg in, then the other, and jerked his bedroom door open, determined to have it out with Wylie once and for all. If the guy thought he could take advantage of Charlotte's restlessness and steal into her bed just because Marcus wasn't in it, the bastard had another think coming.

"Geez, I needed this." Her breathy whisper came from the dimly lit entryway.

Damn, was the asshole taking her against the wall?

Marcus rounded the corner at a run and stopped in his tracks. The red-faced grinning teenager, probably sixteen if he was a day, stared at Charlotte with calf-like eyes as he backed into the hall. His gaze shifted to Marcus, and the smile on his face slipped. He swallowed and returned his gaze to Charlotte. "If there's anything else I can get you, Ms. Reese, you be sure to let me know."

"Mmm," she moaned again. "Thank you, Tim."

The door shut, and Marcus waited for her to turn around. When she did, her eyes collided with his and rounded. "I'm sorry. Did I wake you?"

Marcus felt as if he'd been sucker punched. He'd been so concerned with the boy he hadn't noticed her appearance. Her face, scrubbed clean of makeup, held a healthy glow. Her long lashes and perfect brows were only a shade darker than her hair, her lips a pale pink. Her blonde hair was brushed into a ponytail at the back of her head, wisps hanging in disarray around her face and ears. The white cotton nightgown was thick enough he couldn't see through it—maybe why she felt comfortable answering the door in it—with narrow shoulders straps and tiny buttons from the center of the low-cut bodice all the way to the ruffle at the top of her knees.

She was the picture of virginal innocence, and he had never wanted her more.

"Marcus?"

"Uh, no, I—" He cleared his throat and clutched the towel around his neck. "I was taking a shower."

Her gaze skittered over his bare chest, making him wish he'd grabbed a shirt, and lingered on the top button of his jeans he'd left undone. He quickly rectified that error, which drew her attention back to his face for a brief moment before she swept past him, muttering something about needing chocolate.

He did a one-eighty and followed her to the bar as if she held him by some imaginary leash. Once there, she flipped a switch on the wall and soft light filtered over them from the lamp above the pool table. She perched on a high stool and proceeded to stick her finger into whatever concoction the bellhop had delivered.

Mesmerized, he watched her insert the goo-covered finger into her mouth. She closed her eyes with what could only be described as orgasmic bliss as she sucked. His mind screamed for him to run, but his feet remained stationary, rooted to the spot as she slid her finger out and licked her soft pink lips. So much for a cold shower.

"Mmm, this is so good." She wiped her hands on the paper napkin she pulled from a plastic packet along with utensils. With the spoon, she nudged a cherry to the side of the large bowl.

Against his better judgment, he ventured closer. "What is it?"

"A hot fudge sundae with extra, extra, extra fudge. Next best thing to sex." She scooped a heaping spoonful into her mouth.

Another moan of pleasure escaped her, firing Marcus into retreat across the room before he proved her theory wrong. He really should leave her to the dessert, but for the life of him he couldn't. Instead, he began assembling the balls on the pool table. Anything to stay active and keep his focus off her while he kept her talking. "What is it with women and chocolate?"

"Well, if you can't have sex..."

He jerked a glance over his shoulder, sure her open-ended statement was an invitation but found her once again savoring the ice cream. He tried his damnedest to drag his gaze from her, but it refused, same as his feet, giving in only enough to stray to the low-cut bodice of that damned virginal white gown. It lay open, several buttons undone, to reveal the valley between her breasts. Had it been unbuttoned earlier?

Charlotte smiled as Marcus grabbed a pool stick and turned his back on her to make the break. She slipped off the barstool, taking her hot fudge sundae with her, and padded barefoot toward him.

When he'd suggested they turn in early after such a long day, she'd labeled the night a bust. With thoughts of Natalie wearing on her confidence, she hadn't bought his excuse. The sting of yet another rejection had demanded chocolate.

The decadent dessert seemed to be working its magic, but his inability to keep his eyes off her did more to soothe her wounded self-esteem than the fudge.

Settling on the arm of an overstuffed leather chair, she indulged in another taste of vanilla ice cream and hot fudge, licking the spoon to get every morsel. A heated awareness filled her. She peered from beneath her lashes to find him watching her again. His eyes, darkened with lust, traveled from her lips to her crossed legs, caressing them with fire. Her favorite nightgown—not one she would have selected for seduction, definitely not the black satin she'd hoped to surprise him with—had ridden up to mid thigh.

A few inches higher, moisture gathered and a slow throb began. She uncrossed her legs and re-crossed them, squeezing her thighs tight to ward off any command her body might make for her to hurry. Marcus wasn't the type she could rush even if she wanted to. "Would you like some?"

His fiery gaze flew to hers, and she was hard pressed to keep her expression innocent as she held out a spoonful of ice cream. "You keep watching me. I thought you might want some."

Frowning, he leaned against the stick and shook his head. "Not what you're offering. I want it all."

"You ask too much." Uncertain they talked about the same thing, she added, "You should never try to separate a woman from her chocolate."

That got her a smile. And oh, what a smile. "I'll play you for it. A game of eight ball."

"Pool?"

When he nodded, she stood and made her way to his side of the table. Propping a hip against the edge, she said, "I didn't have you pegged for a chocolate lover."

"I'm not."

"So why do you want the whole thing?"

"Because"—he raised a hand to palm her jaw, releasing all the tiny butterflies in her belly—"watching you eat the damned thing is a sexual orchestration I'm not sure I can endure."

She didn't move as his thumb grazed the underside of her bottom lip and came away with a smudge of chocolate fudge. He stuck the digit into his mouth and gave a nod of approval. "Not bad. Not bad at all."

Then just like that he resumed his game while she stood breathless, longing to glide her hands over his chest. To trace that little line of feathery black hair down his rock-hard belly and lower.

From the hard ridge she'd palmed through his tuxedo pants the night of the bachelor auction, she knew she wouldn't be disappointed in what she found. And from the bulge there now, his words weren't idle chit-chat. She hadn't come onto him, yet she'd turned him on. And he wasn't running.

Charlotte didn't bother to analyze the how or why of the situation but considered his challenge and the opportunity it presented. She could turn his wager around and get what she wanted if she played her cards right. Or rather…her balls.

Suppressing a giggle, she followed him around the table, trailing a finger along the edge of the green felt. "I'm not very good. It was my father's game, so I didn't take it up."

Okay, so she wasn't playing fair, baiting him with information he'd seemed to covet throughout dinner.

Stopping beside him again, she added, "Besides, I don't know if I want to give it up. It's really good." She took another mouthful, playing up her enjoyment to prove her point.

He bent to study the angle of his next shot. "You never know. You might beat me."

Oh, she intended to. No matter who won the game. "And what if I do?"

He tilted his head to look at her, causing a lock of inky black hair to fall over his furrowed brow. "What do you mean?"

"What would I get out of it? The ice cream is already mine."

He grinned and turned his attention back to his aim. "The satisfaction of winning."

Fascinating, the way the muscles of his back and shoulders bunched and stretched under his smooth tanned flesh. And if he moved just right, the waist of his jeans slipped below his tan line, offering a glimpse of white skin. No tanning bed had ever seen this body. More likely he'd gotten his golden and well-toned form working weekends on his family's ranch.

He made the shot and straightened, one hip cocked. "Well?"

She shook her head. "You'll have to do better than

that."

"How about I buy you breakfast in the morning?"

"It's on the house, remember? Part of the package?"

"Oh, yeah." He doused the end of the stick with chalk.

She edged closer. "I have something a little more interesting in mind."

"You do, do you?"

"I'll accept your wager, but on my terms."

"Which are?"

The spoon made another trip to her mouth as did his hungry gaze. His nostrils flared as the utensil eased from between her lips. She waved it at him. "For every ball you pocket, you get a bite of my sundae."

"And you? What do you get?"

"For every one I make, I get one minute of complete and utter control over you."

He blinked, and she could almost see the images her words conjured in the reflection of his dark green eyes. Then he laughed. "I don't think so."

"I'll let you go first."

"Uh-uh."

She shrugged. "I didn't think you'd go for it."

"I'm not crazy."

"No, you're the most reserved, in-control person I've ever known. Whether one or a dozen—"

"Seven—eight if you pocket the eight ball to win."

Hmm, eight minutes. She could work wonders with that much time. Of course, she had to win to get them, and she had her doubts about that. But she'd done a lot in less time than that. She waved her spoon at him again. "However many balls there are, I should have known you'd never give me complete power over you."

"What's that supposed to mean?"

"Nothing."

Rubbing the dark stubble along his jaw, he stared

at her long and hard, then planted a hand on his hip. "You don't think I can handle eight minutes of anything you could possibly dish out?"

She shrugged. "It doesn't matter what I think."

And if he agreed, it didn't matter if she won or lost. She had him in the bag.

Make that in the pocket.

Chapter Twelve

Marcus circled the imaginary hook Charlotte baited so cleverly. He would be a fool to bite, knowing the sharp barbs he'd encounter and how deep they would dig.

"Look." She settled a hip on the edge of the pool table, and the hem of her gown rose to give him a tantalizing glimpse of the tender flesh of her upper thighs. "I just thought maybe you'd loosen up for once, you being the better player and all. I mean, what could I possibly do in so short a time?"

What indeed? Her terms left little doubt she was intent on seduction, and he'd been capable of pole-vaulting unassisted across the room since finding her in her nightgown. Yet if there was ever a time to prove not all men wanted her only for her body, this was it.

And he'd withstood her before. He could do it again. Even if it killed him.

She dug into the ice cream once more, and he clamped a hand around her wrist to stop the spoon from reaching her open mouth. "Uh-uh."

A frown creased her brow. "What?"

"You're eating my winnings."

One brow lifted. "Does that mean you accept my terms?"

"Yes, and I want there to be something left *when* I win." Laying his cue on the pool table, he reached for the bowl. "I think the freezer is a good place to hold the prize."

The grin that split her full lips could have blinded him as she shoved the bowl in his hands and jumped to gather the balls. "You said I'd only have eight minutes if I won, so I'm assuming the most you'll get is eight bites. If you want the whole sundae, maybe we should play several games."

Heading to the kitchen area, he laughed at her not-so-subtle attempt to gain extra minutes of control over him. Though he expected to run the table, there was always a chance she'd succeed in making a few shots. He wouldn't push his luck. Or his stamina. "One game is enough. I'll take big bites."

"You'll get brain freeze," she called out.

He stowed the sundae, turned around, and groaned. She stretched across the table to retrieve a ball, the neckline of her gown hanging open. The gentle curve of her breasts sent his blood rushing south. If she angled a little farther to one side…

Marcus closed his eyes. What the hell was he doing? He would never survive this game if he allowed his imagination to run wild. It was hard enough dealing with the enticement of reality. Hard being the operative word.

Drawing a long breath, he strode forward purposefully, and with no small amount of difficulty, determined not to let her distract him. "Not like that. That one goes in the middle." He took the eight ball from her before she could drop it in the top position. "I'll do this. You go pick out a cue."

"A stick?"

"Yes, over there." He pointed to the rack holding several cues and waited for her to give up the five ball she held in her other hand and move aside.

"What difference does it make what ball goes where?"

"It just does, okay?"

"See, always in control," she said with a wry smile before relinquishing the ball and strolling to the cue rack. She surveyed several then picked one that was too heavy for her.

"You'd be better off with the smaller one, second

to the end."

She slid him a sideways look. "If I didn't know better, I'd think you were trying to help me."

He turned his back on her and finished rearranging the balls. Grabbing the cue ball, he rounded the table and placed it on the head spot. "Just trying to be fair."

When he glanced her way again, she was once more perched half on, half off the far corner, this time with a pool cue between her legs. Several buttons at the hem of her gown were loose, and one strap hung down her arm. She might not know how to play pool, but she sure as hell knew how to play him.

Forcing his gaze from her shapely thighs, he asked, "Still want me to break?"

She eased to her feet and sauntered toward him. "First, I think we should seal the deal." When she stood toe to toe with him, she leaned forward, her lips close to his. "With a kiss."

He stepped back and held out his hand. "A shake will do."

She smiled and placed her hand in his, her eyes dancing with mischief. Or was it triumph? "I have your word? Complete and utter control?"

He smiled back, slightly shaken but still confident. "You have my word."

Nodding, she released his hand. "Then let's get started."

Marcus bent over the table, bracing his fingers on the felt, and tried to concentrate, almost impossible with Charlotte leaning on one elbow beside him. Close enough that her breath brushed his shoulder. He angled a look at her. "Do you mind?"

Her eyes widened in innocence. "Oh, sorry. I wanted to see how exactly you hold the stick. You did say you were trying to be fair."

"Yes, I did." Sighing, he focused once more on his target and pulled back the cue to shoot. Her fingernails grazed the flat of his stomach just above the waist of his jeans. He jerked. His arm shot forward, the cue hitting the side of the ball. He stared slack-jawed as it skidded to one side and into the left center pocket.

"Is that what's called a scratch?"

"I'd call it cheating."

"Now, now," she said, circling to the foot of the table for the cue ball, a giddy grin on her beautiful face. "All's fair in love and getting your just desserts."

"Very funny."

"Oh, come on. It's not like this is a high stakes game."

Maybe not for her, but he'd just lost the upper hand and some of his confidence that he could run the table.

Returning to stand next to him, she placed the ball on the head spot and used her hip to nudge him aside. She took aim, a bit awkwardly perhaps, but well enough for him to wonder if she'd played before or was just a quick study.

Then his attention strayed to the nature of her position, and he wondered other things. Like what she'd do if he stood behind her, close enough to feel her heat through his jeans. What if he diverted her attention as she had his by running his hands up those satiny thighs beneath her gown to slowly peel her underwear away? Would she arch her back, wriggle against him?

"Am I doing it right?"

She rocked back then forward several times, pumping the cue through her spread fingers.

He wanted to close his eyes to maintain what little control he had left but didn't dare. He couldn't trust her not to cheat. "I think you know exactly what you're doing."

****

Charlotte hid her grin, enjoying Marcus's discomfort for a moment before focusing on the white ball. She might know how to play the game of seduction, but she didn't know squat about billiards. She hadn't had the stomach for it after her father bragged to his friends that he'd banged someone's wife on the pool table at home while her mother had been in the hospital.

With a joust meant to release the rage the memory stirred, she rammed the small end of the stick at the center of the ball, shattering the silence. The triangle of colorful spheres dispersed in myriad of directions, but the force of the break was insufficient and most stopped after traveling only inches. She held her breath as one neared the right corner pocket and slowed to a crawl.

"Come on," she whispered, willing the solid green ball to keep moving. "Just a little farther." It teetered then disappeared down the hole. She didn't bother to hide her grin this time as she turned to Marcus. "That's one minute."

"Lucky break," he said, with a teasing smile and careless shrug, no doubt meant to convey his lack of concern. His rigid stance and white-knuckled grip on the stick, told her otherwise.

"Maybe." She leaned close enough to smell the clean fresh scent of soap. "But it's a start."

"Okay, Ace. Get on with it. Call your next shot."

"You mean I have to tell you which ball I'll hit?"

"And where."

She circled the table and pretended to consider several possibilities, making certain Marcus got an eyeful in the process. A cluster of balls, mostly solids, sat semi-close to the left corner. Surely, one would go in if she hit them hard enough. But the angle of the shot looked tricky with the white ball surrounded by others. How was she supposed to get her fingers in between them?

"Orange ball in the left corner," she said, twisting to get the best position.

"Solid or stripe?"

Damn. She had hoped he wouldn't ask that. Either was possible. "Solid. I've never looked good in stripes."

She heard him chuckle as she made her shot. The white ball hopped over the blue one in front of it and landed smack in the middle of the cluster. A red solid raced to the left corner and fell in followed by the orange one.

Charlotte let out a whoop and spun to find Marcus, arms folded over his chest, frowning at her. "What?"

"Are you sure you've never played."

Laughing, she held up her right hand. "I swear."

His expression remained skeptical as he unfolded his arms and motioned for her to continue.

Anticipation bubbling inside her, she scanned the table again. The closest solid was on the other end with a host of stripes between. But hey, hadn't she just worked a miracle?

Her excitement dissolved into disappointment when the end of her stick grazed the side of the white ball and sent it spinning in place. "Does that count?"

"Fortunately for me, it does." Grinning, he chalked the end of his stick and moved into position across from her before she could think to distract him. "Nine—left side pocket."

Two balls crashed into the hole in front of her. Damn. She would have to get busy if she wanted another turn.

"Excuse me," he said beside her. "Twelve—right corner."

She stepped back, waited until he was ready to shoot, then moved in and blew in his ear. He shivered and shook his head, reminding her of a dog out of the tub with his hair still damp. He turned a scolding look on her.

She propped a hip against the table inches from

his. "Hey, a girl has to take every advantage."

"I'd say you've got more than your share." His gaze drifted to the open bodice of her gown before returning to the game.

She smiled to herself and meandered to his other side, trailing a fingernail down the taut muscles of his back, causing him to shudder. "You've got a few of your own."

His jaw clenched, but he didn't look up. She pressed further, palming his ass through his jeans. He jolted upright and pointed to the opposite side of the table. "You—over there."

Laughing, Charlotte wandered slowly, weaving her fingernail over the green felt between balls to stall his play. On the opposite side, she leaned her stick against the table then braced both hands, the inside of her wrists forward, on the edge and balanced her weight on them, thrusting her breasts forward. He liked them so much, let him have a good look.

But he wasn't looking at her breasts. Bent over, his gaze was level with her hips. She wondered if he could tell she didn't have on panties. The way his green eyes darkened before he looked away, she thought he might. Oh, this was fun.

He made the shot, sinking the purple-striped ball, and straightened. "Speaking of advantages, I've often wondered how you fill your days."

Well, that came out of nowhere. Was he trying to turn the table on her, distracting her to keep her from distracting him? Then it hit her. He'd often wondered. How often was often? And did he wonder anything about her other than how she spent her days?

She shook herself mentally. Now was not the time to get lost in wayward thinking. She lowered her voice to a purr. "As opposed to how I spend my nights?"

A telling flush stained his face beneath the tan, making her smile. "I meant, since you have so many advantages, what do you do besides Friday morning story time at the hospital?"

Other than fantasize about you? "Oh, this and that."

"Fourteen — same pocket." He aimed and tapped the white ball, which sent the green ball rolling toward its destination with success. "You obviously don't have to, but have you thought about finishing college?"

"Who says I didn't?" The question sounded defensive even to her ears. It was a topic dear to her, but not one she wanted to share. At least not with him.

"Did you?"

"Not with Avery if that's what you mean."

He pointed to the head of the table. She grabbed her stick, and together they rotated, she to the head, he to the foot. Shadow and light faded in and out of the valleys and plains of his upper body as he moved. She envied them, couldn't wait for her three minutes.

"Why not?"

"Huh? Oh, I flunked a few classes." Most of them her freshman year when she'd wanted to piss off her dad for forcing her to major in business.

"Too much partying?"

It didn't surprise Charlotte that Marcus had jumped to the same conclusion as everyone else. But tonight, his assumption disappointed her, and she felt an overwhelming need to explain. She fought it. It wouldn't change anything.

"There was that." She lifted a shoulder and let it drop.

His gaze darted to the strap of her gown that hung low on her arm then shifted back to the table. "Eleven." He indicated the pocket to her right with his stick. "What else was there?"

"I changed my major three times."

The white ball crashed into the red one, which banked off the left side, sped for the corner pocket beside her right hand, and clattered on its way down. Marcus picked up the chalk and sauntered toward her. Without instruction, she moved in the opposite direction around the table.

"Ten." He nodded toward the corner pocket on her left.

"This one?" She planted one butt cheek above the designated pocket and swung a leg up to rest a foot on the edge of the table. With her knee bent, her gown barely covered the essentials. In case it wasn't enough, she smoothed a hand up her calf and down her thigh then fingered the ruffled hem.

The heat of his gaze as it journeyed from one end of her to the other, stopping briefly in strategic areas, was unmistakable and sent her pulse racing. She wished he would just forget the damn game and accept the attraction between them as inevitable. All this foreplay was great, but she was ready to move on.

"What did you end up with?"

"Huh?"

"What did you finally major in?"

Damn his stubborn hide. Here she was working herself up into a fine state of need and he wanted to talk about education. If he didn't cave soon, she would be wouldn't get any sleep tonight. "I thought it was obvious. Sexual Behavior Science."

He blinked and shook his head. "Why do you do that?"

"Do what?"

"Hide behind innuendo."

She arched her back and angled her shoulders toward him. "Does it look like I'm hiding anything?" When he didn't answer but once more raked her body with hungry eyes, she added, "Want to play hide and seek?"

****

Laying his cue alongside Charlotte's on the green felt plain, Marcus leaned against the table and waited for her to return with his prize.

Having stood just about all he could, he had quickly pocketed the thirteen ball and then the eight to end the game. He'd wanted to get the consequences of this foolish wager over so he could take another cold shower. Hell, he doubted anything short of throwing himself headfirst in a damned snowbank would relieve the aching hard-on behind his increasingly tight jeans.

He struggled not to cover himself, letting his arms hang at his sides. He'd given up trying to hide his condition after the third time he'd caught her blatant stare. To try now would only call attention to it.

Bare feet crowded his view of the carpet in front of him, startling him out of his erotic thoughts. He tried to ignore the length of her slender legs and the desire that swamped him to have them wrapped around his waist as he dragged his tortured gaze upward. It stalled again at the golden flesh peeking over the top of her gown.

She stepped between his spread feet, and he jerked his head back. He'd half expected to see a satisfied smirk at his obvious condition. Instead, her top teeth chewed the lush fullness of her bottom lip and her soft blue eyes held uncertainty. It quickly vanished, replaced by the same sensual aggression he'd seen her use a number of times to put him off.

Marcus took the bowl and set it on the corner of the table. "You have three minutes."

She leaned closer, placing both hands on the table behind him. The beaded tips of her breasts grazed his chest. Her scent swirled around him. "You want me to go first? Aren't you afraid your ice cream will melt?"

Managing to draw a breath, uneven though it was, he nodded. "You lost the game, so technically you would get to break first if we played again." He wasn't about to tell her he might need the ice cream to cool down after she was through with him.

When she straightened, Marcus braced himself for her touch. Her soft hands flattened on his chest, and he nearly jumped out of his skin as they smoothed a path up and along his shoulders. Her sweet lips followed, pressing hot kisses in their wake.

"Complete control," she murmured and looked up at him. "We shook on it."

Control. The key to proving it was keeping it, and yet he'd promised to give it. He ground his teeth and nodded. "You have my word."

She slid her hands down his chest over his ribs to splay across his stomach. "There's a clock over the bar. Let me know when my time is up." She tilted him a sultry smile. "If you can."

He glanced at the black square on the wall with big red digital numbers. Eleven seventeen. All he had to do was focus on the time, and he could endure his debt. Especially when she seemed content to explore his chest. She hadn't even tried—

The buttons of his jeans gave way, the loosened denim dragged open. Cool air hit his straining erection just before her warm fingers wrapped around it.

"Ah, shit." His gaze swung forward. She was on her knees. "No, don'—"

Her mouth closed over him.

"Oh, God."

Hot, wet, slow insertion. Even slower withdrawal. Marcus couldn't imagine any sweeter torture. Her tongue circled his head, once, twice, and he discovered otherwise. He closed his eyes against the pleasure, but that only intensified it.

Opening them, he focused on the clock rather than Charlotte and what she was doing to him. Eleven eighteen. He'd never survive another two minutes. He had to stop her. Now.

He reached blindly for her as she tugged his jeans lower. His fingers fanned the sides of her head, felt the cool strands of her silky hair at their tips and, of their own accord, thrust deep into the tightly bound thickness. She gave a soft whimper, and something popped. He looked down to see the gadget holding her hair back flutter to the floor and her silvery blonde mane spill around his hands to cover her face and brush his thighs. A fantasy fulfilled, but one he couldn't allow to continue.

Then she cupped his balls, her middle finger applying gentle pressure behind them. His knees buckled, and he had to let go of her to grab the edge of the table. His head fell back as shards of heat rippled through him. He would allow himself this one moment of heaven. He would stop her soon.

He heard her ragged breathing. Or was it his? She took him deeper, and the buzzing in his ears grew louder, drowning everything else out. He looked at the clock, vaguely wondering if this was a dream and the alarm was about to go off. If it didn't, he was.

Eleven twenty. Time to stop.

Marcus closed his eyes. He didn't want to stop. He wanted to ride it out, to be right where he was when he came. Just the thought brought on the familiar tightening that warned him release was near. If he didn't stop her now, there would be no turning back.

"Char—" His voice cracked, and he attempted to swallow but didn't have any spit. He tried again, desperate to make her hear him. "Charlotte, stop."

When she didn't, he gave up his hold on the table and grabbed her upper arms. He tried to move backward but couldn't, which meant she had to. Before it was too late. Before he took the very thing he'd told her she shouldn't have to give.

He pushed at the same time he bowed at the waist, a painful but effective move that freed him and sent her tumbling backward. She gaped up at him, clearly startled by his rough actions. Hell, he was, too. But at the moment his attention was required elsewhere.

****

Charlotte blinked as Marcus jerked his jeans up and over his hips then turned away to brace one hand on the edge of the pool table. The other she was certain he used to prevent him from coming. With his head hung low, his back rigid, shoulders shuddering, she knew the difficulty it caused him.

Yet, it was her own reaction that shocked her. She'd done this before but never particularly liked it or been so excited as a result. She certainly hadn't meant to go that far. Just far enough to nudge him past the point of no return so he wouldn't argue when she pushed him onto the table and straddled him. That had been her plan.

But she'd gotten lost somewhere along the way, become consumed by him and his response. She'd wanted to give him everything and take all he had to give.

"Sorry," he said, breaking the silence. "I didn't mean to hurt you."

She pushed off her elbows and sat up. "You didn't. Are you okay?"

"I just need a minute."

A minute for what? To rein in his libido so they could move on to other, more rewarding pleasures? Or simply continue with the rewards of their wager.

Certain either would lead where she intended them to go, she rose to her feet and stood directly behind him. She laid a hand on his back.

He flinched. "Don't."

So, they would be taking the long route as usual.

Sighing inwardly, she picked up the bowl and hopped up on the table beside him, her thigh against his. "Open up. This will cool you down."

Buttoning his jeans, he looked at her, then averted his glassy green eyes and backed away. "I think I'll turn in."

Uh-oh. She couldn't let him escape now. "You can't."

"Why not? Our bargain is finished."

She held up the bowl and dangled the spoon. "You haven't claimed your prize."

He turned and started for his room. "I forfeit."

Setting the bowl aside, she jumped off the table and darted around the chair to block his path. "Forget the bet. You are not walking away from me like this. Not again."

He stared past her, his body stiff, hands clenched at his sides. "Charlotte, if I stay out here, things are going to happen that we'll both regret in the morning."

"Believe me, I won't regret a thing."

His eyes narrowed and locked with hers. "I won't use you."

"Then let me use you."

He snorted and brushed past her.

Rage, hurt, and pure need all battled for the upper hand within her. "I can't believe you're going to leave me hanging like this. I'm in the same shape as you."

Almost to his door, he offered, "Take a cold shower. It's what I plan to do."

Planting both fists on her hips, she thrust her chin forward. "That's right, Marcus. Walk away. Leave it for another man to take care of."

That stopped him. Knowing the barb she'd thrown had hit its mark almost brought a smile to her lips, but she fought it as he turned to face her.

"What's that supposed to mean?"

"I'm sure Grant wouldn't mind another go for old time's sake."

"You said there was nothing between you and Wylie."

She lifted a shoulder and let it drop. "There isn't. But it's been my experience men are faithless and won't pass up an adventurous night of hot sex with a woman who knows what she wants." She pivoted on her heel and marched toward her room, satisfied she'd given him something to think about.

The room suddenly tilted as he caught and spun her around. His strong fingers dug into her forearms, painful yet exhilarating in a way she couldn't explain. Same as his dark expression.

"Don't you get it? Yes, you are a beautiful, desirable woman, but you're so much more. You don't have to do this. There are men who will want you for who you are, not for what you can do for them, if you just give them the chance."

"It's you who doesn't get it," she almost shouted. "I don't want that kind of relationship. And right now, all I want is for you to finish what we started."

"What *you* started."

"You can't tell me you didn't enjoy it, that you don't want me. You're so hot you're shaking, hurting." She splayed her hands at the base of his ribs and slid them upward through feathery black hair to thumb the coppery disks hidden there. He shuddered, and she looked up at him. "I can make it stop."

He closed lust-shadowed eyes but quickly reopened them and stared into hers. His jaw worked, until she thought it would break. He was weakening. She knew it and licked her lips in anticipation.

He groaned, her only warning before his mouth slanted over hers. His tongue demanded entrance. She opened to him. His arms encircled her. One wide palm cupped the back of her head, angling her for deeper penetration, the other splayed at the small of her back, almost crushing her. It was a desperate kiss. One meant to purge himself of her.

Oh, no you don't. Charlotte groped for something to cling to as she mimicked his actions but found only the smooth skin of his back and shoulders. Reaching higher, she clutched his thick black hair then thrust her hips against his, moaning at the feel of his hard dick against her belly.

But he broke the kiss, resting his forehead against hers, eyes clenched tight, his breath rushing in and out, hot against her cheek. "I can't."

"Don't do this." She hated the desperation in her voice, hated that she sounded as if she were begging, but damn him, she would. She ached to have him inside her, even if only his tongue in her mouth. "Please?"

Standing on tiptoes, she tried to coax him with her lips to continue, but he pulled her arms from around him and set her at arm's length. Gently, he palmed her face with both hands, his fingers spread. "I do want you, Charlotte. God knows at this moment almost more than anything in the world."

He lowered his head, but the kiss he pressed to her lips was all too brief. She whimpered when he drew back and dropped his hands to his sides. "But there's one thing I want more."

Breathless and stunned, by both his tenderness and his refusal, Charlotte couldn't move until the door shut quietly behind him. Then she stomped her foot. Damn him, he'd done it again. Turned the tables on her. Staggered her with a kiss and left her wanting. And totally confused.

What did he mean there was one thing he wanted more than having sex with her? What did he want? He'd said she had more to offer a man than her body. Was that what he wanted? A relationship? With her?

A tiny thrill raced up her spine, but she squashed it. If she'd learned anything from her father, it was that men took their satisfaction at whim. Even men like Marcus.

So why did he try to convince her otherwise? Was it part of the game? Was she a challenge he couldn't resist and denial part of his strategy?

And why did her heart try to convince her that wasn't the case? Maybe because Marcus *did* continue to walk away from every pleasure she offered. Maybe he *was* different from most men. Hadn't she suspected as much from the beginning? Wasn't that why she kept him at a distance for so many years?

Or maybe he simply doesn't want you.

The thought cut deep, but Charlotte thrust it aside. He did want her. He'd said so. And she'd felt his desire as surely as she'd felt her own. Something she hadn't been prepared to face.

She fingered her lips, still warm and moist from his kiss. In the past, she'd lost herself in his touch, but tonight, she'd lost herself in touching him. The realization that Marcus's enjoyment could inflame her own response, one of passion and not just of physical need, scared the hell out of her. She'd begged him, for fuck's sake. She'd never done that with another man. She'd never had to.

From the start, she had known any involvement with Marcus, other than sexual, wasn't an option. Now, the stakes were higher than ever. She had opened herself up to lure him in and would likely end up licking her wounds when the weekend was over and he moved on to someone else. If she were smart, she would forget everything and be on the first plane home.

But she couldn't forget her obligations to the benefit, the sponsors and most of all, to the children. She could, however, forget this ridiculous plan to seduce Marcus. She could suffer the moments they were together, make it through one more day and night and get back to life without him in it.

Because if she continued in the direction she'd meant to go, she might never find her way back.

****

Marcus braced his weight against the door. Not because he thought Charlotte would try to follow him. In fact, if the icy glint in her blue eyes was anything to go by, he'd be lucky if she said three words to him tomorrow. And those would probably be "go to hell".

No, he leaned against the door because he didn't think he could make it to the bed without his legs collapsing. His whole body shook from the inside out, and not just from the aftershock of having her glorious mouth around him. Though he doubted he would ever forget those four long and incredible minutes.

It was the bomb that exploded in his brain halfway through that soul-wrenching kiss that had him shaken. If he'd made love to her tonight, she would believe him the same as every man she'd known. After all he'd learned about her, his goal no longer had to do with her perception of other men and what they wanted from her.

It was about him. And what *he* wanted.

He wanted to know the Charlotte she hid from the world. He wanted those little moments when she lowered her guard, when the world disappointed her and she needed someone. He wanted to be that someone, to convince her he wouldn't let her down. That they had more than a physical attraction in common. That she could trust him.

No matter how much she denied wanting that kind of relationship, Marcus was beginning to suspect that she yearned to the depths of her wary soul for something more than a sexual encounter. He just had to make her see she had nothing to fear. At least not from him.

But first, he would have to pass whatever trials she put him through. The anger in her eyes, along with the history of his experience with Charlotte, assured him she would turn up the heat and there would be many more tests like the one he'd just endured.

One he'd damned near failed.

Chapter Thirteen

Fire crackled in the gas fireplace behind them, casting a warm glow throughout the living area of the suite. Steam rose from identical mugs of hot cocoa. Yet neither came close to thawing the stiff-backed woman seated beside Marcus on the bear skin rug.

The camera whirred from several feet away then stopped. Slick Rick motioned to him with one hand. "Can you get a little closer?"

"If I get any closer, I'll be in her lap." Braced on one hand, Marcus faced Charlotte, angled so that his hip pressed against her jean-clad thigh. His bent knee brushed the sleeve of her icy pink sweater every time she sipped from her cup, dragging the wide collar farther over a sunkissed shoulder.

"You're supposed to be lovers on a romantic rendezvous in a hotel room," the photographer said. "You should be close enough to whisper sweet nothings in her ear."

From somewhere behind the lights, Wylie said, "Just pretend we're not here."

"I should be so lucky," Marcus muttered, which earned him a frown from Charlotte, her first real response to him this morning.

He'd been right to worry about retaliation for leaving her unfulfilled the night before. But he'd been wrong about the tests she would put him through. Instead of the increased sexual aggression he had anticipated this morning, she met him with a cold and indifferent stare. As if the previous day had never happened, the closeness they shared disappeared.

Him right along with it.

What dug at him most, like a burr wedged under a saddle, was that while she ignored *him*, unless forced otherwise, she flirted with Grant Wylie, hung on his every word. Even Slick Rick, with his meaty hands and leering eyes, was granted the warmth of her smile and an occasional quip.

Rick cocked his head to one side. "Let's lose the cocoa. It's distracting."

"Good idea." Wylie stepped forward to relieve them of the mugs and winked at Charlotte. "She's enough distraction."

"You didn't used to mind."

Before Charlotte and Wylie launched into another nostalgic story, of which Marcus could neither participate nor stomach, he placed a hand at Charlotte's waist and hauled her against him, hip to hip. He tucked his legs behind her, one wedged against her butt, the other drawn upright at her back, and rested his free arm on his knee, essentially trapping her.

Not that she tried to get away. She could have been a statue; she sat so still. If he hadn't felt the muscles in her back go rigid when he touched her, he would have really been worried.

"Good," the irritating shutterbug said. "Now, Ms. Reese, put your arm around his neck."

She complied easily, but Marcus felt her tension.

"Okay, now put your other hand on his upper arm."

Her hand seared his bicep through the black cashmere pullover he'd picked out for the shoot. Her fingers tightened around his muscle then relaxed, and all he could think about was how they'd flexed around his cock the night before.

"Good. Now Mr. Preston, move in just a bit more."

Marcus hesitated then eased forward. She might have flinched when his chest grazed her breasts. He couldn't be sure. But she did turn her head away as his face came within inches of hers. Close enough to smell the chocolate on her breath, reminding him of hot fudge ice cream, of Charlotte enjoying both, her pink tongue swirling...

The shutter on the camera snapped in rapid succession. "Sweet nothings, remember?"

Marcus cleared his throat *and* his mind, casting out the erotic visions that threatened to unman him. He focused instead on cool blue eyes and the goal he'd set last night. One she seemed hell bent on refuting. "Why wouldn't you have breakfast with me this morning?"

"I don't eat breakfast." Her smile was at odds with the chill in her voice.

He didn't believe her for a moment but decided not to press the issue. "Then how about lunch?"

"No, thank you."

"You do eat lunch, don't you?"

"When I'm hungry."

Her tone said she wouldn't be, and Marcus sighed inwardly. She wasn't going to make this easy. Still, he had to keep trying. He wouldn't let her freeze him out. "Would you like to do something special this afternoon? More shopping?"

"I'm done." She shook her hair over her shoulder. It tickled his fingers, and they automatically threaded themselves into the thickness at the back of her neck. Her eyes fluttered shut, and he felt her quiver.

Something inside him — most likely the ego she'd trampled all morning, hell, from the moment they'd met — responded to the tremor. Before he could stop himself, he touched his lips to the underside of her jaw. Her fingers dug into his arm again. "We could go for another ride." He nuzzled the sensitive spot below her ear. Her pulse raced against his mouth. "You seem to enjoy that."

She jerked her head back to look at him

He gave her what he hoped was an innocent smile. "Riding horses, I mean."

Ignoring his suggestion, she turned to the cameraman. "Can we take a break?"

Rick released an exasperated sigh. "It was just starting to work. Can't you wait five minutes?"

"As much as I adore Marcus, you can hardly expect me to be at my romantic best when I'm hungry." Bottom lip protruding, eyes pleading, her gaze cut to him then back to Rick.

The photographer didn't stand a chance. "All right. Take five."

"Thanks. I missed breakfast."

"Why you little—"

Charlotte pushed out of his arms and, without a backwards glance, headed to Wylie. Marcus let her go. Short of causing a scene, there was nothing else he could do.

"I've got something for every craving," Wylie offered, guiding her to the assortment of fruits and pastries laid out on the bar.

Marcus ground his teeth as he rose to follow them. He knew he shouldn't let their playful banter get to him. For all her teasing, flirtatious or otherwise, he suspected she only did it to make him crazy. And while Wylie matched her sometimes saucy repartee, nothing in his body language indicated sexual interest.

Maybe that's what bothered him. They had some kind of connection beyond their physical past that he couldn't understand. Or share. He was the outsider again. And still uncertain of their relationship, no matter what either of them said.

Easing behind Charlotte, Marcus settled his hands on her waist. She tried to squirm away under the pretense of making a selection, but he held tight until she realized he wouldn't be denied and finally settled on a bite-sized pie with peach filling. She popped the morsel in her mouth and moaned her approval, probably as pay back, then devoured another before reaching for a stem of grapes.

Wylie held out a bowl of cherries. "Want one?"

A knowing look, one that spoke of another shared memory, passed between them, and irritation knifed through Marcus. "She doesn't like cherries."

She twisted to look at him, her eyes wide with a mixture of annoyance and confusion. "How did—"

As she clamped her glossy red lips together into a thin line, he wondered if she realized he'd been watching her when she pushed the cherry in her sundae to one side last night. Then again, maybe her frown meant she recalled the things that had happened—or rather hadn't happened—much later.

She turned back to Wylie, all traces of anger gone from her expression. "And you, my friend," she said, shaking her finger, "know very well why."

Wylie dangled a cherry by its stem. "Can you still do it?"

"Let's see." She bent forward, mouth open, and guided the cherry Wylie held into her mouth, stem and all, with her tongue.

To his credit, Wylie didn't seem the least bit aroused by the sensual act as he grinned at Marcus. "The fraternity held a stem tying contest," he explained. "Charlotte came in second with forty-two successful knots, cherries intact. It took her an hour."

Marcus was mesmerized as she worked the fruit around in her mouth, cheeks sucking in and out, tongue probing. His body tightened. He'd been in that mouth the night before, knew exactly how that tongue felt, but for only four minutes. What heavens could he reach in an hour?

"Probably swallowed more than she tied." Wylie's voice filtered into his fantasy.

Swallowed? God, he'd never look at a cherry the same way again.

Charlotte took Wylie's hand and gave the fruit one last suck before letting it slide from her moist lips onto his palm, its stem in a knot. "I've still got it."

Wylie laughed and dabbed the red juice from her chin with a paper napkin. "Remember how stained your lips were?"

She made a face. "No, but I remember how sick I was after."

"I hope it taught you a lesson," Marcus grumbled.

The heated look she shot over her shoulder told him he'd just stepped into something deep. "Yes, I learned to save my talented tongue for other, much more pleasurable moments."

Wylie choked on one of the damned cherries, but Marcus ignored him. Same as he did the slow burn that started in his groin. He was far more interested in the fact that she had slipped up. He'd gotten to her, made her mad enough that she'd switched gears and fallen back on the defensive pattern he knew so well. One he could deal with. And take advantage of. At least in public.

He grinned as he took the grapes from her and slipped an arm around her. "Sounds like a promise to me."

If making her mad enough to speak without measuring every word was the ticket to understanding and eventually winning her, so be it. And if it got her away from Wylie, even better. He pressed his lips against her temple. "Come on. Let's get this shoot finished."

"But I'm still hungry."

Her pouting mouth belied the tension beneath her soft curves. He sure as hell felt her fingernails digging into his flesh. And heaven help him, the weight of her breasts on his forearm. "I'll feed you, darlin'." He glanced at Wylie and winked. "How's that for romance?"

Wylie grinned and rubbed his hands together, for a moment reminding Marcus of Avery. "I'll break out the bubbly for the hot tub shoot. It needs to breathe."

"Sounds heavenly," Charlotte murmured.

"It's too early for me." Marcus had watched her repeatedly pick up her wine glass during dinner the night before only to swirl it in her hand then place it back on the table. When she was actually thirsty, she drank from her water glass. He'd added that to the fact that she never actually consumed that blasted drink at the bar and finally realized she'd been telling the truth when she said she didn't drink.

It had also suddenly struck him that he might very well be the only one she'd ever admitted that to, since she insisted on hiding her decision to abstain. For that reason, he wanted her to know he believed her, and she didn't have to pretend to please others. Especially him. "I figured you might use champagne in the photos, so I had a bottle of ginger ale sent up this morning. It's in the fridge. Do you mind?"

Wylie looked at him with surprise—probably because champagne was actually considered a breakfast beverage—but he recovered nicely. "Uh, sure. I don't think anyone can tell the difference."

"Thanks."

As soon as Wylie's back was turned, Charlotte twisted free of his embrace to face him. "What was that all about?"

Marcus bit back a smile, enjoying her befuddlement, glad it was her and not him for a change. He tucked a stray lock behind her ear. "Just looking out for you."

"I don't need you to." She swatted his hand then belatedly darted a look at the two men across the room, one occupied with his equipment, the other with his head in the refrigerator. "I can take care of myself. And you can stop being so nice to me while you're at it."

His amusement faded at her words. "You didn't seem to mind yesterday."

"That was before."

"Before what?"

Her chin rose. "Last night."

He couldn't help the sharp bark of laughter that escaped. "What? If I don't sleep with you, I can't be nice to you? That's pretty distorted."

"Ms. Reese, Mr. Preston," Rick called from a across the room. "If you're ready?"

Marcus snagged her hand and pulled her several feet to the rug, determined to hang on to his temper. Right or wrong, he could see only one way to keep her from withdrawing from him again. He had to keep her rattled. "Lie down."

"I don't—"

Marcus placed a finger on her lips and shifted so that he stood between her and the two men. "It was your idea to pretend we're lovers, not mine, but I'm trying to do what you asked. So, if you don't want everyone to find out we've lied, you'll do as I say. Now shut up and lie down." His last command came out a little louder than he intended, and from the look on her face as she darted a glance over his shoulder, the others heard.

Quick to cover his mistake, she gripped the front of his shirt and peered up at him from beneath dark lashes, sultry invitation in her bold eyes for the others to see. "I know this is taxing, baby, and we didn't get much sleep last night, but if you say that again later, I'll make it up to you in ways you can't begin to imagine. And maybe some you can."

The withering glare she shot him before lowering her lithe frame to the fur rug didn't stop the shudder that slid under his skin at the sensual promise. It didn't matter that it was false.

Marcus glanced toward Wylie, who looked back at him with amused sympathy. Having suffered the same look from his brothers, he shrugged off Wylie's pity and turned to Rick. The man practically licked his lips with unconcealed lust, nothing Marcus hadn't seen other men do, but something he feared he would have to learn to live with if he wanted to retain his sanity.

And with what he was about to do, he had to be grateful for the audience.

Stretching out beside her, Marcus propped himself on one elbow and set the grapes on her stomach. Plucking one, he glanced at the cameraman. "You ready?"

The man straightened and lifted his camera.

Marcus turned his full attention to Charlotte. She lay perfectly still and so goddamned sexy, with one hand above her head, the other on her belly, one knee thrust upward. He almost lost his nerve. "How about you?"

She gazed up at him, still angry but unable to conceal a bit of uncertainty. "How about me what?"

He touched the grape to her mouth, words forming on the tip of his tongue that would likely stir a fire better left to cool before one of them got burned. "Are you ready for *me*?"

Her lips parted, he suspected in shock, but her eyes flared with the same telltale desire he'd witnessed the night before. It dawned on him that he'd never seen it in her eyes when she looked at Wylie. Caring, humor, mischief, and yes, sometimes sensual invitation, but never the heated passion he invoked on the occasions they'd been together. The sudden knowledge gave him hope even as it warned of the danger that lurked in the direction he headed, audience or not.

He held another grape ready. "What's really bothering you?"

She paused in her chewing then swallowed. "Besides you?"

Marcus chuckled and rubbed her lower lip with the seedless fruit. "What is it about me that bothers you so much? Other than the fact that I won't have sex with you." *Yet*.

"It's not you personally." She tried to snag the

grape with her teeth, but he pulled it back. She sighed. "I told you last night I don't want the happily-ever-after kind of relationship you're talking about. I don't believe it exists."

"I think you do." He fed her the grape and placed a hand at her waist to tug her closer. Sliding a knee between hers, he rested his thigh on hers. Vaguely aware of the camera's whir, he ducked his head until his lips hovered mere inches from hers. "I think you're just afraid."

"That's ridiculous." Her words came out in a soft whisper as her hand slid up his arm to his shoulder and her fingers touched his hair.

"Is it?" He nipped her lower lip and tasted the sweet juice from the grape. "What about your fascination with fairytales?" He tilted his head back to look at her. "You tell them to the kids at the hospital. Are they not supposed to believe in them either?"

"Those are for entertainment. They're not real."

"Maybe, but many of them relay the promise that love conquers all."

Her gaze drifted to a spot over his shoulder. "I'd say most show how much love hurts."

"Is that what you're afraid of?"

She chewed her bottom lip for a moment then lifted dewy eyes to lock with his, searching for something. "Marcus, this thing between us...I'm—"

"That's a wrap." Rick's voice penetrated the quiet. "I got what I wanted."

Marcus muttered a curse when Charlotte shoved him off her and bolted upright. He rolled to his back, an arm over his eyes, and released a long breath. "Glad somebody did."

He'd been close. But not near close enough.

****

He'd been *too* damn close.

So close Charlotte had forgotten the others in the room and fallen completely under Marcus's spell. She hadn't even heard the arrival of the woman at Grant's side. Worse, she'd let down her guard and nearly revealed things she hadn't even wanted to admit to herself.

"Hi, I'm Robyn Jeffreys, Grant's fiancée." The animated redhead rushed forward. She ignored the hand Charlotte thrust forward and pulled her into a hug. "I can't tell you how much I've wanted to meet you."

"You have?" Charlotte felt rather than saw Marcus climb to his feet, sensed the well-contained frustration that ran beneath the surface as he stood beside her.

"Yes, of course." Robyn stepped back to capture Charlotte's hands in hers. "I owe you a debt I'll never be able to repay."

"You do?" If she sounded like an idiot, it was all Marcus's fault.

"Oh, goodness, yes." The woman's head bobbed up and down. "If not for you, Grant would never have made it through some of his classes."

The floor shifted beneath Charlotte's feet. She didn't have to look to know Robyn's announcement had piqued Marcus's curiosity. Again, she blamed him. If she'd been thinking straight, she would have anticipated the direction of this conversation and headed it off.

She sent Grant an imploring glance. "But he did get through and that's all that counts."

"Yes, but—"

"Robyn," Grant interrupted. "This is Marcus Preston."

"Of course, it is." She let go of Charlotte to clasp Marcus's hand. "Who else would be on the verge of devouring our Charlotte?"

"Who indeed?" Marcus drawled, sounding amused.

Charlotte met his very interested gaze and tried not to grimace. He obviously realized Grant's fiancée contained a wealth of information about her past. The look in his eyes told her he intended to glean whatever knowledge he could from the chatty woman.

Robyn rambled on, oblivious to Charlotte's dilemma. "You must be so proud of her. I know Grant is. After Avery called to say she was coming, all I heard was Charlotte this and Charlotte that." She laughed. "I was quite jealous until he told me about their agreement."

"Agreement?"

Charlotte waved off his question. "It was nothing you'd be interested in." She looped her arm through Robyn's and tried to tug her toward the sitting area. "Why don't we all sit down, have a drink?"

Robyn wouldn't budge. She looked from Charlotte to Marcus and back. "You mean he doesn't know?"

"It didn't seem important. Now, there's a delicious—"

"Not important? Why it is to me. If you hadn't tutored Grant, he might never have made it through college. Then he wouldn't have gone to work for my dad, and I'd never have met him." She pulled free of Charlotte and moved to link arms with Grant, who shrugged as if to say, "I told you to tell him."

Marcus slung an arm over Charlotte's shoulder. "So, you helped Grant with his studies?"

"Mmm, we locked ourselves in his room for hours." She slid him a sideways look she hoped conveyed that studying had been the last thing they'd been doing. It was all well and good for Grant to spill his guts to Robyn. He didn't have near as many secrets as Charlotte, and she wouldn't give them up without a fight. Too much was at stake.

"Oh, don't tease the poor man." Robyn leaned to pat Marcus's arm. "You don't have anything to worry about from Grant. They were *never* lovers."

"That's good to know."

Charlotte refused to look at Marcus but felt the

deep rumble of his voice all the way to her toes.

"That's what I thought, too. I wouldn't be here now if Grant hadn't told me everything." Robyn laughed, squeezed Grant's arm, then winked at Charlotte. "Not that I'd blame you if you had slept with him. He's very good—"

"Robyn." Grant tempered his warning with a tender smile.

"Sorry, I *do* tend to run off at the mouth. It's a bad habit, and I've tried to break myself of it, but when I get excited, I ramble. Like right now." She clamped a hand over her mouth.

"No, please, I'd like to hear more." Marcus disengaged himself from Charlotte. The Preston charm he'd never deigned to use on *her* literally oozed over Grant's fiancée as he moved to her side. "Charlotte is so modest. When it comes to talking about herself, she clams up."

Robyn let go of Grant and shifted her full attention to Marcus, who started them on a slow stroll across the room. "Well, it's really quite confusing."

He glanced over his shoulder at Charlotte. "Is that so?"

"Yes. You see, Charlotte wanted to discourage the nicer guys who wanted to date her. Which really is tragic because she's a wonderful person."

"She is, isn't she?"

Charlotte groaned and shoved Grant toward them. "Geez, would you do something? Call her off, muzzle her—something?"

He held out his hands palm up and shook his head. "Once she gets started, I can't stop her. Nobody can. She doesn't mean any harm. She's just brutally honest and believes everyone else is. Or should be with those they care about. And I told you to tell him the truth. He has a right to know. Besides, I'm getting tired of being on the receiving end of his bad side."

"And why do you think she did this?" she heard

Marcus ask as the two drew near.

She held her breath, waiting for Robyn's answer, certain the bubbly woman had run out of information to ruin her with. What else could she possibly know?

"Oh, my, I don't know. Ask her. She's the one with the psych degree. Two, or is it three of them?"

"Please, no," Charlotte whispered, drawing Marcus's questioning gaze.

"But then you already know that." Robyn's excitement increased, as did her rambling. "I'll bet you have big plans to celebrate her turning in her dissertation. We'll have to order champagne at lunch. It's not every day someone you love becomes a doctor."

Charlotte closed her eyes and hung her head, the fight completely sucked out of her. Except maybe for the small part of her that wanted to kill Grant's fiancée. In one breath, she had single-handedly dispensed with most, if not all, of Marcus's misconceptions. She'd known he would find out sooner or later, especially after she opened her practice, but she'd hoped to have miles between them when he did. As for her pact with Grant…

Geez, how was she going to explain that?

"Dr. Reese, I presume?" Marcus's deep voice startled her out of her contemplation of murder. His dark speculative eyes stared into hers, as if trying to read her thoughts.

She searched for a lifeline, but Grant had finally harnessed Robyn and led her across the room. A little too late as far as Charlotte was concerned. "Not until May. Contrary to reports, I haven't finished writing my thesis."

"And after that?"

"I'll be working at the hospital for a while."

"With kids like Amy."

It wasn't a question, but she answered anyway. Why deny it? "Yes."

"What about your agreement with Wylie? Were you lovers or not?"

So, he wasn't entirely sold on Robyn's story. Maybe she could salvage something. She flattened her palms on his chest and leaned into him. In a breathy whisper, she asked, "What do you think?"

"Charlotte." Unlike Grant's warning, his came with a blistering gleam of impatience.

Okay, so that didn't work. She stepped back, folded her arms across her chest and tilted a stubborn glare at him. "It's really none of your business."

He mimicked her stance. "So, did Wylie fabricate the story to keep his fiancée from getting jealous?"

Charlotte wanted to let him believe that, but Grant had proven a friend to her and deserved better than to get caught up in another one of her illusions. "No, it's all true. Grant couldn't get a handle on English Lit."

"And you needed a cover. Why?"

"We've gone over this." She started to turn away, but he grasped her arm.

"Why?"

"I don't owe you an explanation." She called to Robyn. The woman was good for something if only a diversion. "Come help me decide which swimsuit to wear for the hot tub shots."

Marcus released her as the pretty redhead hurried toward them, but his frown threatened retribution. "We'll finish this later."

"That's what Grant and I were just discussing," Robyn said.

Charlotte lifted a brow. "Swimsuits?"

"No, silly. We were talking about later. This afternoon." She turned to Grant who had followed her. "Tell them."

"Robyn arranged an outing after the ski lodge promo."

Marcus shook his head. "We're not free."

The woman's face crumbled. "Oh."

Charlotte wanted to object to his assumption that he could speak on her behalf, but she let it go. She'd been about to decline herself, having no wish to spend any more stress-filled time with the Little Miss Chatterbox. No telling what else Grant had confessed.

"I'm sorry." Marcus pinned Charlotte with a determined gaze. "We have business to attend to."

On the other hand, when faced with the alternative to spending an afternoon being interrogated by Marcus, maybe Robyn wasn't so bad after all. She wound her arms around his waist and gave him her best pout. "I know I promised, but we can do *that* anytime. Who knows when we'll ever see Grant and Robyn again."

Robyn seemed to take her cue from Charlotte. She latched onto Marcus's arm and tugged. "Please say yes. Whatever it is you and Charlotte were going to do can't be nearly as fun as what I've planned."

A deep scarlet crept up Marcus's neck and face, and Grant coughed to cover his laughter. "Well, I guess—"

Robyn launched herself at Marcus. "Thank you so much." Like a whirlwind she released him and turned to Charlotte. "Avery told us you spend time in Vail every year, so we've been dying to show you what Aspen has to offer."

"Oh? You have a shopping spree planned?"

The annoying little redhead laughed. "No, silly. We want to show you the slopes."

Where Marcus's face had suffused with color moments ago, Charlotte was certain hers was now bleached white. "Skiing? You want to go skiing?"

"Isn't that what one does at a ski resort?"

Robyn's voice echoed around Charlotte as if from the bottom of a well. Her palms grew clammy. Yes, she'd been to Vail every year since she turned fifteen. And yes, she'd learned to ski. But she'd never been higher than the bunny slope because of her inexplicable fear of heights. The one time she tried, she'd ended up jumping out of the lift before it got five feet off the ground. She'd stuck with the towline after that.

Marcus touched her arm. "Are you okay?"

Staring up at him, Charlotte considered her options. Risk Marcus's interrogation or certain death on a mountain?

She forced a smile and turned to Robyn, "Show me the mountain."

Chapter Fourteen

"Ohmigosh, I thought the two of you were going to spontaneously combust this morning."

Charlotte gripped the arm of the chairlift, her teeth clenched, every muscle in her body tight. Not because of Robyn's continued personal observations. She'd gotten used to the woman's perky chatter. It kept her mind off more important matters. Like how the hell she was going to get down this mountain.

She had manipulated the seating arrangement for the ride up, stressing her desire to get to know Robyn better. Mostly to avoid Marcus and his questions, which she'd succeeded in doing regardless of his attempts to get her alone, but also to prevent him from discovering her phobia of heights. He had learned too much about her already.

Purposely dropping her ski pole prior to liftoff hadn't gained her the excuse to stay behind either. But a pair of eager teenagers dressed in neon orange had cut when Marcus stepped out of line to retrieve it, which put him and Grant two chairs back instead of right behind her. At least she would have a moment to compose herself before he arrived.

Robyn released a dreamy sigh. "It's so romantic. The way he looks at you—like he could eat you up."

Like a certain ice cream sundae. "Like Grant doesn't worship the ground you walk on," Charlotte said, bracing herself as they bounced through the last pulley connection.

"But yours is such a fairy tale romance. Announcing your feelings for each other in such a public way, bidding on Marcus to keep him from another woman's clutches. And he's so clearly in love with you."

Charlotte's heart skipped several beats then pounded faster. Her stomach flipped right side up and back again. For a moment Robyn's words made her forget where she was, that her feet dangled over fifty feet in the air as they neared the drop-off point at the top.

Then common sense returned, jerking the reins on any runaway notion that Marcus could love her. They'd played their part as lovers well. Apparently, too well. Even she was getting confused. The sooner they ended this farce the better.

"End of the line," Robyn announced, reminding her that "sooner" meant *after* she dealt with her current predicament.

Forced to let go of the chair, Charlotte managed to stay upright as her skis hit the slippery ice-packed ground. In awkward sideways steps she maneuvered a safe distance away to the softer, fresher snow and sucked in a calming breath.

"They're almost here," Robyn said, beside her. "I can't wait to hit the slope today. All that fresh powder we got last night. You're gonna love…"

Robyn's mouth kept moving, but Charlotte couldn't hear anything for the growing roar of an engine. A snowmobile with a bright red cross on the side careened to a stop on the other side of the tiny building that the lift cable wrapped around. The driver, a broad shouldered, blond in a red parka with EMT on the sleeve killed the motor and lifted his goggles, revealing white raccoon-eyes on a sunburned face.

His interested gaze swept her from head to toe before settling on her face. He flashed a grin and dismounted.

Her spirits lifted as she smiled back, pleased she still had on the powder blue bib and matching sweater she'd worn for the ski lodge promo. They were skintight and emphasized her eyes. If she played her cards right, this Nordic god would be the answer to her prayers. And her way down this mountain.

A quick glance at Robyn showed her occupied with a buckle on her ski boot. Turning back to the lift, Charlotte saw the brightly dressed teenagers bobbing in their chair like a caution light on a windy day as they approached all too quickly, Marcus and Grant not far behind.

Without hesitation, she used her poles and the vaguely remembered leg action to slowly glide toward the rescue vehicle and its rider. She was a bit rusty, but like riding a bike, she would soon regain her confidence as well as her balance.

Until she looked over the edge of that first slope. Then both would desert her.

Just a peek in that direction and thinking about the sheer drop off she would face on this expert run made her head spin and her knees weaken, causing her to wobble when she stopped in front of the snowmobile. Not the most graceful of maneuvers, but it lent credence to the excuse she intended to use to enlist the medic's aid.

"Whoa there," he said, reaching for her.

"Sorry," she said, grasping his arm. He was probably used to women falling all over him—physically and metaphorically. But he seemed to enjoy the contact. Maybe a little too much. She let go and pushed the hair from her face. "I'm so glad you're here."

"Is something wrong?"

"Yes." She squeezed one eye shut and read the name embroidered on his coat. "Blake, is it? I lost a contact on the way up and everything is a blur." The only blur she saw was one of orangey-yellow as the young couple whizzed past, increasing her urgency for escape. "I'll never make it down in one piece."

He gave her another once over. "We wouldn't want such lovely pieces rearranged."

She resisted the urge to roll her eyes and instead released a genuine sigh of relief. If they hurried, she might just make it before Marcus arrived. "Thank you."

"I just have to check on something, and then we can leave."

"Please hurry. I'm starting to feel nauseous."

He started to turn away then stopped, his smile fading as his gaze shifted to something behind her. She didn't have to look to know what—or rather who—he saw.

Strong fingers gripped her arm from behind. "Are you okay?"

Marcus's deep voice, husky with concern, shattered all hope of escape. Pivoting carefully, she saw the same apprehension radiating from his emerald eyes. A rush of warmth spread all the way to her frostbitten toes, but she ignored it, refusing to be lured by false emotions. Hers or his.

He wasn't concerned for her well-being. He wanted answers and obviously wouldn't let her out of sight until he had them. But they were none of his business.

She twisted her arm from his grasp. "I'm fine. We were just having a little chat, but we're all done now. Aren't we, Blake?"

He gave the poor medic a measuring glance then dismissed him. "You ready then?"

"I thought you needed a ride." Tilting his head to one side, Blake frowned. "It's not a good idea to ski with one contact."

"Contact?"

She blinked one eye in rapid succession. "It must have rolled to the back of my eye. It's in place now. Sorry to bother you."

Without a word to Marcus, she trudged to a small

area of level ground, focusing on a nearby thatch of evergreens and pines rather than the precipice where Grant and Robyn waited only a few feet away. Just the thought of joining them made the imaginary nausea she'd complained about to Blake real.

She sucked in a calming breath and inhaled the scent of pine, reminding her of the man beside her. For once, she was grateful for the distraction his presence brought, just as she had been on the airplane yesterday.

Geez, was that only yesterday?

"What was all that about?"

"Nothing."

"It didn't sound like nothing. He said you asked for a lift. Are you sick?"

Okay, so maybe she wasn't so grateful. "I'm fine. Did you bring my pole?"

He passed it to her, and her hand shook as she took it from him. His fingers manacled her wrist. "You're not fine. You're trembling."

Charlotte twisted free and tucked the pole under her arm with its mate, then tugged on her gloves with a few quick jerks to hide her shaking hands. She had to get rid of them if she wanted to make another attempt at a ride on the medic's snowmobile. "I need to make a couple of adjustments, but you three should go on. I'll catch up."

Marcus turned to the waiting couple. "Go on without us. We'll meet you at the bottom."

Robyn glanced longingly down the steep slope that made Charlotte's stomach heave. "Well, if you're sure."

She nodded. "I promise I'll be right behind you."

"*We'll* be right behind you," Marcus interjected.

Her stomach sank as Grant and Robyn disappeared over the edge of the mountain, leaving her alone with Marcus, suspicion etched on his face. "All right. What's going on?"

His voice echoed, not from the cavernous walls of rock around them, but from inside her head. She swallowed, hoping to clear her ears, but it didn't help.

Then his eyes grew wide. "Can you ski?"

"Yes." Her answer came in a whisper, making his frown deepen. She had to get a grip before she totally lost it in front of him.

"You're pale and shaking."

"I'm cold." *Probably from shock*.

He dropped his poles in the snow beside him and shifted closer to slide his hands up her arms, gently rubbing. "If you're not sick and you know how to ski, what's the problem? Why did you need a ride? And don't tell me some lame story about a contact. I know you don't wear them."

His soothing tone was a balm to her fragile nerves as was the hand that cupped the side of her face. His thumb grazed back and forth along her cheek. "Talk to me, Charlotte."

She looked into his hypnotic eyes and recognized the coaxing patience in them. Damn him and his controlling nature. How dare he use it to seduce answers from her when she was paralyzed by fear? She thrust her chin forward and tossed her hair over her shoulder. "If you must know, he was hot and interested, and since you weren't—ouch."

His fingers circling her arm dug into her bicep. "Don't go there."

His anger sparked her own, and it felt a hell of a lot better than the fear that threatened to overwhelm her moments ago. She leaned into him. "Jealous?"

"I'm not buying that crap anymore. You might have flirted with him to get a ride, but something else is going on."

"Poor Marcus. Ever the suspicious one."

He released her to run a hand over his face. "Look, I know you're mad about last night and you're upset about Robyn giving all your secrets away, but sooner or later, we're going to talk. About everything."

Like hell we are. Straightening, she tossed another shank of blonde hair over her shoulder. "Fine. I have nothing to hide."

"Then why have you been avoiding me?"

"Not everything is about you, Marcus."

With that, Charlotte pushed off and over the edge of the first slope. Her anger vanished as she sped down the vertical path. All thought of getting away from Marcus went with it when she hit the first mogul and her skis met air. The ground rushed up to greet her, and the impact knocked her off balance, but somehow, she stayed on her feet.

The steepness increased as did her speed. Panic grabbed her by the throat. She couldn't breathe. And forget snowplowing. Her muscles refused to obey even the most instinctive commands.

"Charlotte, slow down."

Risking a glance over her shoulder, she caught a brief flash of Marcus's silver parka a good distance behind her. Just as she turned back around, one of her poles was ripped from her hand. Flailing, she veered to one side toward a stand of trees. The tip of her ski dug deep in the snow, and she heard Marcus yell her name as she flew forward.

Well, if she broke her neck, at least she wouldn't have to answer his questions.

****

Charlotte's scream ripped through Marcus like jagged glass. Helpless to stop her, he could only watch while she tumbled head over heels down the steep slope. Her skis dislodged from her boots—she'd lost her poles before her fall—and she rolled several times to land perilously close to the thick trunk of a cedar.

He raced forward, slicing over the snow but felt as if he moved in slow motion and would never reach her. Then all at once he was skidding to a halt and popping loose from his skis. Falling to his knees beside her, he caught the slippery ends of his nylon gloves with his teeth to free his hands. "Charlotte, are you all right?"

She didn't answer but lay lifeless on her back, one arm flung over her face, the other at her side. Her legs were sprawled at natural angles. Nothing looked broken, but there could be internal injuries.

"Fuck." He looked around for help, his mind suddenly blank with fear. His heart, already thudding in his chest, pumped jackhammer fast. He could go for the medic, but they'd come too far down the slope for him to climb back up. Besides, he wouldn't leave her.

A whimper brought his attention back around and forced him to calm the panic that gripped him. There was no one else. It was up to him.

"Charlotte, can you hear me?" Again, no answer. He ran a tentative hand up her lower leg, careful not to move her.

She jerked when he reached her knee. "Don't."

Her voice sounded choked and watery. She kept her arm over her eyes but tears trickled from the corners, down her temples, and into damp, ice-caked hair. He applied light pressure to the spot he'd just squeezed. "Does it hurt here?"

"No."

"Where does it hurt?" He hated to think of her in pain, wanted to take it all away, onto himself if he could. "Is it your arm?" She hadn't moved the one at her side at all.

He had barely touched her again when she slapped his hand away and tried to sit up. "I said, don't."

He pressed a hand to her shoulder, holding her down as gently as he could for fear of hurting her further. "You shouldn't move until we rule out injury."

"I'm fine." She shrugged from under his grasp and pushed up to lean on one hand, angrily swiping her cheeks with the other. "I just don't want you to touch me."

Marcus sat back on his heels, relieved yet uncertain of how to handle her outburst. She could be trying to cover her pain by lashing out at him. He was even more uncertain as to how to deal with her tears. He'd suspected a softer side to Charlotte, but until now, it was only that. An abstract version of her.

She curled her legs to one side and rose to her hands and knees, moaning with every move.

"Here, let me—"

"I don't need your help."

At the glare she shot him, he pulled the hand he'd instinctively extended. "Sorry."

"You should be." She began brushing powder from her lank, matted hair. Her designer knit hat was somewhere up the slope. "This is all your fault."

"I beg your pardon?"

"If not for you, I'd be kicking back in front of a cozy fire with hot chocolate and a good book. But no, you have to control everything, forcing everyone to do what you want to do."

Confused by the accusation but allowing for her pain, Marcus pointed out, "You're the one who insisted we accept Robyn's invitation."

"Now, I'm stuck up here with no way down this mountain," she continued, as if he hadn't spoken.

"I thought you said you weren't hurt."

"I'm not."

"Then we can ski down. We'll take it a little slower to be on the safe side, but it shouldn't take long." He stood and brushed off his knees.

She obviously wanted nothing else from him. He would see her down then leave her alone. Maybe he would go home early. That way she could enjoy her visit with Wylie and his fiancée.

He straightened to find her on her feet, hands on hips and shaking her head. The look she gave him was incredulous. "You don't get it, do you?"

After having the life nearly scared out of him, his patience was wearing a little thin. "It seems I'm kind of slow when it comes to reading between the lines these days, so I guess you'll have to spell it out for me."

"There's no way I can ski down this mountain."

One hand on his hip, he pointed up the slope. "Do you mean you stood up there and lied to me about being able to ski?"

"Skiing isn't the problem."

"Then what the fuck is?"

Chewing her lip, she stared at him, as if debating with herself over whether to answer. Finally, her watery gaze cut to the trees. "Yesterday, you thought I was afraid of flying. It wasn't the flying. It was my fear of heights."

"I don't understand. You were—"

"Afraid of crashing, okay? It's a long way down." She sniffed and ran a hand under her nose before lifting her chin. "And it's not that I don't like to ski. I do. I just prefer the bunny slope. I don't get dizzy."

"Are you telling me you came up here, on a slope for well-seasoned skiers, a slope with not only breakneck turns but almost ninety-degree drop-offs, knowing you'd have this reaction?" Marcus spoke calmly and slowly despite the rage that consumed him. When he thought about what could have happened, he wanted to throttle her.

Her chin rose another notch. "Yes."

"Of all the lame-brained, idiotic— You could have been killed."

"I know that."

"You know that? You fucking *know* that?" The truth once again slapped him in the face. "So, you'd rather get yourself killed than spend the afternoon with me."

"You were bent on interrogating me. As if my life was any of your business. What was I supposed to do?"

"You lie so well, you could have made up something to get out of it anytime during the ski lodge promo or later during lunch. A headache, stomachache, cramps, anything."

"You wouldn't have let me get away with that. You'd have followed me back to the hotel and started in with your questions."

"What is it you're so afraid I'll find out, Charlotte? Is there something other than your degree and your non-affair with Wylie you don't want me to know?" Her blue eyes rounded with fear, like a rabbit cornered by a fox. He went for the kill. "Everything about you is a lie, isn't it, Charlotte? Because you're afraid. And not just of heights."

"That's not true."

"You don't drink, yet you pretend to."

"It's what society expects."

"It's what you want them to believe. You couldn't maintain your image if they thought you were sober, could you? You couldn't be the party girl."

Waving a hand in dismissal, she turned away. "You think you know everything."

He caught her arm and pulled her back around. "If I'm wrong, then why bother making everyone believe you had an affair with Grant Wylie when in fact you were tutoring him? Doing something constructive and admirable?"

She stared at him for almost a full minute, then threw her hands in the air. "Geez, Marcus, weren't you listening? Robyn told you why." She flipped a hunk of wet, limp hair over her shoulder. "I needed a break between men."

"That's not what she said. She said you were trying to discourage the nicer guys."

"Same difference."

"I don't think so. Now that I think about it, other than Wylie, you've never had a relationship. I always thought it was because you wanted to be free to be with whoever caught your eye. But I think you're afraid of intimacy."

"Hardly." She laughed bitterly. "I've been *intimate* on a fairly regular basis."

The carelessness with which she bandied about her reputation added to his fury. "Fuck, Charlotte, you know what I mean. I'm talking about commitment."

"What do you want from me, Marcus?"

"I want you to be yourself. The intelligent, caring, beautiful woman you are. The one you let the kids at the hospital see. The one who played in the snow with me yesterday."

She snorted. "You want me to be a woman easily taken for granted. To let others walk all over me. Well, I won't do it. My mother let emotions rule her life and look where it got her."

"You're stronger than your mother."

"You don't know that. I might be just like her. I might fall so hard that I lose myself in trying to hang on to some faithless bastard like my father. I can't—no, I *won't* take that chance."

Her voice broke, and most of the steam went out of Marcus's anger. Except for the bit reserved for her parents. They had really done a number on her. "You can't go through life believing every man is like your father."

"Aren't they?"

"I won't lie to you. Some are. But not all." *Not me.*

She stared at him, telling him with her eyes she wanted to believe him but wouldn't allow herself. He wanted to tell her how he felt about her, but he wasn't quite comfortable with the idea yet. He hadn't even known himself until he saw her hurtling head over heels down the mountainside and thought he'd lost her.

The buzzing of an engine echoed behind him. He glanced over his shoulder as the medic pulled the snowmobile to a stop a few feet away. He held

Charlotte's poles and toboggan in one hand. "Is anyone hurt?"

"No."

"Yes."

They spoke in unison. Marcus indicated Charlotte should go first. She folded her arms across her middle. "I'm fine."

"She took a pretty bad spill. She needs to be checked out." He wasn't about to let her stubborn pride stand in the way of common sense when she clearly couldn't ski down the mountain. And he still worried about internal injuries.

The medic looked from him to Charlotte. "I'll take you down and have Doc Murphy take a look at you."

She hesitated, and Marcus busied himself gathering her skis. She'd revealed so much of herself in the past few minutes; admitting one more weakness, especially in front of him, had to be killing her.

He handed the skis to the medic, and while he bungee-corded them to the snowmobile, Marcus waited beside her. She refused to look at him, so he faced forward. "Make sure the doctor is thorough. Let him prescribe something if you need it."

"I will." She sounded resigned now.

"And make Wylie get a taxi or drive you back to the hotel. I don't want you walking." The hotel was only a block from the ski lodge. They'd walked over after lunch.

"Okay."

"A hot shower might help any aches and pains the medicine doesn't."

"I'll be fine."

He glanced sideways and caught her wiping a tear from her cheek. Aching to take her in his arms, yet knowing she'd hate him if he did, he turned away. "Just in case, I'll—" He cleared his throat. "I'll be there as soon as I can."

The medic motioned her forward, and Marcus

watched until she climbed on and they disappeared over the next ledge. Then he turned away, slowly making his way to where she'd fallen, and picked up his gloves. He'd promised to hurry, but really, what was the point?

Charlotte didn't want his company. She'd said it a hundred times and a hundred different ways over the years. He'd respected her wishes in the past, and he'd do it again. Their weekend was technically over. So was the affair they'd never begun.

She didn't want his help either. The woman had more pride than he'd ever suspected. That and fear. He finally understood why she did the things she did. She had an image to maintain, a wall of enormous proportions that she thought would keep her safe from the pain love sometimes brought.

One thing was clear. If she didn't want his company, his help, or even his sympathy, she sure as hell wouldn't want his love.

Chapter Fifteen

Her bags were packed and waiting at the foot of the bed. There was a flight out of Denver at midnight — she'd missed that one — and another around four in the morning, though that one took a less direct route with a two-hour layover in Chicago. After that there were no departures until their original flight at ten.

Still, Charlotte couldn't make herself leave. Too much was at stake.

She twisted from her perch at the end of the bed to glance at the clock on the nightstand, wincing as her strained muscles protested. Eleven thirty-nine. Two minutes later than the last time she looked. Midnight seemed eons away.

Flopping back on the bed, she wondered how it had come to this. Her plan to knock Marcus off his high horse had started out so simple. Seduce him, prove he was ruled by his libido just the same as any man, and get him the hell out of her system.

But Marcus had demonstrated more will power than any man she'd ever known and turned the tables on her more times than she was willing to admit. Geez, all he had to do was kiss her, and she melted in his hands, forgetting all else. Including her objective.

He seemed to have his own agenda. From the very beginning he had prodded and pushed until he had her so upset and confused that she lost it and confessed almost everything. What she hadn't told him, he'd guessed.

She had seen the pity in his eyes when he'd tried to convince her she could be herself. He believed society would accept her; she would be safe in letting down her guard. Not every man was like her father. Yet, after all was said and done, he hadn't been able to look at her.

Oh, she knew her way of thinking—hell, her whole way of life—was distorted. She didn't need psychology books and professors to tell her that. She had major issues with trust. Especially when it involved men, thanks to her father. But if she tried living as Marcus suggested, she doubted anyone would believe the transformation. She'd lived the lie far too long.

So, she sat in her room. In the silent darkness. Waiting for Marcus to fall asleep so she could convince him he was wrong about her. She behaved the way she did because that's who she was. She couldn't let him go home believing otherwise.

Marcus had to have flown down that damned mountain. He had returned to the hotel almost as soon as she had. The medic had insisted she see the doctor at the emergency clinic, who then took forever to release her, especially after she declined x-rays. Grant and Robyn had found her while she was there, escorted her to the hotel and refused to leave until she was safely out of the shower and settled for the night.

She had no more locked herself in her room than Marcus entered the suite. He had immediately knocked on her door and called her name. She ignored him, hoping he would think she was asleep, then realized in her panic she forgot to turn off the bedside lamp. When he called out to her again, louder and with a hint of concern, and actually jiggled the knob, she knew she had to answer, or he would never go away.

Through the door, he'd asked if she was okay, if she was hungry, if she needed anything. She told him she was fine and just needed a good night's sleep. A few minutes later, she heard his shower running. It was still early then, only seven o'clock, but she'd hoped he would turn in anyway. Instead, he called room service from the phone in the living area and settled on the sofa to watch television. He'd finally gone to bed an hour ago.

Another glance at the clock showed eleven fifty-two. Not long now. Only eight more minutes before she could set her new plan into motion. A plan that would destroy everything between them and bring to an end any thoughts he might have of pursuing a relationship.

With a weary sigh, Charlotte pushed off the bed. Time to get him out of her system once and for all.

****

A whisper of a touch. Soft, light, desired. And yet something was different, not quite right.

Marcus resisted the pull of consciousness. He didn't want to wake up. He wanted to remain in the dream, to finish it this time. He never allowed himself to entertain thoughts like this during the day. Not while his conscience demanded rigid control. The least he deserved was to thoroughly enjoy the fantasy while he slept.

So, he slipped back into the realm of subconscious, where he was able to be whoever he wanted, do whatever he wanted with whomever and without guilt. Without remorse. Without consequences.

His *whomever* was always the same or had been the last five years.

Charlotte.

Charlotte's lips smiling, sensual, parting.

Charlotte's body, naked, dewy, and writhing. Always writhing.

Charlotte's hands, soft, knowing, touching.

He could feel them now. Stroking the top of his foot, caressing his ankle. That was the difference between this dream and others. She'd never devoted so much attention to his feet. Not that he was complaining. It felt good. Damn good.

She must have known how much he liked it

because she stopped. She did that a lot, stopped when he started to enjoy it. But she always came back to tease him with more. It was only when he tried to take control that she vanished. Just like in real life.

A sudden bright light pierced his eyelids, jolting him from the sensual haze of the dream. He turned his head away from its brilliance. It couldn't be morning already.

"Time to wake up."

He opened his eyes, squinting through the glare of his bedside lamp—not the sun—to the figure at the foot of the bed. "Charlotte?"

When she didn't answer, Marcus came wide awake. She wasn't an apparition; this wasn't a dream gone in some strange new direction. Something was wrong. Charlotte needed him.

He bolted upright, only to have his shoulders almost wrenched from their sockets when his arms wouldn't follow his body. "What the fuck?"

One corner of her mouth lifted, and he knew. She was up to something. Slowly, almost afraid to take his eyes off her, he tilted his head back to look.

"Holy hell." His wrists were bound together with a brightly colored scarf—like the ones he'd purchased in the gift shop—and tied to the ornate spindles he hadn't even noticed in the headboard. One of his favorite fantasies brought to life, only in reverse. He yanked to test its strength and felt the silk tighten.

"Hell?" she said. "Hell is the cat and mouse game we've played this weekend. But I'm changing the rules, and you can consider yourself caught."

He looked back at her to ask what she meant; he thought they were through with games after this afternoon. But his jaw went slack as she whipped the pink sweater she'd worn during the morning shoot over her head. Her breasts stretched upward with the movement, nearly spilling over the top of a lacy pink bra before settling back into their cups when she lowered her arms.

Tossing the sweater on the chair in the corner, she reached for the waistband of her jeans. A quick tug at the button and a slow pull of the zipper, and she shimmied out of them. They went the way of the sweater, leaving only a scrap of pink lace that matched her bra in their place. He knew all too well the pale curls that lay behind that triangle.

Marcus forced his gaze upward, reasoning that if he focused on her face, he could pretend she wasn't half naked and convince her this was a mistake. Not friggin' likely when she looked at him with hungry cat-like eyes, as if she were about to devour him. "What are you doing, Charlotte?"

"Isn't it obvious?"

She grasped the sheet near his feet, and he instinctively tried to twist to one side. Silk bit into his ankles, strangling his attempt, and the panic that had idled under his skin revved to full throttle. He wasn't wearing anything beneath the sheet. Worse, he still suffered the effects of the dream, not to mention a hurried but provocative strip tease. "And just what do you hope all this will achieve?"

One shoulder lifted and fell. "An orgasm."

His erection jumped beneath the sheet, along with his desperation. Images of the night she'd come apart in his arms in the mayor's garden swirled in his head. He mentally closed the door on them and jerked on the restraints. The one at his ankles made a tearing sound but held. If he could stall her long enough… "Look, you don't really want to do this."

"Oh, but I do." She pulled the sheet the rest of the way off, and her eyes zeroed in on the part of him that would eagerly relinquish control if he let it. "By the looks of things, you want it, too."

He had never denied that fact before, and he couldn't deny it now. Not even if he wanted to. His mouth simply wouldn't form the words as she hooked her thumbs under the pink elastic hugging her hips and, with excruciating slowness, slid the lace down long, tanned legs. Her panties pooled at her feet, and she stepped out of them.

Fingers spread, her hands smoothed up the sides of her hips over her belly and ribs, seductive in their movement. One arm twisted behind her back, and an instant later, her bra loosened. She slipped her hands under the cups, palming the fullness beneath. Her back arched. Her head lolled to one side. "Mmm, feels so good. But I can't help wishing you were the one touching me."

Oh, he'd love to get his hands on her all right. Right around her pretty neck. "Then untie me."

"I would if I thought you'd actually go for it. But you won't." She shrugged out of her bra, revealing pink-tipped breasts. Pert, firm, mouthwatering. She massaged the underside where the underwires had left indentions. "So, I've taken the decision out of your hands." Her thumbs flicked the beaded nipples, then looked down at what she was doing. "Literally, it seems."

Her knee met the mattress.

"Wait." He strained once more against the silk bindings. The one at his wrists slipped again but held tight. Damn. "Let's talk about this."

"That's part of your problem, Marcus." She placed her hands on either side of his legs to crawl up his body. "You analyze things too much. You need to let things happen."

Marcus squeezed his eyes shut and ground his teeth against the sensation of her warm skin brushing his, her hair trailing over his legs, his hips. "Some things aren't meant to happen."

"This is."

And it was. But not yet. Not until… What? What was so damned important that he couldn't take the pleasure she offered? God knew he ached for it.

"This wouldn't be necessary," she said, settling between his thighs, "if you'd have just let go of that damned control of yours. We could have ended this last summer and moved on."

There it was. The reason. He could no more have moved on then than he could now.

He'd loved her all these years and never known. Or maybe he'd known but fought it. Either way, until this afternoon, when he'd stood alone and watched her vanish over the mountain's edge, he hadn't understood.

Grasping hold of the thought with all his might, he opened his eyes. "But this thing between us didn't start last summer, did it? It started years ago."

Her hand hovering above his cock stilled. She peered up at him from beneath a veil of silvery blonde hair, her gaze startled.

"Admit it. The attraction's been there since the night we met."

The shock faded from her eyes as they narrowed. "I'm beginning to wish I'd gagged you as well." Full pink lips stretched into a smile. "But I know how to shut you up."

Her fingers encircled his dick, warm and tight. His hips thrust upward involuntarily. She laughed as she lowered her head and he tried to sink into the mattress.

Don't think about what she's doing or how good it feels. Concentrate on something else.

Wet kisses rained up and down his shaft.

Count.

Count what?

Her tongue slathered him from root to tip.

Ceiling tiles, the spots in front of your eyes, the beats of your heart, anything. Just count.

One, two, three…

Her lips slipped over his engorged head.

A low groan choked him, and his back came off the sheets. His arms strained against the silk around his wrists. But nothing could stop the sensations her mouth created. He slammed his eyes shut and started counting again, faster this time. One, two, three, four…

Wasn't working. Backwards maybe. One hundred, ninety-nine, ninety—oh, God that felt damn good. Like…like…nothing he could describe.

No, it felt awful. The worst. Like having a tooth pulled. He needed drugs.

She stopped and sat up.

Marcus expelled a lung-full of air. Thank God. His body went limp, the tension easing from his cramped muscles. Resisting was getting more and more difficult.

He had to think again why it was so important to keep fighting her. Why couldn't he give in to the pleasure his body craved? He wouldn't be using her as other men had. He loved her.

Ah, but that was it. He loved her. And damn if he hadn't almost given up on that love once today. He'd been halfway down the mountain when he realized he couldn't do it. He had to try again. Had to show her how much he loved her. For the woman she was, not what she could give him.

Giving in to his physical needs now would be worse than if he'd taken her last summer. For her sake, she had to trust him first. For his, she had to love him.

She leaned forward, regaining his attention. Her hair tickled his shoulder. Her breath feathered his jaw. Cracking one eye open, he found her stretched above him, fumbling for something on the nightstand. Then she backed up, one hand pushing off his chest, to resume her position between his legs.

He followed that hand as it held the thing she'd been searching for. A flat, black packet with gold writing.

"Charlotte." His strangled warning went unheeded as she tore the foil open and pulled out a dark purple condom.

"Marcus." She rolled it carefully down his

sensitive flesh. "This *is* going to happen."

She bent and kissed his belly next to his towering erection. Her tongue lashed out to wet the spot she'd kissed. Then she blew softly. Pleasure rippled straight to his balls.

Silk bit into his wrists and ankles as he renewed his efforts to free himself, jerking and twisting. He concentrated on that pain rather than the sweet torture of her mouth as it traveled up his stomach, his chest. Or the feel of her soft thighs straddling his hips. Or her hot, wet center pressing against his throbbing cock.

"Fuck." He thrust a leg up, hoping to unseat her. One foot ripped free of its bindings.

"Yes," she breathed and tilted her hips, taking the head of his cock inside her.

The thudding in his ears grew louder, faster, whether from his struggles for freedom or from the pulsing desire rocketing through his body.

"Yes," she hissed again as she rose above him and slowly sheathed him to the hilt, then paused. "Be still, Marcus. I'm too close. I want this to last."

Marcus froze, afraid to move, as her muscles tightened around him. This was good. Better than he'd ever dreamed. His whole body was on fire, screaming for relief.

Yet as good as it felt, it wasn't enough. It was still only sex. Not at all what he would have wished for once the time came. He wanted to run his hands over every inch of her soft flesh, to follow their path with his mouth, to make her feel the same sweet pleasure she made him feel.

He wanted to make love to her.

A tremor traversed through her, encompassing him. He shivered and watched her as she came to grips with her body's need to surge ahead.

Damn, she was beautiful. Sooty lashes fanned flushed cheeks. Equally rosy breasts peeked from behind moon-kissed hair that spilled over her shoulders. Her delicate hands gripped the top of her thighs, nails digging into soft flesh.

He closed his eyes, shutting out the vision, just as she shifted, taking him deeper. He moaned. She moaned. Then ever so slowly, as if testing against the threat of climax, she moved, lifting herself until only the tip of his cock remained inside her.

He groaned as she engulfed him once more and began to ride, slowly undulating, rotating with each rise and fall. "For fuck's sake...don't...stop." *Don't stop. Don't ever stop.*

She'd done it. Stripped away every last shred of his control. There was no turning back. He was too far gone.

Now, if he could just get his hands on her.

****

Sex with Marcus wasn't working.

Charlotte tried to focus on the pleasure his body brought her, but her mind refused to let her. And her heart simply wasn't in it. This wasn't what she wanted.

She had ignored his pleas, even closed her eyes to the obvious pain she inflicted. She had manipulated his body's response with moves only a eunuch could resist. But it wasn't enough. She wanted—no, needed—his participation. She needed him to want her as much as she did him.

Pausing halfway through an upward stroke, she looked at him. Judging from his contorted features and the way he strained against his bindings, that was never going to happen. He would fight to the end.

She couldn't do it. She couldn't force him to have sex with her. What would that prove when it was so clear he didn't want to?

The weight of her body, not to mention her shame, carried her back down until he once more filled her. She'd wanted him for so long and hated to give him up. Yet, over and over again, he'd said he didn't want this.

But why?

There's one thing I want more.

Panic filled her. Was he still holding out for a relationship? Why wouldn't he just accept what she offered? Intimacy without commitment. Sex without strings. Wasn't that what all men wanted?

But then, Marcus wasn't like most other men. He would never force a woman once she made it plain, as he had done, she didn't want to continue.

A bucket of ice water couldn't have chilled her more as she realized she was no better than the men she loathed. Instead of turning into her mother as she'd feared, the unthinkable had happened. She had turned into her father. This was the exact sort of thing he would condone.

Sickened, she reached over Marcus's head to untie his wrists. The moisture of unshed tears stung her eyes, making it difficult to see. His continued struggle didn't help either. "Stop. You're just making the knot tighter."

"Hurry, damn you."

His eagerness hurt, but she tried to do as he asked. "I'm sorry." His chest heaved with each breath, making her wobble. "Let me get up."

"No, don't," he bit out, apparently still close to the edge and fighting it. The knot began to unravel, and he yanked one hand free.

"There." She sat back, desperate to leave now, before he had the other untied. She couldn't face his disgust or another deserved rejection.

Marcus sprang upright, startling her. One arm snaked around her waist, hauling her flush against him. His other hand fisted in her hair. "Damn you for this."

His mouth covered hers, his tongue plunging deep, mimicking the thrust of his hips. Her cry of surprise turned to a whimper of ecstasy when he repeated the action. It occurred to her that she should stop him, tell him she'd changed her mind and was ready to give up this foolish game of seduction. All it would take would be to remind him he really didn't want this, that she'd driven him to it. But his kiss was like a drug and her body, still burning, refused to obey.

Joining his tongue in its mating dance, the low simmer in the pit of her belly rose to a slow boil. She wrapped her arms around him and tried to grind her hips.

"No," he growled as he tore his mouth from hers. His big hands gripped her waist, lifting her to unsheathe himself.

She wanted to scream. Was it his intent to deliberately feed her desire, then leave her empty and aching? It was no more than she deserved, but still. "Please, Marcus."

"Not yet."

He moved her slightly over and grunted when his hard length jabbed her left butt cheek as he settled her, still straddling him, into the crevice of his hip. He eased her back until she reclined against his freed bent knee. One hand retained its hold on her hip, the other spanned her belly then smoothed its way between her breasts. "So beautiful."

The rough pad of his thumb circled her puckered nipple. She shivered. "Marcus?"

His dark green gaze, filled with want and promise, met hers. "Soon."

Charlotte closed her eyes. Even if he denied himself, as he had that night so long ago, he would give her what she needed. It wasn't what she wanted, for herself or for him, but at this point, she couldn't argue.

Yes, she would hate herself later, but right now, all that mattered was the hot need that rippled through her as he rolled one nipple between his thumb and forefinger and laved the other with his tongue. She arched her back and grabbed a handful of his thick black hair to urge him closer, but he continued to tease her, cupping, molding her breasts to his desire, nipping with his teeth, licking then blowing softly. Finally, he took her fully in his mouth and sucked hard.

Shards of fire splintered through her, converging between her legs. She moaned and squirmed in his lap, searching for relief. She found a moment's ease by rocking against his hip before he once again gripped with both hands and held her still.

She whimpered in protest, confused as to why he would prolong his own agony. It didn't make sense when she was clearly on the brink of orgasm. One touch and she would explode. He would be free to walk away.

His mouth left her breast and grazed a path to the base of her throat. His breath fanned the side of her neck then her ear. "I want you, Charlotte. I need you."

Her heart fluttered, but she reined it in. He'd admitted wanting her so often then held back, she couldn't allow her hopes to skyrocket, only to plummet when he rejected her again.

Yet she wouldn't discourage him either. "What are you waiting for?"

He raised his head, pinning her with a fiery stare. "I've waited five years for this."

"Does that mean you're—we're—"

He rolled to his side, taking her with him, and suddenly, she was on her back with him nestled between her thighs. His fingers twined with hers beside her head. "It means I'm not rushing things."

His lips slanted over hers in a kiss that stole her breath. Hot, wet, coaxing her return to the pinnacle where she'd stood moments ago. He angled his hips, and she felt the head of his erection penetrate her opening.

"I want it all." He pulled out and pushed forward again, stopping halfway this time before retreating. "I want everything."

He plunged to the hilt. Her muscles clamped around him. She bit back a moan, waiting for him to withdraw again. He kissed her again, slow and sweet. "Everything, Charlotte. No more holding back."

He held her gaze and began to rock. Though frightened of the intensity she saw there, she drew her knees up and opened herself to receive him more fully.

He groaned. "That's it. But I want more."

Untangling their fingers, he braced himself above her and drove deeper. A jolt of icy-hot fire shot down her thighs. She dug her heels into the mattress and met his agonizingly slow thrusts.

"More."

She fisted the sheet and threw back her head, afraid to let go, yet just as afraid — if not more so — to resist. The pleasure was almost painful. But not near as painful as the crack forming in the hard shell around her heart.

"Don't fight it." Each gravelly word strained between clenched teeth. Perspiration beaded his forehead, chest, and straining arms. "Give it to me. Everything you are."

She shook her head. He didn't know what he was asking. "It's too much."

"It's not enough." He reached between their bodies. His thumb found her clit and pressed. Her muscles contracted around him. He plunged again and again, increasing the pace, rotating, thrusting, slamming into her. "It's not enough."

A wave of ecstasy crashed in on her, originating at the place he touched deep inside and spiraling outward until her entire body throbbed. Then something even greater burst inside her. Something that had nothing to do with physical satisfaction. Something so achingly sweet and beautiful, it hurt to look at him.

Yet she couldn't not look. He was magnificent, his sculpted features dark and sensual as he watched her watching him, postponing his release until hers began to ebb. Then he thrust one last time, threw back his head and shouted her name.

When the last shuddering pulse faded, he lowered himself to his elbows and buried his face in the crook of her shoulder. "It'll never be enough."

Chapter Sixteen

It'll never be enough.

Charlotte stared at the ceiling, Marcus's weight pressing her into the mattress. He was right.

In all her experience, which wasn't as much as he believed, she'd never known anything close to what they had just shared. No one had ever made her feel the closeness, the almost spiritual bonding he had. And now that she had known his most intimate touch, this brief moment with him would never be enough.

What a fool she'd been to think making love with Marcus would get him out of her system. Instead, he had burrowed deeper, made her want more. So much more. He'd made her consider the impossible, such as exploring the relationship he'd hinted at so many times. It probably wouldn't last, but then a short time was better than no time with Marcus. And she might even succeed in finally ridding herself of this irritating attraction.

Definitely a fool. And yet…

Biting her lip, Charlotte lifted a hand to caress the damp hair at the back of his neck, but he rolled off her to sit on the edge of the bed, elbows on his knees, head in hands. "I can't believe I did this."

Her hand fell to the sheet as guilt rose again to choke her. Geez, how could she have forgotten how hard he'd struggled to maintain control of his body's needs? She didn't have to close her eyes to picture his face, pinched with anger, before he'd given in. He might have enjoyed the sex once he let go, embraced every moment of passion with fierce abandon while it lasted, but he regretted it now.

Just as she had intended.

Shrugging off her doubts, she dismissed the insane notion of forgoing her original plan. This wasn't the time to start second guessing herself. She needed to make sure he didn't change his mind. Or hers.

She swiped away the tears she'd fought all night and forced a satisfied purr in her voice. "I can't believe it either. You really are as good as they say. Better actually."

His hands stilled in his hair, fingers tightening at the roots. The taut muscles of his tanned back and shoulders, damp and glistening in the lamp light, stiffened.

"And if it wasn't enough for you, I'm good for round two anytime you're ready." She swallowed the rising nausea and waited for his reaction. When none came, she rolled to her side and laid a hand at the base of his spine. "I could tie you up again."

He shot off the bed. "Don't."

"Is that a no?" Watching him discard the condom in the waste basket and grab his jeans off the floor, she heaved an exaggerated sigh and reached for the sheet to cover herself. "Too bad. I'd hoped for more."

As he fastened the button at his waist, he came to stand over the bed. His dark eyes, filled with such tender passion moments ago, blazed with barely controlled anger. "It wasn't supposed to happen like this."

"Really?" She stretched, sore muscles making themselves known again now that the euphoria of their lovemaking had faded, and covered her mouth to yawn. She really was exhausted. "Did you have another position in mind? You should have said something."

"You know what I mean." His hand slashed toward the bed. "I didn't want this."

That much was painfully clear. She studied her fingernails with a raised brow. "I could have sworn you did. It certainly felt like you participated." Looking up, she met his gaze. "Fully."

"Dammit, Charlotte, you tied me up and tortured me until I broke. Only a saint could have resisted, and I'm no fucking saint. There's only so much a man can take."

Before he could see how much the reminder of what she'd done hurt, she rose from the opposite side of the bed, taking the sheet with her. "What's the big deal, Marcus? It's *just* sex."

He flinched, his head jerking back as if she'd slapped him. The heated anger slowly drained from his eyes, replaced by a cold fury. "Well, it sure as hell should be about more than that."

"What else is there?"

"Love, damn you. There should be love." He strode to the chair in the corner to swipe his shirt from beneath her sweater and jerk it over his head. "I guess you wouldn't know anything about that."

Love? Was that the one thing he wanted? Surely, he didn't mean he wanted it from her. Her heart beat faster at the prospect, though she couldn't be certain what caused it, excitement or fear.

Geez, a relationship was one thing, but love? She couldn't. She didn't. Or did she?

She'd tried so hard to ward off that destructive emotion, built a world for herself, an intricate web of lies, all for protection against it. Marcus had breached most of those barriers when he learned her secrets. Had he also slipped into her heart when she wasn't looking?

Charlotte shook her head in denial, then caught herself, glad he had his back to her so he couldn't see the shock and confusion she felt. This was crazy. She was crazy. She couldn't allow herself to think about it. She had come too far to turn back now. She had to finish what she started.

"Sex is a game to you." He raged on, jamming his

feet into the brown cowhide boots he seemed to favor, oblivious to her dismal thoughts. "With new players in every round."

Sucking in a fortifying breath, she relaxed her tense shoulders and schooled her expression into one of boredom. "What can I say? I like variety."

He straightened from lowering his jeans over his boots and stared at her, his face growing almost purple at her taunt. "You've—hell, I'm wasting my breath. You'll never change."

"I don't want to. I told you that."

"Yes, you did. And I'm sorry I didn't listen." He snagged his coat on his way to the door. "I need some air."

"Go ahead, leave," she called after him. "I got what I came for anyway."

The door to the suite slammed a second later, and Charlotte wilted, a sob catching in her throat. She might have gotten what she came for—more than she'd bargained for, really—but she'd lost so much more.

Her self-respect was in tatters after what she'd done to Marcus, and the wall around her heart had been nearly decimated. Only the portion that had kept her from begging his forgiveness remained, and it was crumbling fast. Even now, she wanted him to come back and take her in his arms, to call her bluff and demand she admit he was right about her all along.

She'd lost her secrets, most of them anyway, and her reason for keeping them. Her decided lifestyle had always been the burden she'd carried to keep men at a distance, and for the past five years, her efforts had all but gone to one man. Now that she'd driven him out of her life for good, she'd rid herself of that burden, too.

After all, why bother keeping up the charade when, no matter how much or how often she denied it, she'd lost her heart.

****

Shoving his way through the revolving door, Marcus entered the hotel and shook the snow from his boots. In his haste to get away from Charlotte, he had forgotten to put on socks and his feet were freezing. But two hours spent in the cold night air had done the trick in cooling his temper and clearing his head. He could deal with her now, say some of the things he should have said and take back some of the things he had.

With determined strides, he crossed the lobby and boarded the elevator, ignoring the curious stare of the night clerk. No doubt the man thought there was trouble in paradise with the bachelor and his lady. He punched the correct button for their floor and leaned against the back wall.

Rubbing a hand over his face, he went over all the things he'd said to her. Things meant to hurt. He'd been so damned furious at himself for failing to *prove* he loved her, he'd forgotten to tell her.

He'd been angry at her, too, for forcing him beyond his control. He hadn't thought, just lashed out, throwing her past in her face, when it wasn't at all what he'd believed it was before coming on this trip, only a fabrication, an enhanced and sometimes distorted version of the truth.

He should have realized she only reacted the way she had out of fear. Hell, he'd known he loved her before they made love — and it damned well was making love, not just sex. Yet even expecting to feel something extraordinary, he'd still been scared by the depth and power of the emotion that consumed him. And he'd seen the same sentiment reflected in her tear-filled eyes. It had to have frightened her.

That didn't mean her words hadn't cut him to the quick. They'd come too close to those she'd uttered that night in the garden beneath the gently swaying willow after he'd stroked her, made her whimper with need, and held her as she shuddered through an orgasm.

That was a real treat, Preston, but next time you're coming with me.

He'd told her then that there wouldn't be a next time; he wouldn't join the ranks of those who had gone before him. Yet he hadn't been able to stay away. He had used his need to apologize as an excuse to be near her at the auction, to hear her soft voice, touch her satiny skin, breathe in the scent of her exotic perfume.

He wondered if he would have seen the same emotion in her eyes had they made love that night in the garden. Would he have recognized it, known sooner that she loved him? That she only pushed him away because she was afraid to love and be loved? Probably not.

But he understood it now. No one made love like that if they didn't care to some significant degree. Even if she was only at the dawning of love, he could work with that. First, he had to confront her, confess his feelings, and make her admit what was in her heart. They weren't going home until she did.

Stepping off the elevator, Marcus hurried toward their suite. He let himself in and shrugged out of his coat. All was quiet. What had he expected? For her to wait up for him?

He moved quietly toward her closed door, lifted his fist to knock and hesitated. Now that he was here, he hated to wake her, especially after the fall she had taken. She needed her rest. He started to turn away then stopped.

Dammit, he'd waited long enough. They could catch a later flight, and she could sleep all day if she wanted, preferably in his arms. But they were going to have this out. Now.

He thrust the door open. As light spilled into the room, slicing over an empty bed, awareness snaked through him. He didn't need better lighting to know the rest of the room was as empty as the bed.

His gut twisted into a hard knot as he stepped farther into the bedroom. Her clothes were gone from the closet, suitcases, too. A glance inside the bathroom and at the uncluttered counter confirmed his suspicions. She was gone. Only the lingering scent of her perfume remained.

I got what I came for.

He turned away from the room—and the thought—and headed across the sitting area with determined strides. Her leaving was just another one of her evasion tactics. She was running scared again.

Well, he'd be damned if he let her go without a fight. She hadn't even tried. He deserved that much from her. They both did. He could probably catch up with her at the airport if he hurried.

But when he entered his room, he stopped short. His heart twisted in his chest as he took in the rumpled sheets. In the center of the headboard, a bright blue scarf hung limp, as if innocent and denying any part of what had happened. The smell of sex, along with the underlying scent of her perfume, reached out, drawing him closer until his knees hit the bed.

I got what I came for.

Well, maybe she had. Maybe he'd been fooling himself and the love he thought he'd seen in her eyes was only wishful thinking on his part and nothing else. She'd tried to tell him she wasn't looking for more than a good time, but he had wanted her to be wrong, so he hadn't listened.

Marcus sank to the edge of the mattress, and his fingers brushed something cool and soft. The scarf he'd torn loose from the footboard and later removed from his ankle before rolling Charlotte beneath him. He fisted it in his hand and brought it to his face. Closing his eyes, he inhaled. She was there, vaguely, but enough to reawaken his need and his heart.

It sickened him to think he'd almost told her he loved her. That if she'd still been here, he would have told her and maybe even begged her to give them a chance. God, she would have laughed him out of the room. At least he could be thankful for something.

He clenched his jaw and rose to his feet. She'd made her decision. And now, as much as it killed him, as much as he wanted things to be different, he had to make his. Hell, what difference did it make what he wanted?

She was already gone.

Chapter Seventeen

"How do I look?"

Charlotte wiped a tear from her cheek—the last she'd shed today if it killed her—and turned from the window and the man outside, who unknowingly held her heart. She'd cried enough in the two weeks since returning from Aspen to last her a lifetime. And Christmas Eve was not a time for tears.

Still wearing the cranberry silk bridesmaid gown, she glided across the tiny dressing room to stand behind Melody at the full-length mirror. "You look like a happily married woman."

"She does, doesn't she?" Melody's mother straightened from tugging the hem of her daughter's going away suit, a pink wool skirt and jacket with a winter white blouse and matching three-inch heels. "And she owes it all to you. If you hadn't told her about the position available at Preston Enterprises, she never would have met Spencer."

"That's true." Charlotte lifted the pearls she'd let Melody borrow and draped them around her neck to finish off the outfit. "And I'll cash in on that debt someday. Just you wait."

Melody let her chestnut hair fall into place and caught Charlotte's hand over her shoulder. "I'll never be able to repay this one."

The glow of her friend's face and the love shining in her eyes made Charlotte's eyes burn. She blinked against the threatening tears and failed. Just as she had during the ceremony.

It had hit her all at once as she watched Melody and Spencer repeat their vows. He loved her. Really loved her. Spencer would never betray Melody as Charlotte's father had her mother. He would remain forever faithful.

That was when this particular stint of tears had begun as she also realized Marcus was the same kind of man. Family meant everything to him. He would never hurt someone he loved, would cling to his vow once made. Glancing at him across the steps of the altar, their eyes had met, his stone cold, and she'd known the realization came too late.

Seemed she was her mother's daughter after all. In love with a man who could never love her in return. She'd seen to that. He'd never forgive her for all she'd done to him.

"Oh, are you crying again, dear?" Mrs. Jamison handed her a tissue.

Heat flooded her cheeks as she took the tissue thrust into her hand. Geez, she really had to get a grip. "I always cry at weddings."

"Liar. You hate weddings." Melody met her gaze in the mirror. "I quote, 'Love is only found in fairy tales. I give them two years, and they'll be divorced.'"

"Yeah, well, I must be getting soft, because I believe you actually found a genuine Prince Charming."

"Goodness, you are getting soft."

"Don't worry, dear." Mrs. Jamison beamed as she fussed with her daughter's collar. "From the looks passing back and forth between you and a certain groomsman today, I'd say your prince isn't far away." She stepped back and sighed, then suddenly burst into tears.

"Now, Mom, don't do that. You're going to make me ruin my make-up."

Melody pulled her mother into her arms for a hug that Charlotte would have envied if she hadn't been so rattled. If Melody's mother noticed how often her gaze had strayed to Marcus, had anyone else? Had *he*?

"We certainly can't have that," the older woman teased as she released her daughter and dabbed at her eyes. "I'd better go find your father, so he won't miss saying his good-byes."

"See if you can find Spencer and hurry him along. I'm ready to go." Melody waited until her mother was gone before crossing her arms and tapping her toe. "Well?"

Charlotte turned away and began packing Melody's makeup in her overnight bag. "It was a beautiful ceremony."

"How do you know? You cried through the whole thing."

"Don't you start, too."

"Charlotte Reese, I've known you since forever. I'm your best friend in the whole wide world, and I've never seen you cry. Ever. Then you return from your trip with Marcus, and suddenly, you're crying all the time."

"Not all the time."

"You went through an entire box of tissue and half a roll of toilet paper Friday night."

Charlotte turned to imitate Melody's stance. "May I remind you we rented six hours worth of tear-jerker movies? And I wasn't the only one bawling."

She had wanted Melody to have the best bachelorette party possible, but truthfully, having anyone else with them while they celebrated would have felt like an intrusion. So, they had spent the night as only true friends could. Painting each others' nails, eating pizza and ice cream in their pajamas, and watching movies until the early hours of the morning.

"So, what's your excuse now?"

She shrugged. "I'm losing my best friend."

Melody frowned, as if wanting to broach the subject Charlotte was determined to dodge, then sighed and turned back to the mirror to fiddle with an earring. "We'll see each other as often as we do now.

And you know lunch on Friday will always be yours. After my honeymoon, that is."

Grateful, she squeezed in beside Melody and smoothed her fingers over her own hair, readjusting curls she had painstakingly arranged in a pile at the back of her head. It was almost like they were kids again, playing dress up, sharing the mirror, and experimenting with make-up and hairstyles. Only this time, one of them was really a bride. "And speaking of the honeymoon... Did you pack my gift to Spencer?"

"Uh-uh. I'm wearing it."

"You better hope he doesn't find out or you won't make it out of town, probably not even the parking lot." Several months ago, Charlotte noticed her friend stocking up on underwear every time they went shopping, thongs in particular. She'd finally wheedled the reason out of Melody; Spencer had a tendency to tear them off during their more passionate encounters.

Melody gave her a sly wink. "Hey, the honeymoon can happen anywhere."

Laughing, Charlotte backed up and moved across the room to close the hanging bag that contained Melody's wedding dress. "Has he told you yet where you're going?"

"No, but I'm counting on your gift to help me entice it out of him." She swiveled a grin over her shoulder. "Can you see him out there? Is he waiting?"

Knowing she would see Marcus again, Charlotte hesitated, then steeled herself and returned to the window facing the parking lot. A crowd had gathered around Spencer's silver Jag decorated with shoe polish, streamers and something that looked a lot like condoms. Still, the Preston brothers were easy to locate, standing heads above most. "Yes. He's there."

She heard Melody scurry around behind her but couldn't turn away when Marcus embraced Spencer and laughed at something he said as he handed him over to Avery. Then Nick took his turn but wouldn't let go, which had them all laughing while Marcus tried to pry them apart.

He was so natural with his brothers, so easy going, just as he'd been with the children at the hospital and throughout the reception with his friends and family. It hurt to think he couldn't be that way with her, that he stayed guarded in her presence. But then she'd never been open to him either. Not entirely.

Melody joined her at the window and smiled at the brotherly antics taking place. "They can be such idiots when they're together."

Charlotte had never known what it was like to have siblings. Melody hadn't either, but at least she'd had two loving parents. Charlotte hadn't even had that. Though she had to give her mother credit for trying lately. "You're lucky to be a part of that closeness now."

"Yes."

"And I might have been whining earlier, but I'm really glad you found Spencer. He's a good man."

"Marcus is a good man, too."

"I know."

"Then why don't you talk to him? Try to work things out?"

"Because it's too late. I screwed things up." Pushing him away this time had torn her heart in two. Not even the pain of her childhood had hurt as much as this.

"I wish you'd tell me what happened between the two of you. He won't talk to anyone either. Not even Avery."

"No, he wouldn't. Marcus isn't like that."

"Then why—"

"Suffice it to say I was my usual self."

"You're being too hard on yourself. And so is Marcus. He's thrown himself into his work. He's there till all hours of the night. And when he's not at the office, he's out at the ranch. Everybody can see he's hurting and holding everything inside. Just like you."

Charlotte suspected he wasn't hurting so much as he was punishing himself for what he thought he'd done wrong, which only made her guilt increase. "I hope this isn't your way of trying to make me feel better."

"He loves you, Char. That's what I'm trying to tell you."

Melody's soft words slammed into her heart. She wanted so desperately to believe them.

"I see it every time he looks at you. And Mom's right. He couldn't keep his eyes off you today."

"Funny, I stood five feet across the altar from him, but I could have been invisible for all he seemed to care."

"Men act that way sometimes. I don't know if he's too proud, hurt, or just afraid, but I know he loves you. Don't ask me how. I just do."

Even if he did, even if he could forgive her, the fact remained she could never be the woman he deserved. She had too much baggage, too many issues to deal with. He'd do better to find someone who could give him what he wanted.

All these years she'd pushed her reputation to the limits, spitting in the face of propriety, her only objective to remain safe. That same wall of defense now held her prisoner. Society never forgot and neither would he. He would always wonder how many there had been before him and how many there would be when he wasn't looking. He would never trust her.

And she would never be good enough for him. He deserved someone better. Someone good and wholesome. A woman he could be proud of. She might be acceptable to socialize with, but she could never be family.

"Talk to him. Please. As a wedding gift to me?"

"Geez, I already gave you your wedding gifts, emphasis on the plural. How many do you want?"

"Just this one more. Show him who you really are."

"I've been playing different roles for so long I'm not certain *I* know who I am anymore." She'd been trying to figure that out since she got back from her trip. One thing was certain, there was no point in continuing the charade meant to keep anyone from getting too close and breaking her heart. It was already broken.

"Promise or I'm not leaving."

She rolled her eyes. "Okay, okay, I'll talk to him." *Someday.*

"Today."

"Geez, Mel, I—"

"Today. The longer you put it off, the worse it will be. I mean it. Promise me."

"Okay. But not until everyone else is gone." The least she could do was apologize. Make him understand he had done nothing wrong. She was to blame. And to let him know he had nothing to fear from her. She would never tell anyone.

"Melody, honey?" Connie Preston's voice had them turning to the door. Her warm hazel eyes lit on Charlotte. "Oh, I didn't mean to interrupt."

"I was just leaving." Charlotte grabbed Melody's overnight bag, her heart racing around in her chest. Facing Marcus's mother wasn't something she wanted to do. She'd caught the woman watching her during the reception with eyes that said she was as aware as everyone else in the family of her son's distant mood and who had caused it. "I'll take this out to the car and tell Spencer you're ready."

"Chicken," Melody muttered under her breath.

"Please don't leave on my account."

Skirting the woman, Charlotte forced a smile. "A maid of honor's work is never done."

She shut the door behind her and leaned against it to calm her palpitating heart. Though why she bothered she didn't know. The promise she'd made her best friend would grind the tattered organ to a painful halt.

****

Bird seed pelted Marcus as his brother and new sister-in-law emerged from the gauntlet of well-wishers lining the church steps. Spencer opened the passenger door of the Jag then stood back, waiting for his bride to finish her good-byes, the first of which was to her maid of honor.

Charlotte's face tightened with emotion when Melody hugged her. After a few whispered words the two parted. Melody shook a finger in that lecturing manner he'd come to know, and Charlotte nodded, wiping away another tear as she moved aside for the Jamisons.

Her eyes met his across the hood of Spencer's car before she turned to climb the church steps. But in that brief moment he saw a wealth of pain and regret.

"She's sure been crying a lot."

Marcus shrugged, not bothering to ask who Avery meant. He hadn't been very discreet in his observations this afternoon. She seemed different somehow, more in tune with the woman he'd thought to uncover. Still, he'd tried to harden his heart against her; what was left of it anyway. "Women cry at weddings."

"No, I mean since you two got back from Aspen. Mel told Spencer she cries all the time now."

Marcus dragged his gaze from where she'd stopped at the top step to watch the progression alone. "What do you want me to do about it?"

"Talk to her."

"Believe me, she doesn't want to hear anything I have to say."

"Not if you keep acting like a prick."

Spencer rounded the front of the car, saving Marcus from having to reply or kick his brother's ass, and Nick stepped forward to hand him a twenty-five-pound bag of rice. "They won't let us throw this stuff anymore, but I couldn't let you get out of here without making sure you're set for the future. We want lots of nieces and nephews."

Avery thrust a brown paper sack forward. "And this is to make sure you get to enjoy your marriage for a while before all that fertility kicks in. I figure these might last through the honeymoon."

Spencer looked inside at the box of condoms and laughed. "Only twenty. Doesn't say much for what you guys think of my stamina."

"It's not your stamina we're worried about. It's actually your impatience. Any protection you have is probably packed in the trunk, and we didn't want you to use the decorations off the car."

Marcus slipped an envelope from the inside pocket of his coat. "And last but not least."

"What's this?"

"A list of hotels in every town between here and Galveston where you can find a room already reserved and paid for under the name of Mr. and Mrs. Spencer Preston. In case you can't wait until you board the ship."

"Come on, guys. Let him go," Melody shouted over the cacophony of noise around them. "I promise to bring him back in one piece."

Laughter burst from all four, and Spencer slid behind the wheel. "You guys are the best."

Marcus stood silent beside his remaining brothers, already feeling the separation from Spencer as he drove out of sight and into another phase of his life. He wondered if Nick was remembering the day he'd married Julie, if he still hurt from her betrayal and resulting death. And Avery, well, there was usually only one thing on his mind. He was probably lamenting Spencer's loss of bachelorhood and the ability to live for the moment.

There wasn't a doubt in Marcus's mind that Spencer would be happy with Melody. They shared a love so special, it was almost impossible to watch them and not ache for something even remotely close. Until recently he never believed he would settle for anything less.

He risked another glance at the top of the church steps, but she was no longer there. After today, he doubted he would see her much. Just as well.

"I need a drink," Nick said, yanking the tie from around his neck. The bitter edge in his voice confirmed where his thoughts had been.

Avery slapped his hands together, rubbing them briskly. "We'll toast Spencer's marriage and the fortunate fact that we're still single. What do you say, Marcus? You up for a celebration?"

Hell, he could use a drink or two. Anything was better than the alternative, which was going home to stare at four walls and think about all the mistakes he'd made with Charlotte. "Sure, but I'll have to catch up to you. I promised Natalie a ride home."

Both Nick and Avery lifted a brow.

"What?"

Nick stuffed his tie in his pocket. "You should distance yourself from that one before someone gets hurt."

"Nat's just a kid."

"With a rack like that?" Avery snorted. "Come on."

Nick nodded. "She was like a hound at your heels during the reception."

At the ranch, too. He'd been meaning to talk to her, but somehow never found the time or the right moment. "It's just a ride home. But you're right. I'll talk to her on the way."

"I'll call and let you know where we end up." Avery peered past him, his brown eyes crinkling, and waved. "How about you, darlin'? Want to shake up the city with us?"

Marcus turned as Charlotte, now wearing a coat over her bridesmaid dress, strode toward them. Her gaze locked with his, determined, solemn, searching, even after she stopped in front of him.

That's how she'd been throughout the reception. When she wasn't directing the catering staff or doling out punch, she'd kept to herself, quiet, almost subdued. Not at all the Charlotte from before.

"Uh, okay then," Avery said behind him. "We'll leave you two…to it."

The silence continued to grow even after his brothers left. Finally, he cleared his throat. "You look lovely." It wasn't what he meant to say.

Her eyes flickered over the parking lot, her cheeks flushing pink. "Thank you."

"I saw your mom. How is she?"

She fiddled with the strap of her purse. "Taking one day at a time."

Aren't we all? "She didn't stay for the reception."

She shook her head and looked down at the sidewalk. "No, she's only been home a few days and wasn't ready to face the champagne. I'm staying with her through the holidays or until she gets her bearings."

"Do you need a ride home?"

Her head jerked up, surprise evident in her expression. Right. Probably not a good idea with the kid in tow. Maybe he could get Avery to take Natalie home. He indicated with a nod to the parking lot. "I didn't see your car."

Emotions flitted across her face so fast he couldn't be sure, but he thought he saw hope in her pale blue eyes then disappointment before they went blank.

"No, I traded the Corvette in last week." She pointed to the lime green Volkswagen Beetle parked a few cars away. "I like this better."

"Ah." What else could he say? The sleek red sports

car had been her trademark ride for so long he had a hard time picturing her in anything else. He wondered if it was one of the many things she'd hidden behind.

"Melody said you picked up several new clients last week."

So, his sister-in-law had made it her mission to keep Charlotte abreast of the happenings in his life. Much like Spencer had done the past two weeks with him. Even a certain little blonde angel had filled him in on her comings and goings at the hospital. He pretended otherwise, but he relished every bit of information relayed. "Only one is new. The other three were actually returning clients."

"Ones my father stole."

He shrugged. What was the point in stirring an already dead issue? "So did you finish your dissertation?" He knew from Spencer she hadn't, but he was reluctant to end the conversation.

"I have a little more research, but I'm looking at early spring."

He nodded and couldn't stop himself from tucking that stray curl behind her ear. "I'm proud of you."

Her gaze lifted, and she stared at him with a yearning that made him want to throw caution to the wind. He couldn't hurt any more than he already was.

"Charlotte, we—"

"Marcus, I'm—"

She bit her lip and darted a glance toward the church. He'd never seen her so unsure of herself. Nervous fidgeting wasn't her style. Obviously, she had something on her mind. Did she regret how things ended in Aspen? Maybe she wanted to work things out, take the risk of letting him love her. Maybe even love him in return.

His heart pitched, but he quelled it with reason. More likely she was looking to ease her guilty conscience. If so, he wouldn't make it easy for her. He thrusts his hands in his pockets to keep from reaching for her and waited.

Finally, she looked at him, hers eyes filled with uncertainty.

"I-I wanted to apologize for what happened in Aspen. I shouldn't have done…pushed you to…"

He swallowed the resentment welling inside him. He didn't want her apology. But neither did he want her to make herself sick over it. He wanted to tell her to forget it. That he really hadn't done anything he hadn't wanted to do since the moment he met her, which was nothing short of the truth. "What happened was—"

She held up her hand. "No, please. Let me finish."

But again, she only stared at the ground, at her hands, anywhere but at him, and he couldn't stand it any longer. He couldn't wait for her to trample his heart again. Better to get it over with. "It was inevitable. The chemistry between us was too strong."

She blinked, her lips parted in a soft gasp, and he waited once more while she struggled to form words, wanting them to be the ones he longed to hear. "Yes, well, I thought maybe you could—that we could try to— Oh…" More of the light in her eyes dimmed. "You said *was*."

"Is." He ran the back of his knuckles across her cheek, hating to see her so vulnerable. He thought he knew where she was going, or at least he hoped he did, and now he wanted to ease the path for her. But carefully. "I don't think it'll ever die."

Those lips, painted dark red to match her dress, lifted slightly. "Me either."

Okay, so he'd dive right in. "Before you say anything else, I have something I need to tell you."

"Marcus, your mom wants to talk to you before we leave."

At the sound of Natalie's voice, he jerked his hand to his side. Charlotte looked from him to Nat and back again, the uncertainty he'd seen moments ago back tenfold. "I'll be there in a minute."

"She needs help getting your grandmother to the car. Nick and Avery already left, and she doesn't want your father or Melody's dad trying to lift her."

Charlotte straightened the strap of her purse on her shoulder. She looked ready to bolt. "You should go."

He glanced toward his parents' car parked in front of the church then to the top of the steps where his mother and grandmother waited. He couldn't leave his grandmother in the cold and Nat was right. Grandma Preston could be a bit ornery when she was in one of her moods.

Turning back to Charlotte, he said, "I'm sorry. This shouldn't take but a minute."

"That's okay. I need to get home anyway."

"No." He pinned her with a look he hoped conveyed his need for her to stay. "I'll be right back. Don't leave."

Charlotte nodded. "Don't keep your grandmother waiting."

Marcus turned and sprinted across the street and up the steps of the church, pausing once to look back at her as if he were afraid she would disappear. She might have smiled had Natalie not stood watching her. Instead, she met the girl's serious gaze and forced a smile. "Thank you for manning the groom's table."

"I didn't mind at all. Spencer's like a brother to me."

The subtle reminder of Natalie's connection to the Preston family found its mark, bringing with it the envy Charlotte had tried to suppress over the last week.

She'd forgotten about her curiosity over the girl's familiarity toward Marcus and his brothers during the benefit until Melody's cousin called, unable to make the wedding, and Connie Preston suggested Natalie serve at the groom's table. Later, she'd learned from Melody that Marcus's mother had taken the ranch foreman's daughter under her wing after the girl's mother died four years ago.

"Yes, well—" She dislodged the little green monster from her throat. "—I know Melody appreciated it."

Natalie folded her arms over ample cleavage displayed above the plunging neckline of the green velvet dress that made her look innocent and provocative all at the same time. "Actually, I wanted to thank *you*."

Perplexed, Charlotte shook her head. "For helping Melody? I wouldn't have let her down to save the world."

"Not for that. For what you did to Marcus in Aspen."

Charlotte's stomach lurched. Had he told Natalie what she'd done? What they'd done? "I'm not certain I understand what you mean?"

"Before the trip, he was distracted. Now he has focus. He's been out to the ranch almost every night. We've spent more time together these last two weeks than in the last six months. Whatever happened between you, and I really don't want to know, I'm grateful."

"So, you and Marcus were…" She choked on the words.

"No, Marcus would never make a commitment if he weren't absolutely free to do so. But I think whatever happened in Aspen is helping him get past the thing that was holding him back. His attraction to you."

Charlotte glanced in his direction and found him watching her as he pushed his grandmother's wheelchair. Was that what she'd been doing? Holding him back? Maybe she had. That *inevitable* attraction had kept her distracted for longer than she could remember. She knew now it was more than a physical yearning she'd felt all these years, but was that all it had been to him? A distraction?

"Look, I don't mean to hurt your feelings, but it's no secret you aren't Marcus's type. He needs a woman he can trust, one who believes in family values. Not one he's ashamed of."

It wasn't something she hadn't thought herself, but hearing it aloud, and from someone who claimed to care for him, stung. Sure, Melody cared about him and had still argued against Charlotte giving up on him, but friends were often blind to one another's faults.

"I guess," Natalie went on, "I'm asking you to let him go and sever any lingering threads."

"So you can step in?"

"I love him."

Love. He'd thrown it in her face numerous times. The last being just before he'd walked out of the suite.

There's one thing I want more.

His words pierced her heart as thoroughly as any arrow. Words she finally understood. He wanted love. But was it Natalie he loved?

She played back the times she'd seen them together during the reception. Had she missed something? Marcus had moved from table to table alone, speaking with everyone and no one in particular. When Natalie had joined the group, he'd stood apart from her and often excused himself soon after. But then Marcus had never been one for public displays of affection. The only time she'd seen him allow it was as part of their ruse in Aspen.

Her gaze drifted across the street and met his worried frown over the roof of the luxury car. Having the woman he loved and a former one-night-stand together probably did that to a man.

She turned back to Natalie, anxious to leave before he settled his grandmother in the car. And before she let loose another round of tears. "Tell Marcus I had to go."

"He'll only follow you. You need to end it here and now."

She swallowed. "I can't. Just tell him I wanted to thank him for making the trip enjoyable and that the sponsors were extremely happy with the layout for the Valentine's promotion. It'll be out the day after New Year's."

"I'll tell him."

About to turn away, she made herself stop. She blinked to clear the blurriness in her eyes. "And whatever you do, Natalie. Make him happy. He deserves that. If I'd known…" She shook her head and backed away. "I never would have…I didn't know."

Charlotte turned away and hurried to her car as quickly as possible without seeming desperate. As she started the engine, she thought she heard Marcus call her name, but she shifted the car into gear and drove away. She couldn't bear hearing him confess he loved Natalie, which was more than likely the "something" he had to tell her. Not when she'd thought he was about to tell *her* those very words.

It all made sense now. The guilty look moments ago when Natalie had interrupted them, the purple tie-dyed scarf he purchased at the gift shop for a young brunette. And though she'd assumed he spent time the last two weeks working while out at the ranch, he was probably spending as much time as possible with Natalie to alleviate some of his guilt.

Guilt she'd forced upon him. Literally.

He had tried to resist. Last summer at the mayor's party, during the auction, and throughout the weekend in Aspen. He'd fought his desires every step of the way and up to the bittersweet end. For Natalie. He might have succeeded, too, if she hadn't tied him up.

How could she have been so stupid? So vain as to think he wanted a relationship with *her*? Of course, not with her. She was the last person he would get involved with. She was a project, a good deed. The

Snow Whites of this world were the ones men like Marcus wanted when it came to settling down and having a family.

Snow Whites like Natalie.

****

The traffic light had barely turned green when Marcus muttered a curse and honked at the car in front of him. As soon as they cleared the intersection, he steered his truck into the right lane and shot past the other driver. Not that he had anywhere to be other than downing a few shots at the bar with Avery and Nick. Pissing drunk. That's where he needed to be.

Charlotte had accused him of being good at walking away, but she was fucking good at it herself. And he'd be damned if he was going to chase her if she didn't care enough to stay and listen to him.

Still, he'd been so sure they were on the same page, that she knew exactly what he wanted to tell her and that she wanted to hear it as much as he wanted to say it.

Sensing Natalie's gaze on him, he glanced sideways. She'd been so quiet he'd forgotten she was there and that he should be using this opportunity to straighten a few things out with her.

He cleared his throat. "We have to talk."

Her brown eyes rounded with what looked like a combination of fear and guilt. "About what?"

"Nat, you're a nice kid, but…" How did he say this without coming off like an ass or hurting her feelings?

The wariness in her eyes faded into defiance, and her chin lifted slightly. "I'm nineteen."

"And I'm twenty-eight."

"So?"

He turned down the side road that led to his family's home, wishing he'd had this conversation with her weeks ago and not now when he was in a piss-poor mood. "So, you should be spending time with someone closer to your own age."

"I'm not interested in anyone my age."

"Well, I'm not interested in anyone *your* age."

She blanched at his bluntness, but he couldn't feel any remorse. Loving Charlotte as he did, there was no room in his life for anyone else. Especially someone as young and immature as Natalie. Charlotte might have her faults, but she was all woman. And he loved every inch of her. In spite of those faults.

Because of them.

"It's Charlotte Reese, isn't it? When are you going to see she's not good enough for you? She's a spoiled and lazy slut."

He took the force of her words against Charlotte as if they were meant for him. In that moment, he understood all she had endured over the years. Granted, it was self-inflicted, but that didn't make the negative opinions hurt any less. "You don't even know her."

"I know she's not right for you. Everyone does." She turned to stare out the window. "Even she sees it."

Marcus slammed on the brakes, causing the truck to skid slightly to the right as it slid to a halt. He turned to his sullen but nervous passenger. "What did she say?"

"Nothing."

"Natalie, what did she say to make you think that?"

A guilty flush stained her cheeks. "Nothing."

"Then what did you say to her?"

"I only told her the truth, what everybody else already knows. That with her reputation, she isn't the kind of woman you could be proud of. You need someone who shares the same values as you. And—"

"Fuck, Natalie, why would you do that? You have no idea what I need."

"Yes, I do. You need someone to love you, somebody acceptable to society."

"I don't give a flying fuck about society."

"Yes, you do." Her eyes flashed. "Otherwise, you would have dated her openly instead of slinking off to screw her in some dark corner when you thought no one would know. Like you did at the auction."

Marcus wanted to deny the accusation, wanted to make her take the words back. Not the screwing part, though it wouldn't have been anything so vulgar had they made love that night. And Natalie wouldn't believe him anyway. No, he wanted to claim he'd never thought about what people would think of him had he pursued Charlotte publicly. But he couldn't, and it made him sick to his stomach to realize Charlotte had known it, too.

Oh, he was sure she'd been aware of his concerns, used them to drive him away, but until now, he'd always believed his thoughts were private, or between them. But to hear Natalie voice what she and everyone else had seen him display in word and deed made him see himself all the more clearly.

He swallowed the bile rising in his throat. He had to make things right. "Appearances can be deceiving. She's not what she seems. She puts up walls, pretending—"

"You're defending her now?" She threw her hands in the air. "Of course, you are. She's got you by the balls and won't let go. Don't you see she's making a fool of you?"

"Natalie," he warned through clenched teeth, trying to make allowances for her age and the hurt he'd caused by ignoring her feelings toward him. And by not setting the example, not showing Charlotte the respect he should have so that this girl and so many others would do the same.

"Stupid me." She ignored him and ranted on. "I thought you'd get your fill of her while you were in Aspen and come back ready to move on." She snorted. "She must be really good. God knows, every man in

Texas wants a piece. Most are probably waiting for seconds."

Marcus grabbed her by the shoulders and shook her once. "Don't you ever"—his shout reverberated through the truck, giving voice to the rage burning inside him—"*ever* say another word against her to me or anybody else. Do you hear me?"

She stared up at him, startled, then with a horrified gasp, she whispered, "Oh, my God. You're in love with her."

He released her and sat back in his seat. He didn't want to discuss his feelings for Charlotte with anyone. Certainly not with a petulant child who had added to the mess he created.

"You are. You're in love with Charlotte. All this time, I thought you were just—but you really…" Her lower lip began to tremble, and a tear spilled down her cheek. She looked down at her lap. "This is so unfair. I love you, Marcus. I have since I was fifteen. I've been waiting for you to see that I'm grown up."

"I'm sorry, Nat. You're sweet, but—"

"But you don't love me."

"No. I care for you, like a kid sister. Even if I didn't love Charlotte…" He trailed off when she burst into tears and searched the console for a tissue. He found a napkin from the last fast-food place he'd driven through and,. with a sigh, put the truck in gear before his conscience overrode common sense and he did something stupid. Like try to comfort her. As much as he hated to see her cry, she would probably take it as a sign that he cared more than he did. Besides, a good cry would help her heal—not to mention keep her quiet. He needed to think.

But his thoughts were a jumble, and clearly, Natalie had more to say. She laid a hand on his arm resting on the console. "She doesn't know, does she?"

He thought back to the minutes following their lovemaking. He'd come near telling her, thought she might have guessed, but he hadn't actually said the words. "No."

"I didn't think so."

Something about the way she said it, the way her voice cracked with shame, made him look at her. "What do you mean?"

She darted a quick glance at him, guilt and remorse shifting back and forth around the hurt in her big brown eyes. She opened her mouth as if to explain, then wedged her lower lip between her teeth.

"Nat?"

"I can't believe I'm telling you this, but I think she loves you, too." He thought he would have to prompt her again, but she shook her head and rushed on. "She gave up too easily. From all I'd heard about Charlotte, I'd expected her to be a vindictive bitch, to sink her claws into you and not let go no matter who she hurt, you or me. But instead, *I* was the bitch. I wanted her to leave you alone, so I let her believe you had feelings for me, that your attraction to her was holding you back."

Sniffling, she turned away. "You must hate me. I don't even like myself right now."

Marcus gripped the steering wheel with both hands and hung onto his patience by a thin thread, afraid she'd start to cry again and never tell him what he needed to know. Like why she thought Charlotte loved him. He prayed she was right. "I don't hate you, Nat."

"It's just that I—I do want you to be happy. That's what she said, you know. You deserved to be happy and to make sure you were. I thought that's what I was doing—would do if you gave me the chance. Anyway, she obviously cares enough about you to do what she thought—or what I led her to believe—was best for you. I'm so sorry, Marcus. Maybe it's not too late."

"Maybe." But if it was, he had no one to blame but himself. He'd been cocky enough to think he could control everything—a teenage girl's infatuation, his attraction to Charlotte, his dick. Well, he'd done about as well controlling those as he had his heart.

But right now, it wasn't *his* heart he was concerned about. Charlotte might not love him, might not care if he loved her, but she had to be hurting after the things Natalie said. He had to find her. He had to make things right.

Luckily, he knew exactly where she would be at seven o'clock on Christmas Eve, the night of miracles.

A little angel had told him.

Chapter Eighteen

Arms loaded with colorfully wrapped gifts, Charlotte backed up to the double doors of the burn unit's game room. She sniffled, the lingering effects of the last breakdown she'd had since leaving Marcus at the church, and sucked in a steadying breath. She couldn't start blubbering in front of the children and upset them.

Butting her way inside, she heard the pitter patter of slippered feet and Sarah's sweet voice. "Charlotte, you came."

"Of course, honey. I promised, didn't I?" She surveyed the room, taking a head count to make sure she had enough gifts for everyone. "Did Dylan go home?"

"Yeah, today."

Good. Children needed to be home with their families at Christmas. She'd take his present to him later in the week.

Squatting at the base of the tree, she lowered her burden to the floor as several children, excited at her arrival and the new haul, ran over to investigate. She looked around for the smallest and most precocious of the bunch. "What about Amy?"

"Oh, she's here somewhere." Sarah danced beside her. "I can't wait to show you what I got this morning."

Charlotte smiled at Sarah's excitement and felt a little of her depression lift. This place—these children—could always do that, make her forget the world outside. "Oh, did Santa come early?"

"You could say that."

She looked up to see the girl's face lit with humor. Brushing the dust off the knees of her jeans, she straightened and slipped out of her hip-length, black leather jacket. "Okay, I give. What's up?"

Sarah took her jacket and draped it over the chair behind her. "We had a visitor after breakfast."

"Yes, I've already got that much. Who was it?"

"Marcus." Sarah beamed. "And look what he gave me."

Charlotte flinched at the sound of his name and suddenly wished she hadn't worn her hair in a ponytail. It left her flushed skin too exposed, even above the turtleneck that peeked from under her sweatshirt. Her gaze followed Sarah's fingers as they ran over the purple tie-dyed scarf tied neatly around her throat. The very scarf she'd thought he bought for Natalie.

"It covers my scar."

"It's beautiful."

"He said you helped him pick it out."

"Yes." Something fluttered inside Charlotte, knowing he spoke of her to the children. Then again, he could have been using her relationship with them to ease the way into creating one of his own. Either way, she was relieved the gift she had helped him choose wasn't for another woman.

"Charlotte!"

Amy's squeal from behind yanked her from the edge of another attack of self-pity. She turned to greet the little girl and stopped in her tracks when her gaze, leveled for the tiny five-year-old, landed on a pair of very masculine, jean-clad thighs. Following them upward, she took in slender hips and a trim waist that expanded into a broad chest covered in a dark green cashmere sweater. Little legs encased in pink thermal pajama pants dangled over wide shoulders.

Unable to breathe for the tightness squeezing her lungs, Charlotte blinked past the face she knew so well to Amy's, peering at her over waves of jet-black hair. "See what Marcus gave me. A snow globe. It has a little town in it."

"H—how pretty." That he'd been thinking of the children while on their trip was another reminder of the kind of man he was. And that she had ruined any chance of happiness with him. That she'd never really had a chance.

"I hope you don't mind me barging in."

Forced to acknowledge him, she took a direct hit to her heart. Geez, it hurt to look at him. "Of course not. The children seem to have formed an attachment to you. And it was thoughtful of you to bring gifts. Where's Natalie?"

If the floor opened up to swallow her, she would have rejoiced. It was the last thing she had meant to ask. Now, she sounded like a jealous ex-lover, exactly what she was.

He shrugged, making Amy giggle, then lowered her to her feet. "I don't know. I dropped her off at the ranch and headed back here. Didn't want to miss the fun."

Fun? He called this fun? Every nerve in her body ached with the need to touch him, to feel the warmth of *his* touch.

Sarah tugged on her arm. "He brought something else, too. The doctors and nurses have been having fun with it all day."

Both the girls began to titter and point above her head. She glanced up and saw a sprig of mistletoe tied to a ceiling beam with red ribbon.

"You gotta kiss her, Marcus."

Charlotte jerked around to find Amy and Sarah pushing him toward her. Shaking her head, she started to back away, but his hands slid up her arms to rest on her shoulders. He leaned close to whisper. "For the kids."

She wanted his kiss, wanted it more than

anything. But she'd made a promise to herself that she would think of him and what he needed. "I don't think we—"

"Then quit thinking," he murmured as his head drifted toward hers. There it was, the same raw hunger in his eyes she'd seen so many times before. But there were other things now—a gentle understanding, a questioning hope, a profound longing.

She closed her eyes, certain her own longings were playing tricks on her, and ducked from under his hands.

"I left something in the car." She started walking backward, toward the exit. "Sarah, you start passing out the presents."

"Charlotte, wait."

His voice followed her into the hall, and she quickened her pace almost to a run. Several nurses looked up as she passed their station, but she didn't care. She could feel the tears welling up and had to make it to the elevator before the dam broke.

He caught her halfway down the hall and matched his stride to hers. "I'll come with you."

"There's not that much." Actually, there were no gifts in the car. And as much as she hated to lie to the kids, she wasn't coming back tonight. Not while Marcus was here.

"I need to talk to you anyway. There are some things I should explain."

"You don't have to. I get it now. I—" To her horror, her voice cracked then wouldn't budge past her throat as the first of her tears tipped over her bottom lashes.

"Oh God, Charlotte, please don't cry."

Swiping the back of her hand over wet cheeks, she lifted her chin away from him and sniffed. "I'm not." Not really. This was nothing compared to what she wanted to do. Would do later when she was by herself.

He stepped in front of her, putting his hands on

her upper arms when she tried to go around him. "Then stop running away."

"I'm not," she repeated the same feeble words, unable to think beyond her need for escape.

"You're not crying and you're not running?" He shook his head. "You used to be a better liar than that." She tried to pull away, but he wouldn't let her. "Not this time."

Hysteria bubbled inside her, and she could feel herself losing the thin grasp she had on her emotions. "What do you want from me, Marcus?"

"I'll answer that later. For now—" Marcus moved her to one side of the hall as two nurses approached with obvious curiosity and waited for them to pass. "For now, I want to start by saying I'm sorry."

"No, *I'm* sorry. For everything. If I'd known—" Her voice broke again, and shame dragged her gaze to the wall behind him.

"Shh, it's okay."

"No, it's not. I made a game out of trying to seduce you. When I couldn't win fairly, I cheated. And now..."

"And now?" he prompted.

She inhaled deeply and exhaled, struggling for composure. "You won. No matter what happened."

"Did I?" When she wouldn't answer, he framed her face in his hands and tipped her head back. "What if I said it was you who won? You got what you wanted and proved I was no different than any other man you've known."

Charlotte grabbed his wrists. She couldn't let him believe she thought that of him any longer. "But you are. You're a good man, Marcus. You're honest, loyal, devoted to those you care about." She was rambling, but now that the words were coming, she couldn't stop them. "I've never allowed myself to look for those qualities in a man because I didn't believe I'd find them. But you made me want to see them. You made me want things I never thought I could have—commitment, marriage, children. You made me want *you*. I fell in love with *you*."

She blanched as the words left her lips. Her throat constricted. "I'm sorry. I shouldn't have said that."

"Why not?"

"I don't want to complicate things any more than they already are."

He brushed the tears from her cheeks with the pads of his thumbs. "You mean with Natalie?"

"Yes. She suspects something happened but from all she said, I think she's willing to overlook it. You can still work things out."

"Charlotte, baby, there never was and never will be anything between me and Natalie. It was a teenage girl's infatuation and my own stupidity in not dealing with her sooner. She told me why you left the church after I asked you to wait. I hate that she said those things to you, but even more, I hate that you believed them."

He lowered his hands to her shoulders and pulled her closer until she was flush against his chest. "Yes, I've been out to the ranch a lot lately. But only to work off my frustration. I've mucked out more stalls in the last two weeks than I have in my whole adult life. There are three hundred yards of new barbed wire fencing and seventeen horses with a brand-new set of shoes. If Nat was around, I didn't notice. I was too busy missing you."

The pain in his dark eyes said he spoke the truth, and for a fraction of a second, she let herself rejoice. He missed her. Most importantly, he wasn't in love with Natalie. Snow White had lied about everything.

Well, not everything.

Marcus might have missed her, might even have feelings beyond the attraction they shared. But that didn't change who she was. Or who she had been. Either way, her past was still her past. She shook her head to ward off the need to forget her doubts and reach for the happy ending. "I'm not the right woman for you. I'm not—"

He placed a finger over her lips. "Good enough? Charlotte Reese, *you* are the only woman for me, the only one I want. I don't care if you wear your clothes too short or too low or too tight because no matter what you wear, you make it look good. And I don't care if you've slept with every man in Houston, which you would no doubt have me believe, though I wouldn't for a minute, so don't even try. As long as I'm the one you sleep with every night from here on out."

"What are you saying?"

"I love you, Charlotte." His lips brushed hers so tenderly, fresh tears burn her eyes. Then he pulled back. "Will that be enough? Will you trust me to love you forever? I will, you know, whether you'll have me or not."

From the time she'd come to understand her parents' relationship, she'd hidden behind the pretense of fast and loose, afraid to let a man near enough to hurt her, determined never to let a man control her the way her father did her mother. And yet, her actions of defiance against men like her father had given him more control than if she'd simply lain down and let him walk all over her.

It had taken Marcus's persistence in Aspen to make her see that. She'd thought it was too late, and she was still afraid, but for the first time in her life she felt free to embrace love and all that came with it.

"I'll have you," she said, sniffling.

A grin split his face. "Good, because from now on, you can have me any way you want me. I'm not fighting it ever again."

Charlotte winced. "I really am sorry about that."

"I'm not. Making love to you is just that. Another way to show you how much I love you." He nibbled her lower lip. "I'd like to spend the rest of my life showing you."

She looped her arms around his neck. "That could be arranged."

"Really? Then I should warn you." He lowered his voice. "I've got some scarves at home with your name on them."

"Such a control freak," she teased even as excitement bubbled through her veins at the thought of being tied to his bed. Releasing an exaggerated sigh, she toyed with the hair at the back of his neck. "Just one of the many things I love about you."

"I thought you hated it."

"Maybe I just like making you lose control."

A low groan vibrated against her lips as he kissed her, showing her as he'd said he would how much he loved her. Applause erupted at the other end of the short hallway, and Charlotte pulled back just in time to see one of the nurses herding the kids back inside the game room.

Sarah wrapped an arm around Amy. "See, Charliss cured Marcocius."

Amy shook her head. "I knew all along Marcus wasn't a beast."

"What about you?" Marcus asked, drawing Charlotte's attention from the disappearing children. "You think I'm still a beast?"

She thought about the scarves and smiled. "I'm counting on it."

Thank you for reading *Bachelor Auction*. If you'd like to know more about Darah's upcoming releases, sign up for her newsletter at:

https://www.darahlace.com/contact-darah/

About the Author

Born and raised in Texas, Darah Lace enjoys a simple life with her husband and two dogs. She loves sports, music, reading/watching a good romance and penning scenes that sizzle. She prefers a hero who demands that ultimate satisfaction and a heroine who isn't afraid to explore her sexual fantasies. The author of erotic contemporary romance, Darah will lead you on a journey of desire, seduction, and forbidden pleasure.

*Darah would love to hear from you.
Connect with Darah at*

darah@darahlace.com
www.darahlace.com
www.facebook.com/darahlace
www.facebook.com/DarahLaceAuthor
www.instagram.com/darahlace/
www.linktr.ee/darahlace
TikTok @Darah_Lace_Author
Twitter @darahlace
Newsletter: www.darahlace.com/contact-darah/

Other Books by Darah Lace

COWBOY ROUGH SERIES
Saddle Broke
Bucking Hard
End of His Rope
Taming the Wildcat (Coming Soon)

PRESTON BROTHERS SERIES
Bachelor Unmasked
Bachelor Auction
Bachelor Playboy (Coming Soon)
Bachelor Betrayed (Coming Soon)

STAND ALONES
S.A.M.: Satisfaction Guaranteed
Getting Lucky in London
Dragon's Bride
Sexting Texas
Yes, Master
Game Night
Wrong Number, Right Man
Yesterday's Desire

Also Available

S.A.M.: Satisfaction Guaranteed
By Darah Lace

Hot off the assembly line, he's the perfect man. Too bad he's not real...or is he?

As the CEO of one of NYC's top ad agencies, Emma Raines devotes her time to stomping the competition in five-inch heels. She has no time for a love life, and her sex life is limited to a quarterly hook-up with a west coast colleague. When her pent-up desire sends her to the discreet offices of Weston Inc., one glance at a picture of SAM—their newest Sexually Animated Male—and she's dying for a taste of the more lifelike toy.

Sam Weston might be the genius behind the biomechanics of Weston, Inc., but the unexplained return of male sexbots by female customers has him scratching his head. When his cousin and co-founder cajoles him into a harebrained scheme to replace Emma's order with himself, the nerd in Sam is convinced research outweighs deception. The Dom in him scoffs at the idea of normal sex. But one night of substandard vanilla sex later, he's determined to take control and give the feisty exec the dominance she craves.

Darah Lace

A Sneak Peek at

S.A.M.: Satisfaction Guaranteed

Chapter One

"So, did you get your sex machine?"

Emma Raines pressed the phone closer to her ear as a surge of heat flooded her cheeks. She glanced around the plush office in the high-rise complex of Weston, Inc., manufacturer of all things robotic, to make sure she was still alone. She'd been escorted to Weston's private office five minutes earlier, but the business mogul had yet to appear. "I can walk out of here right now, you know. I don't have to go through with this."

"Sheesh, I was just kidding." Celeste, the one and only person in the world Emma ever opened up to, sighed. "No one's going to find out, Em. You're not dealing with a backstreet sex shop. Weston's high-end. They only deal with high-end clients. They have too much to lose not to be discreet."

"And that's the only reason I'm here." If any of her colleagues found out she was about to purchase one of Weston's new male sexbots, she'd lose all credibility. Her Queen Bitch of Advertising crown would certainly topple. Showing weakness wasn't an option, and to Emma, her recent increased need for sex classified as a weakness.

She'd done without for the most part while she worked her way up the corporate ladder, but lately, the quarterly hookup with her west coast fuck buddy and the late-night fantasies starring the hot pink silicon vibrator housed in her bedside table weren't enough.

"So, come on, spill," Celeste persisted. "Did you find anything you like?"

"Maybe." Leaning against the edge of Weston's enormous walnut desk—compensating much?—Emma fingered the pictures on the glass top, spreading them out for a better look at the male specimen depicted. Tall and lean, in a three-piece business suit, he was different from the ones she'd seen in the brochure.

This god-like creation was more life-like than the other sexbots. He was beautiful, though not in a way that made him pretty. His hair was dark, semi-long and a bit unruly on top, and short around the sides and back. His blue eyes reflected a deep intelligence and maybe a hint of impatience. A shadow of growth lined his jaw, as if it hadn't seen a razor in a couple of days, which was an odd feature for a sexbot but one she found sexy as hell. With one hip cocked, he stood with the sinewy grace of an athlete. He seemed so alive, so…real.

"Send me a picture so I can drool and be jealous."

"Why would you be jealous? You have a man." She picked up the envelope containing more photos and turned it over to read the label. New Product Promo.

Product. Ugh, that wouldn't do. If she was going through with this ridiculous plan, she couldn't think of him as a product. She slid another handful of photos out and flipped through them. Half a dozen depicted the man on a yacht, dressed in casual clothing—jeans, a cable sweater, and deck shoes. A few more showed him jogging in a park. He didn't look like any product she'd ever purchased.

"Craig is wonderful," Celeste rattled on. "Best

husband ever. But there's just something about the mystery of a new man. Especially one designed only for pleasure."

A man designed only for pleasure. It had been a while since she'd found that with the opposite sex. Matt's last trip to New York hadn't allowed for more than a quickie at his hotel before he took the redeye home. And men hadn't exactly lined up at her door over the last couple years. Those who had come knocking, she hadn't had time for. Relationships demanded too much time and energy, which she didn't have as CEO of one of the largest and most successful ad agencies in New York.

"I'm telling you, Em. This is just what you need."

"You just want me to get him so you can borrow him for a threesome and not feel like you're cheating."

"Hmm, I hadn't thought of that." The wheels were probably turning a mile a minute in that scatterbrain. Emma wasn't sure why she clung to the woman's friendship. They were nothing alike. Celeste had purple hair and more piercings than a pincushion, but she'd grabbed Emma's hand on the first day of kindergarten and never let go.

"Well, forget it. That would be like sharing a toothbrush." Emma dropped the photo and returned to the wingback she'd vacated after being left to cool her heels. Much longer and Weston would lose a customer. She wasn't known for her patience, and what little she had was running out.

Another reason relationships didn't work for her.

The door opened behind her, and something unfamiliar coursed through her. Panic? Fear? Ridiculous. Emma Raines feared nothing.

"Gotta go." She punched the OFF button and shoved her cell in the side pocket of her briefcase.

Emma stood and turned to face a devilishly handsome man, possibly in his early thirties, blond, with eyes that smiled behind black-framed glasses.

"Ms. Raines." He held out a hand. "Caleb Weston. I'm so sorry to keep you waiting."

She shook his hand. "I'm ready to make a purchase. No need for a sales pitch."

He blinked, obviously startled by her forthright approach, then recovered. "Of course."

Settling in the chair, she waited until he was seated behind the desk, then tapped a polished nail on the photo nearest him. The man under her finger looked back at her. The smile drew her in. "Is this one available?"

"Sam?"

"Is that what you call him?" Sam? The others had more modern, trendier names that would be much more marketable. Brett. Gavin. Derek. Of course, this new model very well could make the name Sam popular again. "Is he new?"

"New?"

She glanced up, irritated that he kept answering her questions with questions. "He wasn't in your brochure. I assumed he was a new model." Emma pointed to the label on the envelope. "New Product Promo."

His brows, which had been high on his forehead, lowered over rounded eyes that slowly narrowed. He cleared his throat and leaned forward. "Are you interested in Sam?"

A man who'd do her laundry, cook her meals, and

give her countless orgasms, satisfaction guaranteed or her money back? "I might be."

"Hmm, well…he's, uh…" His eyes brightened for a split second, then dulled, and he shook his head. "He's still in the testing stage."

Before she could stop them, her shoulders sagged, and she murmured a pathetic, "Oh."

"Is there another model you'd —"

"No." She gathered her briefcase and rose, ready to call an end to this meeting. The other sexbots were certainly attractive, beautiful even, but this model sparked a fire in her belly that made her hot, restless, something she hadn't felt in a long time. That alone set off bells — more like sirens — of warning while, at the same time, made the idea of sex with such a creation hard to resist. If he wasn't available, that just meant this whole idea was a mistake. Wasn't meant to be.

"Wait." The head of Weston, Inc. stood, nearly toppling his chair. For a moment, he seemed more like a frightened boy than the head of a Fortune 500 company. Then he squared his shoulders and pushed his glasses up the bridge of his nose. "If you really like Sam, I can probably work something out."

She hesitated, knowing Caleb Weston would bend over backward to get this new sexbot for her if she wanted it. Backing from her agency could open doors for Weston, Inc. Wouldn't do her firm any harm either. Weston was about more than sexbots. The company had a strong background in the medical field with prosthetics and only in the last few years branched into robotics.

Emma's gaze was once again drawn to the pictures on the desk. Her tummy fluttered, and her nipples tightened. Wanted was an understatement. She hadn't felt this way about a real man…ever. She tugged her jacket together, folded her arms over her breasts, and lifted her gaze to meet his. "I'm listening."

"I can offer you Sam—" He swallowed audibly. "—but only on a trial basis. Free of course."

"That's not necessary. I can afford him."

A red stain spread across his cheeks, and he shook his head again. "You'd be, shall we say, taking our newest product for a test ride."

As if contagious, the heat of embarrassment burned her face. Yet, she refused to give him the satisfaction of letting on that both knew what kind of test ride she'd be taking. She lifted her chin. "When can he be delivered?"

"Oh, uh…" He swallowed again, looked at his calendar, then back at her. "Monday?"

Emma nodded. "Just one more question before we discuss the details. Why Sam? Why not something more modern? I'm sorry, professional curiosity. I tend to analyze everything for promotional purposes. Sam just doesn't strike me as marketable. Does it stand for something?"

"Oh, uh, yeah…Sam." He seemed confused for a moment, then he smiled. "S-A-M. Sexually Animated Male." His grin grew wider, and he laughed. "Guess we should have gone with something a little trendier, huh?"

She took one last look at the sex toy in the photo and tried to see him through the eyes of the average female consumer. He actually looked like a Sam. Solid. Manly. Gorgeous. Dreamy. Sexually appealing. Very sexually appealing. Hmm, maybe Weston's people knew what they were doing, after all. "Personally, Mr. Weston, I've never followed trends."

****

Smooth as silk, her skin warmed his palm as he tested the weight of her left breast. She shuddered and pressed into his hand. His thumb grazed the nipple, and he waited for the soft mewl he knew would come. She didn't disappoint. She never did. She was perfect.

The perfect woman. The perfect lover. Delilah could satisfy any man's desires. Except his. She was made for long, slow sensual loving, not the hard-core kink Sam Weston enjoyed. Not many women were.

He rolled the beaded tip. Maybe it was time to move on to Genevieve. She'd be perfect for someone with his appetites.

"Mmm, sugah, that feels so good." The syrupy sweet southern drawl grated on his nerves.

Sam lowered his hand and stepped back from between her thighs. "Her timing sensors are in sync, but we need to rethink that accent before we put Delilah on the shelf."

His lab assistant, Ben, shook his head. "Marketing says a southern drawl rates the highest of turn-ons for men, Russian coming in a close second."

Neither turned Sam on. He preferred something more refined with a bit of an edge when a woman begged him to fuck her.

Ben rubbed the back of his neck. "I can't find anything wrong with Derek."

"Well, there's got to be a glitch somewhere. He's the third manbot returned this month." Sam initialed the inspection form for Delilah, turned her off, and laid his tablet aside. "Let's take a look."

Joining Ben beside the nude sexbot, Sam pinched an earlobe, one of many erogenous pressure points built into the toy. "Derek, my man, how's it hanging?"

The bot closed his eyes, moaned, and the semi-hard erection rose to full attention.

"That well, huh?"

Ben backed up. "Geez, I'll never get used to that."

Sam laughed. "Intimidated?"

"Hardly." Despite his denial, the younger man blushed. "Just not used to eyeballing a man's dick. Feels weird to get paid to handle one."

The sight of a man's cock didn't faze Sam. Half the men at The Red Door, the BDSM sex club he frequented, walked around with their equipment on display. And he'd shared enough women in his adult life to get over any reservations he might have had. One, two, or three men, all pleasuring the same woman, sometimes led to accidental contact, but he'd grown self-assured in his masculinity over the years.

His confidence hadn't come easy, considering he'd grown up the stereotypical, pencil-thin, glasses-wearing nerd. The muscle-bound men at his club reminded him of the jocks who'd terrorized him in high school. He hadn't exactly joined their ranks, still on the slender side, but his body could now compete with those who boasted a swimmer's physique.

"I don't get it." Ben peeled back a layer of synthetic flesh above the bots buttocks and opened the panel covering the motherboard. "Men aren't returning the fembots." He looked up at Sam. "Why don't you just ask the women returning these guys what's wrong with them?"

"We have." No matter what he and Caleb did

physically or programmatically to the male sexbots, the return rate from female customers continued to climb. The average return was within thirty days of purchase with no adequate answer as to what the customer disliked or found lacking. "They don't seem to know. Or they're too embarrassed to say."

Prior to releasing the male sexbots for public purchase, they'd performed the usual research and development, established a test market with a hundred subjects from all social and economic backgrounds. Every volunteer gave rave reviews, couldn't wait for the product to hit the "shelf" and were disappointed to learn the manbots would be in limited supply the first year. A fact both Caleb and Sam lamented.

The highest percentage of sex toy purchases was made by women, and if they could tap into that resource, they'd have a corner on the market. Not that they didn't already with the prosthetics and medical robotics division. But he and Caleb were trying to branch out, to do something more exciting, more innovative, that would launch Weston Inc. ahead of the competition. Yet every return was another setback.

Ben moved aside so Sam could see inside the back panel. The connectors were all in place. Had to be in the programming. Dammit. "Did you run diagnostics?"

"Yeah." Ben handed him the readings. "Caleb thinks we need to figure out what women want."

Sam snorted as he scanned the readings. "Like I said, I don't think women know what they want."

The lab door swung shut behind Caleb as he strode into the lab. "I have the perfect way to find out." His gaze slid over the manbot with disgust.

"Goddammit, not another one?" He held up his hands, palms forward, to ward off an answer. "Never mind that. I have to talk to you." He glanced at Ben. "Can you give us a minute?"

"Sure. I'll take an early lunch."

As Ben hung up his lab coat and grabbed his hoodie, Sam eyed his cousin. The nervous energy radiating from Caleb could only mean one thing. He'd just had one of his famous epiphanies. Occasionally, they turned out to be a good thing. It had been his idea for Sam to combine his design for animated life forms with his overly stimulated sexual imagination. However, more often than not, Caleb's epiphanies led Sam into trouble.

The second they were alone, Caleb slapped his hands together and rubbed them vigorously. "So, the meeting this morning with Emma Raines, CEO of that big ass ad agency…"

"Yeah, how'd it go?" Sam widened his stance, folded his arms across his chest, and patiently waited for Caleb to spill the excitement bubbling inside him. Only then could Sam get back to work and figure out what was wrong with Derek. Maybe hiring a female lab tech was the ticket. The male bots responded to him or Ben without fail, and they'd sold at least a dozen male models to male customers with zero returns.

"She signed a contract."

Selling to Emma Raines had been to Caleb like Christmas was to a kid. Sam understood his excitement. He just didn't feel any himself. Right now, all he felt was frustration for not having a goddamn clue what the hell was wrong with his manbots. "And?"

Caleb rocked from the balls of his feet to his toes and back again. "She wants you."

"I'm sorry, you've lost me." Sam was smart, had an IQ of one hundred eighty-two, but sometimes, even he couldn't follow Caleb's thought process. He didn't have time for this, but he rested against the table behind him and sighed. "She wants me to what?"

A short bark of laughter burst from Caleb, and he shook his head. "No, no. She saw the pictures from your photo shoot on my desk and thought you were a sexbot. She wants you. And when I told her you were still in the testing stage and weren't available yet, but that—"

"Testing stage?" Sam's gut twisted. This was not going to be one of those good epiphanies.

"—she could choose another bot, she almost walked. Sam, we really need this to work because—"

"What to work?"

"—if you can satisfy Emma Raines, her ad agency could help launch the sexbot division and even Weston Inc. to another level. That agency is known for making consumers believe in controversial ideas and—"

"Wait. Stop." Sam closed his eyes and let silence fill the room, trying to grasp the situation he wasn't sure he wanted to grasp. But the overwhelming realization that he was about to be dragged into another of Caleb's harebrained schemes rose to a near suffocating level. Sucking in a deep breath, he opened his eyes and nailed Caleb with a look that usually worked to keep him grounded. "What. Did. You. Do?"

Caleb chewed his bottom lip, first one side, then the other. This wasn't good.

"Caleb?"

His cousin lifted his shoulders in a slight shrug. "I told her you'd be delivered Monday."

"Monday?" Sam stared at his cousin. "Are you insane? Even if I wanted to, I can't design a new prototype to look like me by Monday."

"You're not listening. I told her you'd be delivered Monday."

"You're not making any sense, and I don't have time for—"

"No, don't you get it? You'll pretend to be Emma Raines' sexbot."

The truth of Caleb's plan finally sank in, and the pea-sized lead ball in his gut expanded to the size of a cannon ball. "Jesus, Caleb, you are insane."

"This is it, Sam. This is the perfect opportunity to figure out why women are returning the males. You'll have a chance at firsthand knowledge of what we're doing wrong."

"Oh, no, no, no. Uh-uh, no way." Sam turned back to the open panel in Derek's back and bent to inspect the processor. "You'll just have to tell her you made a mistake."

Caleb rounded the table to stand beside Sam. "I can't do that. We'd look—"

"Crazy?"

"I was going to say unprofessional, but yes, I know what I did is foolish." He paced around Sam to his other side. "We have to do something. And really, how hard can it be? You programmed the males. You know what they respond to and how. You'd know exactly what to do. Besides, we both know you don't care who you fuck so what's the difference?"

Sam was used to Caleb's offhand remarks, but that

didn't stop the twinge of anger that tightened his jaw. He was very careful in choosing his partners, and the club screened all its members, both psychologically and physically. Which brought up another point and hopefully a possible means of getting Caleb to comprehend exactly what he was asking Sam to do.

He straightened and resumed his standard arms-crossed signature pose that usually told Caleb to back off. "Our sexbots don't necessitate a condom, so how do you plan to explain the requirement, 'cause I damn sure won't be having sex with a stranger without one."

The light in Caleb's eyes went from dull desperation to halogen high beams. "Already took care of that. It's in the contract."

"You put a condom requirement in the contract?" Despite the fact he hadn't meant to give the man hope, Caleb's forethought bordered on impressive. He shook his head and crossed the room to his workstation, Caleb close on his heels.

"She didn't even blink, Sam." Caleb almost danced beside him. "I told her it was standard for the first thirty days as a stipulation in the return policy."

"That's probably the smartest thing you've said all day. We should make that the norm for all returns." He took off his lab coat and draped it over his chair. Maybe he'd join Ben and take an early lunch since he obviously wasn't going to get any work done this morning.

"Women don't like clean up anyway," Caleb rambled on. "So, I'm sure they'd be agreeable. I'll have Margo talk with legal about it." Caleb scribbled a note on his palm. His cousin might look like a polished CEO, but, like Sam, he was and would always be a geek at heart. "Any other reasons why you don't want to do this?"

Sam shoved his thumb and forefinger under the nose grip of his wire-rimmed glasses and pinched the bridge of his nose. He couldn't believe he was even having this conversation much less still talking about it. It was too fucking bizarre. "Have you considered the fact that, if we did what you're asking, we'd be breaking the law? Selling a sex toy is one thing, but selling human flesh—my flesh, I might add—is prostitution."

"No, no, not at all. I gave her a thirty-day free trial."

"Oh, you gave her a free trial. Well, that makes it okay then." Sam tossed his glasses on a note pad and scrubbed a hand over his face. Even if he wanted to do this, he couldn't pull it off anyway.

All the male sexbots were programmed for normal partners. And Sam didn't do normal. Any woman with half a brain would figure that out. Which lead to another argument against this idiocy. "Have you thought about what will happen when she finds out I'm not a sex toy?"

"I was hoping that wouldn't happen and that maybe you could pretend to malfunction or something to get you out of there. Then we could offer her another model. But while you're there, you could collect data. And there's a good chance she won't want to have sex with you right away."

Sam just looked at him, because really, what was there to say to that reasoning?

Caleb pulled off his glasses and chewed the end of the earpiece. "Or maybe we can rush a new prototype in your likeness and replace you with another you without her knowing."

"You honestly think I'd allow that?"

"We'll think of something." Caleb waved off Sam's concerns as if what they considered was perfectly normal and began to pace. "If we don't jump on this, we may never know how to fix the problem. If returns keep coming in, we can kiss the sexbot division goodbye." He stopped in front of Sam. "The board is breathing down my neck as it is. They might force the issue and insist on turning our sexbots into soldiers for a more profitable government contract. It's all about the bottom line, you know."

He did know. When they'd first talked about expanding the company to include artificial life forms, he'd been adamant about how the bots would be used. That's when Caleb had suggested sexbots. Once the board was involved, the fight to keep his creations out of harms' way hadn't been easy. The mere thought of Derek, Delilah, or any of the others manning the front line and being blown to bits…

He'd be damned if he would let that happen. But without knowing how to correct whatever flaw women saw in his manbots, that's exactly where they were headed. Perhaps there was merit to Caleb's madness. Perhaps he could pass himself off as a sexbot. But what if he couldn't? "What happens if Ms. Raines becomes another unsatisfied customer? She could ruin us."

"Are you kidding?" Caleb laughed. "I have complete faith in you, oh master of hedonism?"

Sam ignored the jab as his brain ran all possible scenarios. God, was he really considering doing this? "What if she figures it out? I mean, I'm not bragging when I say it's hard to tell the difference if you don't know they're not real, but when you actually start poking around..."

"Then we're screwed." His cousin tilted his head to one side. "Well, technically you'll get screwed. Twice. Or thrice. Or—"

"I'm serious. This is not some fraternity prank."

Caleb sobered and shoved his glasses back on his face. "I could call Ms. Raines and tell her after talking to the head of development, Sam isn't ready for distribution."

"That would be the wiser course. Head off the catastrophe before it happens." And they'd be right back where they started. They'd have to form new test groups, screen new subjects. It could take weeks or even months to gather the information they needed.

"Yeah, I know." Caleb sighed. "I just hate to lose her as a client."

"Maybe she'll change her mind and accept Derek or Brett."

"I don't think she'll go for it. She was pretty set on you." He laughed. "Didn't like the name though. Said Sam wasn't marketable."

"I'll keep that in mind." Again, Sam considered the woman who, from nothing more than one look at a photograph, would consider none of the other bots. Why him? And what was wrong with his name? "You actually gave her my name?"

"It sorta slipped out. Pretty clever, though, if I do say so myself. S-A-M. Sexually Animated Male. Get it?"

Sam rolled his eyes and tried to find humor in the situation now that he was off the hook. But for some reason he felt as if he were still dangling on said hook, the sharp pointy end still lodged deep in his chest.

His grandfather had built Weston from the ground up, beginning with prosthetics then expanding to robotics when Sam's father came on board. Having faith in Sam and Caleb, his father had retired and handed over the reins not long after they finished university.

The company's chief focus had been helping those in need, those less fortunate, and though robots designed for sexual pleasure were hardly necessary to survival, they had let their enthusiasm carry them away. Sam didn't regret the decision, but if push came to shove and the trustees used the loss of profit due to returns to get a military contract, his grandfather would turn over in his grave and his father would…well, he'd be disappointed in him.

As much as he hated to admit it, Caleb's cockamamie plan was the fastest way to get the results they needed. And he was curious about Emma Raines. She sounded like a strong-willed woman who knew what she wanted in a man and how to get it. Well, obviously not how to get it or she wouldn't be in the market for a sex toy. But she'd gotten Caleb to cater to her demands. Maybe she really was the answer they were looking for.

Shit. Was he actually thinking of doing this? Did he really have a choice? He looked at Caleb who seemed to have wandered into his own thoughts. "Do you really think we could pull this off?"

Caleb met his gaze with a resolute confidence. "I know we can. You can."

"There'd be a lot more to fooling anyone than just

mimicking a sexbot."

"So, you'll do it?"

He couldn't believe he was saying this but… "Yeah, I'll do it."

Fist pumping into a deep lunge, Caleb let out a jubilant, "Yes!"

"Don't get too excited. We have a lot to work out. First thing being, how to get me out of this as soon as I get what we need." A malfunctioning sexbot wasn't good for business but neither was a lawsuit for…what? Jesus, he couldn't even fathom the consequences.

"Sure, sure, we'll come up with something."

"And what about food? I can't drink that bio fluid shit."

"Already thought of that."

"Of course, you did." Sam put his reading glasses back on, grabbed a tablet and pencil, and pulled out two chairs. He groaned as he sank into the worn padded seat. He'd finally done it. He'd jumped on the crazy train called Caleb and was riding the rails straight into the realm of insanity.

Darah Lace

You Might Like

If you're looking for spicy fantasy with lots of action and emotion, you'll enjoy this series.

Chasing Time
Bonded Souls Book 1
By Mia Downing

Skye Worthington's quest for family brings more than she bargained for...

My already turbulent life flips upside down the moment Marek Young appears. Nightmares from a childhood jumping between foster homes edge into sexy dreams of a man in leather pants with a simmering magical touch. As Marek is an important client at the bookstore where I work, I can't say no when he asks me to dinner. I didn't expect the pull of desire or the sizzle of familiar energy the first time we touched, but I need more than satisfaction. I need the truth. Yet the truth he offers seems too bizarre to believe...

One fated jump through time destroyed Marek Young's life...

I have only one mission—make Skye love me again. Except the aloof bookstore clerk and grad student has no recollection of me. An emergency jump through time left Skye to grow up in this era with no memory of our adventures...or me. Unfortunately, she's always had a temper, and my time is running out. All I want is to be the man she can fall in love with again.

You Might Like

If you're looking for something on the dark and gritty side, you'll enjoy this series.

Blade
Heller Raiders MC Book 1
By KyAnn Waters

Hana

I hate the Heller Raiders. They betrayed my brother, taking his cut, his bike, and his patch because he chose me over them when our parents died. Back then I was just a teenager crushing on his best friend, but I was too young for the hot bad boy, Blade. I never expected to see him again. He shouldn't feel this good. I shouldn't feel this good. Three years ago, I'd loved him. I'm afraid I still do.

Blade

Hana Vance is my best friend's sister. Off limits. But he's not in the MC anymore and she's grown up. A badass, tattooed hell raiser. I want her on the back of my bike and in my bed, but my life is a wreck, and my club is on self-destruct. I'm going to break promises. My loyalty is going to be challenged. The MC has rules, but I done obeying them.

Heller Raiders MC romance series. Bad boy bikers, dangerous drama, and lots of steamy sex. These are gritty stories including violence, drug use, and graphic language. Get ready for a wild ride. Some readers may find content disturbing.

Printed in Great Britain
by Amazon